of unicorns and phoenixes, of the Minotaur and the Arthurian Questing Beast, of the Fey and their faerie hounds, and, of course, of dragons, are found within:

"Yes, Virginia, There is a Unicorn"—Not everyone can see the mascot of the gift shop The Maiden and the Unicorn. But anyone can feel his bite. . . .

"The Fields, the Sky" —Foolish Theseus left the Minotaur for dead, and the labyrinth's secret door open. . . .

"Father Noe's Bestiary"—Father Noe said he was a wizard, and his shop was filled with paintings of legendary creatures. But why does the painted Caldwurm have to stay in a solid gold frame?

"Nothing but a Hound Dog"—He was just another stray mutt on the streets of New York City. Right? But he had the extraordinary green eyes, white coat, and red ears of a faerie dog. . . .

CREATURE FANTASTIC

EDITED BY

Denise Little

DAW BOOKS, INC.

DONALD A. WOLLHEIM, FOUNDER

375 Hudson Street, New York, NY 10014

ELIZABETH R. WOLLHEIM
SHEILA E. GILBERT
PUBLISHERS
www.dawbooks.com

First Printing, September 2001
1 2 3 4 5 6 7 8 9

ACKNOWLEDGMENT

CONTENTS

INTRODUCTION
by Denise Little

Tales of enchanted and impossible beasties are a mainstay of myth and legend. Until fairly recently, they were even a mainstay of science. Creatures never seen on this Earth populate the margins of early maps—"Here there be Dragons!" The oceans and wild places at the edges of the known world have always been, even for sober and meticulous mapmakers, full of lairs where impossible creatures lived, always ready to stalk the unwary.

Medieval bestiaries were full of tales of amazing animals, presented as fact by the best biologists of their day. Dragons and unicorns, manticores and gryphons, all carefully drawn and classified, make their appearance right next to giraffes and hippos and elephants and zebras. In their own way, the animals we now know to be real had to appear just as outlandish as the creatures that we today relegate to the world of the fantastic.

Perhaps that helps explain why rumors of fantastic creatures appear across all human societies and persist centuries after nearly every nook and cranny of the world has been probed and cataloged. What it doesn't explain is why each society has its own particular boogieman to scare the children into good behavior. Nor does it explain the persistence of specific mythic creatures—like dragons—across nearly all human societies. Most cultures have some sort of dragon myth. I've always wondered whether discoveries of dinosaur bones, which have been unearthed on every continent and which even the ancients had to run into on occasion, didn't serve to begin the myth of the dragon, with subsequent discoveries keeping the myth alive throughout time. It's a theory, anyway.

But no matter how the myths of fantastic creatures got started, there's no denying their power or their contribution to literature. From the Minotaur in his maze to Grendel in *Beowulf* to Thurber's story of "The Unicorn in the Garden," tales of these beasts have fascinated us all. Though the creatures are rooted in myth and legend, that doesn't make them any less real in our minds and hearts. Several classics of modern fantasy, like Mercedes Lackey's great book *Black Gryphon* and its sequels *White Gryphon* and *Silver Gryphon* are built around the existence of these fabulous beasts.

In this collection, we've brought together a fine array of modern writers to add their own special touches to the fantastic creatures of myth and legend. Their stories were influenced by popular mythology (we've got our share of dragon and unicorn and phoenix stories), arcane sources (Mallory's Questing Beast), some mythic (the Minotaur), some thoroughly modern (Nessy), and stories culled from cultures across the globe (we've got two creatures of the Sidhe, a Chinese dragon, a northern horse tribe myth, and a retelling of the Middle Eastern myth of the Phoenix). I sincerely hope you'll have as much fun as I did, searching through the treasures collected here to find your favorite "creature fantastic."

Enjoy!

Denise Little is the editor of several anthologies, including DAW's *Twice Upon a Time, Alien Pets, Dangerous Magic,* and *Perchance to Dream.* She's also a writer, and her work has most recently appeared in DAW's *Civil War Fantastic.* Her other books include *Realms of Dragons, Mistresses of the Dark,* and *The Quotable Cat.* She's an executive editor working with science fiction legend Dr. Martin H. Greenberg, who is even cooler in person than he is in legend. In her spare time, she plays piano wretchedly and spoils her cats.

FATHER NOE'S BESTIARY
by Jody Lynn Nye

Jody Lynn Nye lists her main career activity as "spoiling cats." She lives northwest of Chicago with two of the above and her husband, author and packager Bill Fawcett. She has written twenty-five books, including four contemporary fantasies, three SF novels, four novels in collaboration with Anne McCaffrey, including *The Ship Who Won*, a humorous anthology about mothers, *Don't Forget Your Spacesuit, Dear!*, and over sixty short stories. Her latest books are *License Invoked*, co-written with Robert Asprin, and *Advanced Mythology*, fourth in the Mythology 101 series.

"How can you say you feel sorry for dragons?" demanded Kinsie. "They're killers!"

"Now, now, they're completely harmless if you don't bother them," Father Noe said, from behind his easel. Dust filtered through the light that came in through the big window over his shoulder at the back of the little shop. Except for the ends of his sweeping silver beard and moustache, his grayish, pale, long-nosed face was in shadow. "They want to be left alone, same as you and I would. Can you sit still?"

"Besides," the black girl said, tilting her chin up

so she looked defiantly down her blunt nose at him, "they're fake. They don't exist."

"Oh, you're wrong, dear poppet," the old man said, with a sigh. "They used to live under every hollow mountain and in every deep cave. Or they did. Those times are past." He set down his brush, leaned around the edge of the stretched canvas and turned Kinsie's head so that the colorful beads binding the ends of her elaborately cornrowed braids caught the light. "Now, hold still."

"They weren't ever here," Kinsie said to the wall. Abelard Noe's collection of pictures looked back at her. "Neither were these guys—griffins, mermaids, unicorns, wyverns, manticores. You know. They were just made up to scare kids."

Noe smiled. "I only wish the truth were that simple." He worked for a moment in silence. "Do you know what is the most dangerous, vicious creature in the entire world?"

"No," Kinsie asked eagerly, sitting forward on the edge of her seat.

The old wizard leaned over and daubed a bit of blue paint on her nose. "You are."

"Me?"

"Humans. Mankind. There's never been an animal with such a voracious appetite for other people's land and belongings. People kill for sport. You know that tiger skin at the museum?"

"Yes . . ."

"Well, someone, a man, went to the tropics and slew that tiger, just to prove he could. It wasn't encroaching on his territory or threatening his family. It lived thousands of leagues away. He had to travel to where it was to kill it. That's viciousness. Small wonder the great beasts of the world are afraid of us. Now, sit still. Your mother wanted this done for your grandsire's birthday. It wants time to dry before I put it in a frame."

"You talk very weird," Kinsie said. "He's my granddad, not my grandsire."

The old man's beard was cut to show his mouth, which curled up in a little smile. "One speaks in the language of one's birth. Changes have come and gone since I was born."

"You're pretty old, aren't you?" Kinsie asked.

"Ancient," Noe agreed.

"But you've killed hundreds of monsters! Hundreds and hundreds!"

"No, I have not. Don't talk nonsense."

"But, that's what Gordie Velazquez said about you. You vanquished the fiercest beasts on earth! Vanquished means killed. How did you do it? With a sword? Did you blast them with fire and lightning?" Kinsie's eyes lit up. "I'd like to see you throw lightning."

"Not at all," Noe said, patiently. "I collected them. I captured them in oils or watercolors, appropriate to their nature. You see there? That's the giant of Megarath. Yes, he was a terrible one, indeed. Thousands cringed at the sound of his footsteps booming across the land. Bad temper, that one. Looks lovely in oils, though, doesn't he? I recall, it was a fine September day I saw him first . . ."

Kinsie wriggled in her chair, listening eagerly. She had heard dozens of these stories over the last two years, since Noe had moved in next door. He claimed that he was the last resort for the desperate towns at the mercy of terrible monsters. Where he went, the monster was never seen again. Noe was a little foggy on hard facts, which Kinsie felt was unsatisfying. Most of his stories kind of went to a commercial break, then came back and ended with the monster already gone and the grateful townsfolk thanking him for ridding them of the terror. You never got to hear about the actual fight. She wanted all the gory details.

"All I've done is preserve them for prosperity," Noe went on. He poked at the easel with his paintbrush, frowning all the while. "I love them. I love them all. Here on my walls they are saved for the future ages, when I hope we will be more enlightened. Alas, that will probably be long past my time. Maybe in yours," he said, patting Kinsie on the arm. "Human beings are relentless. The dragon has the advantage of size and power, but humans have the advantage of numbers, and they never forget fear. They presevere until they succeed. Not always for heroic reasons. Sometimes for evil and selfish purposes. They get strange ideas in their heads, like that drinking dragon-scale tea will make one braver, or that unicorn's horn will protect them from poisoning, or that eating the dust of a manticore's claw will make a man's . . . well, you don't need to hear about that, poppet. A dragon may survive a generation, two, three, but sooner or later he will fall to bloody self-interest. Selfishness, really. They're grateful to be preserved like this. They have a chance."

Weird. Kinsie could never figure out why a guy like this with class and obvious money had settled in an area most white folks considered a slum. The news reports all said their neighborhood was the crime center of the city. Kinsie knew that you never

ought to go walking out alone after dark with anything you didn't want to lose. Gunfire could be heard
most nights, and there were bars on most windows.
Noe didn't notice the tension, and he didn't hold
with putting bars on things. He wanted to be accessi-
ble. He said he was indulging a long-time fancy of
having a small shop in the center of town where
people could come to visit him, not up in a tower or
in a cottage on a mountain top. She thought that
sounded weird, too, something out of a fairy tale,
like the way he talked.

He'd said he was a wizard. Unlike most of his
number, he'd told Kinsie, he rather liked people of
all kinds. That was because he'd originally been a
priest; back in the Middle Ages, he had been in holy
orders. That was why he had never married, he said.
He had learned magic to undertake what he saw as
a sacred duty. He considered himself the first conser-
vationist. And he was an artist. Pretty fine, too, Kinsie thought.

No matter what else, he was one friendly old dude.
Animals adored him. Every kid trusted him, even
the gangbangers. His shop was considered neutral
territory in the neighborhood, almost an oasis. No
one bugged him, no one stole from him. He treated
everyone who stopped in with respect, never hanging over a brother's shoulder as if he might walk off
with the goods.

Kinsie and her friends loved the shop. It was a
cool place. It looked kind of like the inside of a castle,
or as Kinsie imagined a castle might look. Noe rarely
used electric lamps, preferring glass hurricane lamps
like the one Kinsie's grandmother had for power fail-
ures. The store always smelled faintly of the oil. That

was kind of nice and old fashioned. Noe hadn't bothered to repaint when he moved in, and the cracks in the walls followed the line of the cinder blocks underneath, making the walls look like old stone. Not a lot else had changed, except for the shiny brass sign outside next to the door that said "Abelard Noe, Lessons and Commissions."

Maybe he wasn't a wizard, but he had something, anyway. Confidence, like he was bulletproof. One day, about a month after he'd moved in, one of the local enforcers had dropped in on him, looking for protection payment. Father Noe had just looked at him long and hard. Kinsie was about to run for her daddy, who was part of the neighborhood watch program, but to her amazement the ganglord was reduced to a stammering child. He apologized to Noe, something that some of the neighborhood folks considered a vanquishment right up there with that of the giant of Megarath, who glared out at the world from a blue frame under the stairs. The enforcer left Noe alone after that.

Noe didn't ask for much, really. He paid his taxes, sat on the stoop and talked with the other old folks on the street, drank in the corner bar at night with the neighbors, bought his vegetables from the grocer. And he painted things. The walls of his ground floor showroom were full of framed pictures of dragons, gargoyles, wyverns, griffins, mermaids and tritons, sea serpents and all sorts of other weird creatures facing either dexter or sinister, sitting couchant or raging rampant. Noe called it his bestiary, which had a short "e," not a long one as Kinsie thought it ought to, to sound like "beast."

She hung out in the shop whenever she could,

going from frame to frame, trying to get into the story that each picture was telling. Her mama admired that somebody with artistic leanings had come to the neighborhood and wanted Kinsie to take lessons. Kinsie did what she was told, but she was happier browsing his collection than starting paintings of her own. She didn't think she could ever do anything as good as his. When she looked really closely at one of Noe's pictures, brush strokes were visible on the surface. If not for those, the subjects on each canvas or parchment looked so real that they could have jumped right out of their frames and eaten you.

Kinsie and her friends were always coming in to see the paintings. Noe didn't mind. He liked showing off his collection. He wanted the kids to get to know their heritage.

"One day," he always said, mysteriously. "One day."

More to pass the time than because he needed the money, Father Noe painted pictures and sold them. He did landscapes, birds, flowers, fruit, and people. Kinsie thought none of these looked as real as the monsters, but her mother cautioned her not to criticize the old man. It was unkind and impolite. Kinsie kept her mouth shut for other reasons. Kinsie had seen plenty of fantasy movies. You never knew what would happen to you if you criticized a wizard. She didn't want to wind up a frog or frozen into a statue. Not that she really believed him, of course, but there was no sense at all in taking a chance. Mama had come up with the idea that Granddad might like to have a picture of her, Kinsie, for his sixtieth birthday. She wondered whether she'd come out looking more like a flower or a monster.

"Ah," Noe was saying, just as the bell hanging over the door jingled. "It's beginning to resemble you. Shall we take a break and greet our visitors?"

In this neighborhood a person learned to have pretty good instincts about whether or not a body could be trusted. Kinsie disliked the newcomers prowling around the front room on sight. One was a mean-looking, leathery-skinned dude with bad teeth and shaggy, kinky hair who could have been black, or Hispanic, or something in between. The other was a white man, much younger, skinny, with a bleached-blond buzz-cut and darting, pale eyes. She didn't recognize either one of them, meaning that they came from outside the neighborhood. They started strolling around the dusty shop, leaning over the cases and peering at the frames on the walls. They didn't look like the kind of men who bought pictures from a wizard or anyone else. The white guy was carrying a big knife in a sheath on his belt. Kinsie was sure the bulge in the other's jacket was a gun.

The dude poked at the pictures on the wall. He stopped before the one that Kinsie liked best, which Noe said was the Caldwurm. The dragon, with scales rippling in color from bronze to green, was pictured couchant, dexter, on a heap of jewels, picking its teeth with a sword. The frame around him was smooth, yellow metal so heavy that the one time Noe let Kinsie and her friends handle it, they couldn't hold it up.

"Nice picture," the first one said. His hands, rough as bark, caressed the frame. "Brass."

"It isn't," Noe said, genially, rocking back on his heels and patting his belly with flattened hands. "It's gold. Solid gold."

"Bull," said the other man. He looked sly. His pale blue eyes kept sliding around, noting where the doors and windows were. Kinsie felt like going for her dad. Keeping a good eye on the men, she started sidling, nice and easy, toward the back door. "Brass. Maybe brass plate."

"I assure you, gentlemen," Noe argued, "it has to be gold. He insisted on it, this one. He wanted lots of gold to live in, or he wouldn't be happy."

"Old fool," one said to the other. "It's brass. But the picture's nice."

"It did turn out well, didn't it?' Noe said, proudly, stepping up to flick a bit of dust off the glass with the edge of his sleeve. He looked so short and fragile next to the street guys. Kinsie wished he'd shut up. "My first watercolor. Douses the flame, you know. Makes him tolerable for the rest of us to live with."

It was obvious the two visitors didn't understand a word he said. "Unh," said the dude. "Give you three bucks for it."

"Sorry," Noe told them. "It's not for sale. That one's part of my private collection. If you are interested in buying a piece of art, I've got these lovely sea anemones I finished just yesterday." He fetched an unframed canvas from behind the glass-covered counter. "Just look at that coral. You could almost touch it."

The men turned their back on him, conferring. A cluster of pictures caught the white guy's eye. "How come these are full of water?" he asked, curiously.

"Oh, you need to keep mermaids in water," Noe said. "Otherwise they dry out."

"Crazy," one man said to the other. They exchanged a glance. The leather dude glanced at Kinsie and gave her a grin that was supposed to be friendly but just looked mean. She froze, holding her breath. The dude looked back at his partner, tilted his head toward her. The other man nodded. The two of them pushed past Noe and out the door onto the street. Kinsie let out the breath she was holding.

"Thank you for stopping in, gentlemen," Noe called after them.

"They didn't steal anything because they knew I was watching them," Kinsie told her parents over dinner. "That's the only reason. If they could'a caught me, they'd probably have beaten us both up and taken all the pictures."

Kinsie's parents looked at one another.

"That old man needs looking after," her mother, Coralee, said. "He doesn't really understand about people. I don't know how many times I've stopped that grocer from cheating him on vegetables."

"Jin Soon is a real tightfist, but I don't think he's dishonest," said Kinsie's father, Darryl, who tended to believe only the best about people. Kinsie's mother was more level-headed.

"It's like Father Noe's playacting being a regular person," Coralee said. "He needs someone to watch over him. He's sacred, not worldly. He's a holy man, and he's crazy. That makes him twice sacred."

"Don't mistake it," said her father, reaching across the table for the salt. "He's not helpless just because he doesn't behave like you or me. Doesn't mean he's being fooled."

"Well, if I were you, I'd spread the word to keep an eye on him. He's good for the neighborhood. He's kindhearted, and he's a good role model. There're a lot of crimes against people who don't know any better. I wouldn't want anything to happen to that man."

So the kids in the neighborhood kept watch over Father Noe. The adults did. The community action volunteers made a point of visiting his shop every day to see if he needed anything. Always friendly, Noe welcomed them all, telling stories and offering tea and cookies to the ones who had time to stop in. Kinsie stayed close. She suspected that they hadn't seen the last of those two men.

About a week later, the tinkle of breaking glass woke Kinsie. She found her alarm clock and peered at it. Two A.M. Another crash came. She sat up in bed. She had *not* dreamed the sound. She slipped out of bed to the window next to the fire escape, to see if she could tell where it was coming from.

It was pretty dark in the back alley, but out of the corner of her eye Kinsie glimpsed a shifting shadow down near the trash cans at the back of Father Noe's store. Burglars! On tiptoe she ran to her parents' room.

"Mama," she hissed. "Someone broke into Father Noe's! I've got to warn him. Call the cops!"

She ran out again, hearing the sleepy voices of her parents behind her.

"The cops? Honey, what's going on? Kinsie, where are you?"

"Call Noe and ask him if he's got a burglar," Daddy said, still half out of it. "No, wait, he hasn't got a phone."

While her parents talked about what to do, Kinsie hurried back to the window. She couldn't see any-

thing. If it was those same two dirtbags, they'd kill
the old man and steal all his monsters. She couldn't
wait for the cops. She ran to her room, shoved her
feet into her sneakers, and threw on her dark-colored
sweatshirt. As quietly as she could, she eased up the
window sash, climbed over the security bars and
slipped down the stairs. She had to warn Father Noe.

The back door was still barred, but that big window had been broken out and a rag thrown over
the frame to let the intruders get in without hurting
themselves. Kinsie hung back, terrified.

What was she doing? She could die, meddling
around like this! Then, by the faint light of the hurricane lamps, she saw the burglars. Her instincts were
good: it was the same two dudes, carrying a big sack.
They were taking pictures off the walls and shoving
them into the bag. The stairs leading to the upper
floor were just a few feet from the back window. She
mentally pushed at the two men, willing them to go
farther toward the front so she could sneak up an
warn Father Noe.

"Goddammit!" the leathery-skinned dude
growled.

"Hey, quiet," the white guy said. "The old man
will hear you."

The dude reached into his pocket and pulled out
a gun that meant serious business. "If he comes
down here, he's dead."

"Hey, here it is," the white guy said. Kinsie quiv-
ered with fear and fury. They were going for the
dragon of Caldwurm. Kinsie knew they couldn't resist it. The white guy took it off the wall. It fell out
of his hand and crashed to the floor. The two men
started, looking around. Kinsie ducked behind the

low wall, then crept up so she could just see over the edge.

"What's with you?" the dude growled at his partner.

"It's heavy!" the white guy whined, stooping to pick up the fallen picture.

"Goddammit, someone will hear us." The white guy stood up, holding the frame in one hand and the parchment with the dragon in the other. "Looka that. A dragon. It looks wussy in those girly colors."

"What'll we do with it?" the white guy asked. "Sell it?"

"It ain't worth nothin'. Hey, we can use it to save power." Kinsie could hear the evil grin in his voice. She had to get upstairs to Father Noe. Watching them carefully, she climbed in through the broken window and crawled on her hands and knees toward the bottom step. She tried not to cringe as she felt shards of glass under her palms.

The dude rolled the dragon parchment up into a tube and swung around to the nearest hurricane lamp. He twisted the little key on the side, causing the flame to leap up. Kinsie watched in horror as he stuffed Father's precious artwork into the narrow glass chimney. Yellow flames licked at the fragile yellow paper, drawing a curved line of black at the corner that spread and spread. Without another thought, the dude went back to stripping art off the walls.

Before he finished turning around, they heard the thin sound of glass shattering.

A shower like hailstones began falling in the small shop. The white guy caught one of the projectiles and held it near the lamp. Even from her crouch near the back stairs Kinsie could see the flash of electric blue as the stone caught the light.

"Look, dude, it's raining jewels! We're rich!"

"I don't believe it!" The two of them scrambled around, grabbing the glittering gemstones and shoving them into their bag. "Look at these!" Kinsie saw something else, too, that made her freeze solid as ice.

"Dude?" the white guy asked, his voice constricted to a bare squeak. "Do you feel something hot on the back of your neck?"

"Uh-huh."

The two men stood up very, very slowly. Together, they turned around.

Looming over them was a scaly bronze head nearly the size of their bodies. Glowing red eyes the size of their heads stared down at them, watching, waiting. It tapped a gigantic, bronze and green foot on the floor. Once, twice, three times.

Feebly, the white guy offered it the sack of loot. It snorted, and actual flames shot out of its nostrils. The men backed away, stumbling on the heap of treasure. The dragon extended its long, snakelike neck and came after them. The floor shook with every step. Whipping the gun out of his pocket, the dude fired the whole clip of bullets straight at the dragon's chest. The giant beast staggered back a pace, then reared its head up to the ceiling, roaring. It lunged toward the men.

Kinsie gasped. Frilled, scaly ears perked up like a cat's. The huge head swung around to meet her, eye to eye. Then, one huge paw came sweeping around and scooped her up in its claws. Kinsie curled into a little ball, too scared to scream. The big paw kept moving up, up, *up*, then Kinsie felt herself tumble off the massive palm as it deposited her on the landing at the top of the stairs.

Kinsie sat on the small platform, gasping. Tears ran down her face. Her heart was beating hard enough to leap out of her chest. She'd been so frightened when that hand came around, but the dragon hadn't hurt her. It didn't do anything to her.

Then the screaming began. Two screams. Two men screaming. Screaming and screaming . . .

The noise galvanized Kinsie. She sprang to her feet and started pounding on Father Noe's apartment door with both fists.

"What? Who is there?" the old man asked, swinging the door open. Kinsie threw her arms around his waist and buried her face in his dressing gown. "God bless my soul."

The two of them got all the jewels picked up and hidden away before the cops got there. Noe bathed and bandaged the cuts on her hands, then Kinsie held the dust pan while Father Noe swept up broken glass. The bag of pictures was on the floor beside the front display case, and the broken hurricane lamp had spread glass and oil all over creation, but Kinsie didn't see a single sign of the intruders.

". . . I'm a very sound sleeper. The first thing I knew about the break-in was when this young lass here knocked on my door," Father Noe said, continuing to clean up while one of the cops took the report. "As you can see, there is a little damage, but nothing of value is missing. The thieves didn't get what they came for, I can assure you."

Kinsie bet they were assured. The screaming had been heard for a block in every direction, and so had the roaring and crashing noises. Everyone crowded into the little store, including the neighbors, her parents, and the police, were keeping a safe distance from Father Noe—everyone except Kinsie. As she saw it, the safest place to be was right next to him. The junior cop was a young Hispanic guy who lived above the dry cleaners a block down. He knew all the rumors about Abelard Noe, and Kinsie knew he believed them.

"I've gotta ask you, Father," the rookie said respectfully, because you didn't piss off a wizard, "did you magic those perps away somewhere?"

Father Noe stopped sweeping and put a hand on his heart. "I swear to you I did not take any action against them at all. May my magic turn against me if I did. I'm a peace-loving man. I am trying to prevent violence."

"Sure sounded like *someone* didn't mind a little violence," said the older cop, a heavyset black man. "We'll keep an eye out for anybody matching these guys' description, but if they're smart, they're in the next county." Of course, nobody who was standing in that shop at that moment thought the crooks were anywhere at all.

"They're in that dragon's belly," Kinsie said, accusingly, as soon as the cops went away.

"Were you watching?" Noe asked mildly, as he started putting his precious pictures back on the wall.

"No."

"Then how are you so certain? Do you want to ask him?"

"Not a chance." Kinsie looked around. "Where'd he go, anyway?"

"He's down in the cellar," the old wizard said.

"I've got to put him back before the meter reader comes tomorrow." He gave Kinsie a thoughtful look. "You can stay and watch, if you want. You've earned the privilege. I had no idea you were so heroic."

"Heroics are only something you do when you haven't got time to think," Kinsie said, wedging herself into a narrow corner behind Noe's easel as yard after yard of bronze muscle and fire wound its way up the basement steps and into the small confines of Father Noe's workroom.

Noe gathered up all the remaining lamps and turned them up to their brightest light. Kinsie could hardly breathe looking at the dragon. It was like special effects in a Hollywood movie, only it was right there, inches away from her, bigger than a truck. She could feel the heat from its breath. If she'd had the nerve, she could have reached out and touched it. She didn't dare.

She watched, terrified but fascinated, as Noe spread out the bags full of jewels and made the dragon lie down on them. He bullied it to do what he wanted, just the way he pushed her around when she sat for him. She didn't dare laugh, but it was funny. The old man was so tiny next to the dragon, who was so huge, but it listened to him as if he was its boss. Kinsie it treated with respectful disinterest. She'd found out that the Caldwurm was not a comfortable person to talk to. Kinsie had never entertained the notion for a moment that it was intelligent, let alone that it could talk. But tonight was a surprise all the way around.

"All right, if you insist, we can try a new pose," Noe was saying, as the dragon used the sword for a backscratcher. "Tch tch. Are you certain you want to go down into history this way?"

"Perhaps not," the deep voice rumbled, just at the bottom edge of sound. Thoughtfully, the dragon stuck the sword point down into the heap of treasure, then curled up like a cat, with its tail around the hilt.

"Very nice, very nice," Father Noe said, picking up his paintbrush. "Very artistic, and rather more comfortable than the last pose, don't you think?" He paused for a moment, raising his thumb to stare over it at the dragon. Then, muttering under his breath, he began to daub bright color on the new, pure white parchment sheet taped to his easel. As he painted each jewel, it vanished from the arrangement on the floor. Kinsie took in every moment as though she was being given a precious gift. Magic. She was seeing magic. When all of them were in place, he began to paint the dragon. Slowly, one scale at a time, the dragon faded from the pool of lamplight.

Just before it, too, vanished onto the parchment, Kinsie heard the dragon's deep voice rumbling.

"Thank you," it said.

"So how old are you really?" Kinsie asked. Noe detached the parchment from the easel. He fitted it into the frame with a new piece of glass.

The old man leaned back a little on his stool, looking up at the ceiling, the picture on his lap. "Nine hundred and sixty eight, next birthday. I prayed God would let me live until the day I can set my charges free. So far He has."

Kinsie no longer doubted his word. "And you

have all the magical monsters in the world on your walls?"

"Not all of them," Noe said. "Only the ones who thought they could bear the confinement. It's boring to be trapped in one's own world like that, bounded by the edges of the canvas. Many beasts chose death rather than preservation and uncertain revival. I know what history will say about me. They'll say that I made the choice for these noble creatures, took their free will away from them, but that's not true. I just had a better idea than extinction. The trouble with nature is that it doesn't always select for intelligence. We have to wait for our chance. I am sure the day will come when they can be free, even if I have to wait for centuries more."

Kinsie looked at the picture. She still loved the dragon, even though it had eaten two people. In her opinion, they had pretty much deserved it. She stroked the smooth frame, looked into the wise, red eyes.

Noe watched her thoughtfully for a moment, then patted her on the shoulder. "Ah, maybe I'm wrong. Perhaps that day is not so far away."

YES, VIRGINIA, THERE *IS* A UNICORN
by Von Jocks

Von Jocks believes in the magic of stories. She has written since she was five, publishing her first short story at the age of twelve in a local paper. Under the name Evelyn Vaughn she sold her first romantic suspense novel, *Waiting For The Wolf Moon,* to Silhouette Shadows in 1992. Three more books completed her "Circle Series" before the Shadows line closed. Her short fiction most recently appeared in *Dangerous Magic,* from DAW Books. The book was selected as one of the top 100 of the year by the New York City Public Library, and her story was nominated for a Sapphire Award. Von received her Master's Degree at the University of Texas in Arlington, writing her thesis on the history of the romance novel. An unapologetic TV addict, she resides in Texas with her cats and her imaginary friends and teaches junior-college English to support her writing habit . . . or vice versa.

The unicorn stared at the T-shirt.

The T-shirt—specifically, the big-eyed cartoon unicorn drawn on it—stared back. The unicorn's own reflection, white-maned and pearly horned, superimposed itself across the store's plate-glass window and the shirt within.

And the unicorn figurines.

And the unicorn calendars.

The unicorn sighed a snort of horsey resignation and shook his head, as though he were getting rid of flies. Not that fantasy creatures tempt flies, since flies were attracted to things on the *lower* end of the vibrational spectrum. Things on the *higher* end—unicorns, dragons, and the like—weren't even visible to human eyes without making an effort to become so.

At the moment, few humans passed by because the mall opened late on Sundays. The unicorn studied the display window of the gift-shop called The Maiden and the Unicorn a while longer. Votive-holding ceramic castles. Pewter wizards raising crystal balls aloft.

And unicorns.

Unicorn jewelry and stickers. Unicorn greeting cards and journals. Plush toy unicorns and unicorn hobby horses. Like a shrine . . . or a sanctuary.

He tossed his head again, satisfied. His long forelock, thick as a Shetland pony's, slid over one eye. It gave him a Veronica Lake kind of look, which he remembered from his days of monitoring the balconies of velvet-seated movie houses. Today, however, he meant to stand vigil over a different kind of innocence.

From the scent of fryers firing up, down by the food court, it was time to check out the covered parking.

Modern-day Maiden Patrol.

Kori appreciated the ride to work and all. She appreciated Tyler walking her to the store, too; the asphalt flooring and concrete supports where they parked echoed darkly, even at noon.

She didn't even mind Tyler looping his wiry, basketball-player arm around her waist as they walked, so that their hips bumped every few steps. But beyond that, the PDAs—or, to quote one of the snootier high school teachers, Public Displays of Affection—kind of embarrassed her.

"*Ty*-ler!" she chided under her breath, blushing, when he started kissing her neck before they even reached the shop. And not just because, with them still walking, his nose kept bumping her jaw. "Not *here*."

The manager across the way, rolling up the cage that protected his Discount Clothing displays overnight, pretended not to be watching them.

"Why not?" Tyler challenged, and nibbled at her earlobe. Unfortunately, he accidentally caught her earring in his teeth, and that hurt.

"*Stop* it!" Kori pulled away and glared at him.

He scowled back at her. "Geez, Kori. Grow up. If you're old enough to move away to college this fall . . ."

Tyler wanted her to attend the local community college—to stay with him. But Kori wanted . . . what?

Unsure, she dug out her key to The Maiden and the Unicorn. She liked that the owner, Dyann, trusted her enough to let her open the store.

"Look," she said, turning the key, opening the door, and punching in the correct code on the security keypad. A scent of candles and incense, as from a church, wafted out of the store and across them. "We've talked about this."

"All you ever want to *do* is talk."

Now he meant more than college, which wasn't fair. They'd done a *lot* more than talk. They just hadn't, well, done it *all*.

"I've got to get to work," she insisted, seeking refuge in responsibility. She turned on the lights. "Are you going to pick me up at six or not?"

"Why should I?" But now he was just being a big baby, and they both knew it. She waited for it to pass. He scowled, ducked his head, and muttered, "Whatever."

"Thank you," she said, and rose on her tiptoes to kiss him.

Tyler, being Tyler, made it more of a kiss. And it's not that Kori *minded*, really. Not even when he slipped his hands into her jeans pockets and flirted his tongue between her lips. . . .

Then Tyler lunged forward, right into her.

"Hey!" he exclaimed, as if *he* weren't the one who'd shoved *her* into the counter.

"Watch it!" she yelped. "Things are *breakable* in here!"

"Something *bit* me!" Tyler turned in a circle, as if trying to see his own rear-end.

"*What?*"

He glared at her, as if *she* were the crazy one.

"What do you mean, something bit you?"

"Right on the ass!"

"Oh, dear," said a third voice from the doorway, amused. "Well, this *is* a shop full of unicorns."

Wonderful. All Kori needed was her boss showing up. "Hi, Dyann," she said, blushing so hard her eyes almost watered.

"Hello, Kori. Tyler." Dyann came into the shop and circled behind the glass counter. "I thought I'd come in early, today, just in case . . . to catch up on work. Shall I run the tape?"

The store's old-fashioned cash register required that they print numbers at the start and end of each day to check against the till. Dyann was an old-fashioned lady in some ways but somehow timeless in others. Kori liked the tie-dyed dresses and flat, strappy sandals her boss wore in defiance of current fashion. She *really* liked Dyann's amiable simplicity.

But still, to be caught making out with her boyfriend instead of doing her job. . . .

"I can do it," Kori insisted.

"All right; I'll be in back." Dyann winked. "As you were."

"Hey, Mrs. Miro?" asked Tyler.

"It's *Ms.* Miro. Or just Dyann. No Mr. Miro in the picture."

Kori marveled at how easily Dyann confessed such a thing, since she had to be, like, forty or something. If *Kori* had never been married by that age, she wouldn't *admit* it.

Tyler once suggested maybe Dyann was gay. Kori knew it shouldn't matter . . . but she sometimes wondered too.

Now Tyler said, "What did you mean about the unicorns, Ms. Miro? What's that got to do with something biting me in the—"

Kori glared at him.

"In the butt?" he edited.

"It's part of the legend of the unicorn, Tyler. Supposedly . . ." But Dyann finally noticed Kori widening her eyes. "I'll let Kori tell you about it."

Kori wilted in relief. Not that Tyler hadn't probably *guessed* she was a virgin. They'd been going steady for half a year and hadn't done anything—or rather, hadn't done everything—but, still. . . .

She didn't want to, like, *advertise* it!

"Pay no attention. She's just being . . . Dyann," she hedged now, as her boss vanished through the curtained doorway into the back room. "Unicorns aren't. . . ."

But she couldn't finish. One of the weirder rules in Dyann's shop was that they were never to question the reality of unicorns out loud. Like maybe unicorns really did exist and spoken doubt would harm them, like Tinkerbell in *Peter Pan*.

"It's all part of some myth about unicorns not liking guys," she finished, only a half-truth. "That's all."

Something blew against her neck, the oddest sensation since Tyler was standing at least two feet from her. Clamping a hand to the ticklish spot, Kori now glanced over *her* shoulder.

Nothing—except, of course, castles and dragons and wizards. And shelf after shelf of unicorns. Nice enough, but hardly consequential.

Tyler frowned, shrugged. "Whatever," he said, rubbing his butt. "I'll catch you at six, 'kay?"

" 'Kay," she agreed.

But this time, aware of Dyann in back, they didn't kiss goodbye.

The unicorn followed Tyler to the covered parking, just to keep the boy paranoid. On his way back to the shop, he paused to snuffle a two-year-old in her big-wheeled walker, while her mom rested from another lap of mall exercise. How many unicorns did this baby's future hold . . . if any?

The child, who of course *could* see him, giggled. Then she tried to stuff her pacifier into his left nostril.

The unicorn nuzzled her, inhaling her sweet, innocent smell, before continuing onward, alert.

Something definitely felt suspicious, today. And not just because of the other, er, maiden.

"Look, Charlie," Bella said, as she pushed open the door from the parking lot with her hip before the guy chasing after her could get all chivalrous. "We had a nice night. I gave you a lift to the mall. I didn't say you could freakin' *stalk* me all day."

But when she turned toward the gift shop where she was working, Charlie trailed her like a damn puppy.

She was beginning to regret going home with him after the party. He'd looked a lot better after several Jello-shots; although, to be honest, he probably looked a lot worse through her resulting hangover.

At least, through some miracle, she'd remembered this guy's name. Not that she had much more use for it.

"C'mon, baby." Still following her, Charlie tried to sound winning, but only managing to sound whining. "You don't have to be at work *yet*, do you? We could have a burrito down at the food court, talk about us—"

Bella stopped and turned on him. So much for being nice. "*One*,"—she poked his muscle-shirted chest—"I'm nobody's *baby*. *Two*, mention food around me again and I *will* smack you, I swear to God. And *three*, there is no *us*. There's just you, going that way, and me, going this way. Got it?"

He blinked at her, like maybe he didn't get it. But

at least when she stalked off toward The Maiden and the Unicorn, he stayed where he was. Bella actually passed the gift store and turned a corner, counted to ten, then peeked to be sure he'd left.

Then she sank against the wall with relief.

She had to find herself a man. A *real* man. One who was great in the sack but didn't get all clingy during the day. These one-nighters were enough to drive her crazy.

But not as crazy as the sight of Little Mary Sunshine in the shop, when she went in. Wasn't that just peachy . . .

"Hi, Bella," greeted the perky blonde co-ed, looking up from a square of cloth the size of a beach towel. "I didn't know you were working today."

That makes us even. "Hey, Kori." Bella used her most friendly, phone-solicitor voice. "Dyann here?"

"In back."

"Thanks." She gave the kid a wave and a chummy grin as she passed, and an uncertain smile brushed Kori's lips in return.

As soon as Bella got in back, she dropped the grin. "What's *she* doing here?"

"Working." Dyann didn't look up from the papers she was examining at her cluttered little desk. Stacks of boxes encircled her like towers on a cardboard castle, a far more realistic castle than the inanity out front. "I'm going to be in and out today."

Normally, Dyann had either Bella helping her or Kori. Rarely both—and for obvious reasons.

"In and out doing what?" asked Bella.

Dyann, with the barest of smiles, said, "Stuff."

Generally, Bella liked Dyann. Dyann didn't take it personally when Bella flipped her off, like right now, for one thing. She was smart, easy-going, even worldly—*nothing* like the kind of woman Bella would imagine having a thing for unicorns, good men, and other fantasy creatures.

For that stereotype, Bella would have pictured Alice-in-Wonderland, out front.

"You *know* she drives me crazy!"

Dyann blew out through her lips. "Bella, I'm not up to this today. Live with it. And try not to bait her."

"*Me* bait *her*?"

But Dyann, at least, didn't take bait. She just looked back at her papers, frowning. "And wear one of the T-shirts. On the house. I don't think halter tops are really appropriate for our image."

Bella had showered at Charlie's place this morning. She wasn't a pig. But she'd been pretty much stuck with what she'd worn to last night's party.

Leather pants and a cutesy T-shirt. Talk about your fashion don't!

"Well," she muttered, "at least the kid's leaving in August, right?"

"Unless her boyfriend talks her into a local college."

Bella scowled. "You just love to torment me, don't you?"

Dyann smiled with an innocence that the co-ed out front could never have mimicked. A *knowing* innocence.

"So what's got you so busy today, anyway?" demanded Bella, propping a shoulder against the door-jamb. Usually Dyann loved being out front, dealing with the kids and kooks who frequented a store full of unicorns.

"You're stalling," said Dyann.

"You betcha."

When Dyann shooed her away with her papers, Bella went back out front.

"Hi, Kori," she repeated brightly. "Not even two months 'til you start college, huh? That must be pretty darned exciting."

Kori nodded, almost wary. *Great. So being friendly just scared the kid.*

Come to think of it, Bella only had three or four years on the "kid," tops.

"So what are you doing?" she persevered, selecting a purple T-shirt off the rack and coming around to where Suzy Sunshine was holding up what turned out to be some kind of faux tapestry.

"Dyann said to choose a piece to display. I thought maybe this one. Since it has a unicorn *and* a maiden."

The tapestry did have both; its medieval design showed the unicorn lying beside the maiden like a dog, his head—horn and all—resting across her lap.

Bella snorted.

"What?" asked Kori, suspicious.

"You gotta admit, it's kind of kinky," laughed Bella.

Kori stared at her.

"The horn," Bella clarified. "Right there on her lap."

Kori didn't even blink.

Bella rolled her eyes. "Geez! You are *such* a little virgin, aren't you?"

"And why would that matter to you, if I were?" demanded Kori.

Bella wanted to laugh again. Then she remembered that Kori's boyfriend wanted her to stay in town.

"Not to me," she said quickly, to Kori's visible surprise. "You go on and save yourself for marriage, and I bet everyone will be happier."

And then all the elves and pixies in Fairyland will hold hands and dance a magic dance in your honor. . . .

She saw Charlie, passing the windows, and dropped quickly behind the counter. While there, she pulled on the T-shirt, with its big-eyed, curly fore-locked cartoon unicorn.

The unicorn loved this old mall. He loved the smell of fries and pretzels and soft-serve yogurt, much of which got left out on tables where nobody noticed them vanishing. He loved the retired folks who came regularly, choosing familiarity over flash. He loved that most of the chain stores had moved out, leaving behind shops with less money but far more personality—health food emporiums, candle shops, used-book dealers, outlet stores. Safe harbors like this, in a world that focused too often on top dollars and bottom lines, didn't come along every decade.

Purse snatchers and pickpockets didn't last long around him. He'd become a legend among the occasional vandals who might otherwise have trashed the place. But his main job, of course, was protecting the maidens and their wares.

Which is why he followed Leo Denarri every step of the way in, from his parked Jaguar to the shop at the heart of sanctuary.

The Maiden and the Unicorn.

Denarri paused outside the door and glanced around with heavy-lidded, suspicious green eyes. He couldn't see the unicorn, of course. But he sensed it—as a hungry lion senses a gazelle.

The unicorn hovered mere feet from him. He'd seen too many of these daily battles to underestimate their power. Over the centuries he'd seen too many losses, no less heartbreaking for their small scale.

But this was the maidens' battle.

With an imperious grin, Denarri entered the shop.

Kori didn't notice the man until Bella moaned happily, as she might at the taste of a delicious cheesecake. Then Kori looked up, too.

Right off, she didn't like him.

The man appeared handsome enough, for someone closer to Dyann's age than her own. He stood tall, brawny, with thick tawny hair, tanned skin, and almond-shaped green eyes. But his smile seemed almost too white. Too toothy.

"May I help you?" Bella made it sound like a come-on. The way she folded her arms on the counter to lean nearer him clinched it.

The man propped his own arms inches from hers. "I'm *sure* you can," he purred.

"Just tell me what you're looking for," she teased back. "Unicorns, or maidens?"

Bella was such a slut. If "maiden" meant "virgin," she was just out of luck. Kori didn't have to speculate. Bella talked about her sex life whether you were interested in it or not.

Not that Kori was *entirely* uninterested. But this. . . .

She ducked into the back. "Dyann? There's a man out front, and . . ."

Then she didn't know what to say. Bella *was* waiting on him. So to speak . . . And he hadn't done anything threatening . . . yet . . .

But maybe Dyann read something in her voice, because she put down the phone, got up from her desk and went out front, touching reassurance onto Kori's shoulder as she passed.

The customer glanced right past Bella to Dyann. "Ms. Miro," he greeted in a deep, rumbling voice. "I'd hoped to find you here."

"Mr. Denarri," returned Kori's boss with amiable coolness. "You are persistent."

"Have you given any more thought to my offer?"

"No less than it deserves."

Bella leaned slowly back and murmured to Kori, "Do you have any idea what they're talking about?" Her breath smelled like cigarettes.

Kori shook her head.

"It's a once-in-a-lifetime opportunity," purred Mr. Denarri.

"Maybe I believe in reincarnation. There'll be other lifetimes."

He laughed a rumbling laugh. "I'll leave another benefits packet, just in case you change your mind."

"I won't," said Dyann. "And I already have three packets."

"Which means you aren't throwing them out." The big man laid a shiny cardstock folder on the counter, nodded at them, and strode out.

Kori hadn't realized how different the shop felt in his presence until he left, and the air stopped ringing. Imagination?

This was the shop for it, she guessed.

"Now *that*," sighed Bella, "is a *man*."

"Don't count on it." Dyann opened the folder, extracted what looked to be a carbon contract, and used their credit-card pen to draw a big "X" through each page.

When she noticed Kori staring, she quickly added, "More like shark, I'd say."

So why did Kori have the feeling she'd meant something more in line with the dragons and gargoyles perched around them?

"What's he selling anyway?" demanded Bella, and slid the folder away from Dyann. "Ooooh! The *supermall*? He wants this store at the new supermall?"

"Among other things."

Everybody knew about the new mall-and-entertainment complex being built across the highway and—conveniently for tax purposes—in a different township. It promised to be beautiful, three stories high with skylights and fountains and even a skating rink in the center. The very best department stores, from Nordstroms to Saks, were moving in, along with cutting-edge eateries and even—so went the rumor—a full-service spa. Its scheduled opening, in the autumn, promised to be such a local event that Tyler was using it to try to lure Kori into giving up her scholarship and staying in town.

She'd figured she could visit for a weekend, instead.

Bella said, "I didn't think *any* of the shops from this rat-trap were welcome there. You mean this guy's already handed you *three* contracts?"

"Most of it's advertisement," clarified Dyann. "The legal part's more like . . . contracting to be contracted. Sign away your autonomy on the dotted line, no blood required up front."

"Shit," marveled Bella, not quite drooling on the shiny floor plan. "What's not to like?"

And Kori, less distracted by Mr. Denarri's broad shoulders than by the increasing sense that something weird was afoot, said, "What *is* not to like, Dyann?"

But all Dyann said was, "Customer."

A preteen redhead towed her mother into the shop. The Maiden and the Unicorn did a lot of business with younger girls. "Can I help you?" greeted Kori.

"I want something that looks like the unicorn out front," announced the girl. "He's sooo cool."

Her mother looked perplexed. "You mean . . . the unicorn T-shirt in the window, like that nice lady's wearing?"

The girl shook her head.

"The unicorn lamp?"

"No, the *unicorn*. Just *outside*."

Even after several months working here, Kori hadn't gotten used to these "unicorn sightings," as Dyann called them. This one, however, tickled at the back of her neck. She slanted her gaze toward the magical creatures filling the shop—dragons and chimeras, winged horses and winged cats, and of course unicorns, painted on shirts and bags, made out of ceramic and crystal and plastic, pressed out of pewter and silver and gold.

She said what Dyann had taught her to say: "That's our store mascot; not everyone can see him. Even I haven't," she added, truthfully.

But for the first time, she wondered if maybe she wasn't just entertaining customers with that line.

Bella always knew Kori was a freak. She was one of those good-grades-in-school, did-what-her-parents-expected, dating-a-ballplayer-without-putting-out kind of teens. The kind who'd made Bella feel so substandard, back before she dropped out. The holier-than-thou kind that made her teeth ache.

But Kori rose a notch in freakdom when, after Dyann headed out to "check some stuff," she asked Bella, "Have you ever seen it?"

For a moment, Bella thought maybe Kori was talking about a certain male body part, which she'd *more* than seen, thank you very much. But she valiantly erred on the side of sweetness-and-light by asking, "Seen what?"

"The unicorn."

Bella laughed. Yeah. Right.

Kori frowned. "Remember the girl who came here, just after Mr. Denarri left?"

"Mmmm." Bella remembered Denarri, anyhow. He'd worn a suit that probably cost more than her car. That she didn't recognize his rich, warm aftershave probably meant it came from a pricy range, too. She'd secretly retrieved the man's business card from the trash, where Dyann had tossed it. Not that she meant to call him—if Denarri was Godiva chocolate, Bella was Nestle's Crunch. No way would she set herself up for that kind of brush-off. But she liked rolling his name through her head, anyway. *Leopold Denarri.*

Compared to him, Charlie-from-last-night seemed downright embarrassing—even if he'd finally stopped trolling the mall for her.

What possible reason could Dyann have for not jumping at the chance to associate with people like Denarri in the new mall?

"The redheaded girl," repeated Kori. "She saw the unicorn."

"Kid," said Bella with valiant patience, "you can't turn around in this store without seeing some freakin' useless unicorn."

"*The* unicorn," repeated Kori, and then Bella got it.

"Oh, please. You mean the, 'That was just our mascot, not everybody's able to see him' unicorn?"

Kori nodded.

Bella sighed. She didn't get paid for this. "Hey, college girl, newsflash. That's *make-believe*. Like the Tooth Fairy and the Easter Bunny and Santa Claus! There's *no such*—"

Kori widened her eyes, so Bella stopped midsentence. "What, you're gonna tattle to Dyann if I say it?"

"If it's only make-believe, why do so many of our customers see it? I've waited on at least four, and I've only been here since May."

"You might have noticed that the folks who see it are usually *children*." Although actually, now that Bella thought about it, she'd waited on some old blue-haired ladies who'd insisted they'd seen the unicorn out front, too. And a thirty-something businesswoman, even.

Not that it *meant* anything. But . . . "Anyway, no, I haven't seen it," answered Bella. "Besides, I'm out of the running. Even if they were real, only virgins can see unicorns."

Just as she'd hoped, Kori blushed.

"And you haven't? Why, *you little slut!*"

"Don't say that!" protested Kori.

"Way to go, Tyler!"

"*Stop it!*"

God, but it was too easy. "I'm just kidding. *Sheesh!* If there really were a unicorn around here—I mean, other than the *gobzillions* that surround us—I'm *sure* you'd see it, okay?" She didn't add, "You frigid little goody-two-shoes," but maybe her tone implied it.

Then Kori surprised her. "I don't see what's wrong with it, if I am."

"What—a virgin?!"

The kid didn't nod, but she didn't deny it either.

"I bet *Tyler* knows what's wrong with it," teased Bella. She'd seen Kori's boyfriend in the store before. He was cute in that bony, big-footed-puppy way that teenage boys had.

"Maybe it's not about Tyler."

"What, you think you're too good for him?"

"No! I just . . ." Kori took a deep breath. "Sometimes it seems people who sleep around want everyone to be doing it, so they don't have to feel bad, is all."

Who *sleep around . . . ?!*

"Trust me," said Bella. "If it feels bad, you're not doing it right."

Unfortunately for her fun, Dyann walked back in then. "Not doing what right?"

"Sex," answered Bella, while little Kori-kins blushed. Again. Maybe that's where all the blood went, if you didn't have sex like *normal people.*

Dyann sighed. "I told you not to bait her."

"She started it!"

"All I did—" Kori turned to Dyann, full of little-blonde-righteous-fury. "All I did was ask about the customers who see the unicorn. Is it true that only virgins can see them?"

"That's one legend," said Dyann slowly.

"Oh puh-leeze," sighed Bella, and dug into her purse. "I'm taking another smoke break now, okay?"

"But some of that depends on how you define a virgin," added Dyann, and Bella couldn't leave yet after all.

"Come *on*. What other definition is there? A virgin is a person who hasn't had sex, which in this day and age is as rare as a freakin' unicorn. A *technical* virgin is someone who's fooled around hot and heavy, but hasn't actually done it. And there's no such thing as a born-again virgin without expensive elective surgery, don't *even* ask. Now are you both up to speed here, or do I need to draw you some diagrams?"

Kori was pouting, honest-to-god. Dyann quirked an eyebrow, patiently waiting for Bella to finish. And all of a sudden, Bella couldn't stand being in this stupid little shop with all its useless, incredibly annoying *make-believe*.

Clutching her pack of cancer sticks, she stalked out—and bumped into someone, child-height. "Watch it," she snarled.

But when she looked down, she didn't see anyone or anything.

She hadn't imagined it. Her hip tingled, remembering the feel of muscled flesh against hers, but nobody stood anywhere near her. *What the—*

Through the display window, a cartoon unicorn on a T-shirt, big-eyed and swirly forelocked, seemed to be laughing at her, both from inside the store and reflected off her chest.

Bella hurried on outside to have her smoke.

* * *

The unicorn followed her.
So did Denarri.

"Why do people who sleep around get so angry if you don't?" asked Kori, watching Bella stalk out.

"Sleep around?" Dyann surprised her by laughing. "Generalizations are almost always illusions, Kori. Being well-adjusted may not require sex, but plenty of well-adjusted people do indulge."

And Kori asked something she'd never have thought she would dare. "Do you?"

"There are three things I never answer questions about," said Dyann, straightening a ceramic unicorn with gilt hooves. "My religion, my politics, and my sex life."

"I'm sorry—"

"Don't sweat it. A policy of discretion just seems the easiest way to keep stuff like the McCarthy hearings from happening again. You were asking about virgins and unicorns, right?"

Now it seemed foolish, but. . . . "You said there was another definition. . . ?"

"The one I like to go by dates back to ancient times, Rome or Greece or even before that. Back then, the word 'virgin' described a woman—or a goddess—who was whole unto herself, not owned by any man."

"*Owned?*" Kori screwed up her face.

"My opinion exactly," agreed Dyann.

"So it had nothing to do with sex?"

"Well . . . I wouldn't say *nothing*. I've read that when women in particular have sex, their brains release a hormone that sort of *imprints* the person they're with onto them. 'Oxy-something: they call it the 'cuddle hormone.' It forms a certain bond. Some women have no trouble moving on after its release—"

Like Bella, thought Kori.

"—but some women have a hard time even existing without a man, sex or no sex. Factor in the pair-bonding, and I doubt it would be easy for them to stay whole-unto-themselves after getting intimate, you know?"

Kori wondered which kind of woman she was. Maybe the point was to at least be sure of that before making irrevocable decisions. "That's a pretty old definition, though," she hedged.

"The unicorn," noted Dyann, "is a very, *very* old animal."

"So . . . you believe they're real," challenged Kori.

Dyann tried to laugh it off. "Virgins, or unicorns?"

And Kori whispered, "Both."

"Can I have a light?" asked a deliciously rumbly, male voice, and Bella looked up from the parking lot's pavement to behold the beauty that was Leopold Denarri.

"You can have anything you want," she teased, tossing him her lighter.

"I may take you up on that," he said, with a flash of white teeth. Despite the shadow of the covered parking, the flame from the lighter gilded his thick mane of hair, the glitter of his eyes.

"Promises, promises."

To her delight, he didn't toss the Bic back to her. He closed the space between them, his nearness warm against her skin, and pressed the lighter into her free hand. "I owe you," he purred.

"Damn straight," she breathed, tipping her head up to capture the kiss he was bending to give.

God, but he kissed beautifully. Somehow he surrounded her with himself, all fine fabric and expensive aftershave and thick, tawny hair and powerful, sensual lips. Within moments they'd dropped their cigarettes to clutch at each other instead. Within heartbeats, they'd moved on to groping. Everything Bella groped thrilled her, and everything *he* groped . . . well.

She'd never felt so turned on.

"C'mere," Denarri growled, drawing her physically around a concrete pillar, deeper into parking shadows. She went with him unquestioningly. She pretty much figured what he wanted, and she wanted it, too. Standing up. Here in the parking lot. Where they could be caught any minute.

She could think of nothing more exciting . . . as long as he wore a condom, anyway. She wasn't *stupid*, after all.

But then it happened. They were deep-kissing, caressing, her hand in his trousers and on his ass, his hand under her T-shirt and on her breast, getting to the really good stuff—

And he jumped. *"Shit!"* he roared.

"What?" It's not like he didn't want her. She could *feel* he wanted her. And she wanted him more, in that moment, than she could remember wanting anyone in a long, long time.

"Where the hell are you?" Denarri bellowed, scanning the parking lot around them as if looking for something.

And with the chilling thought that this guy was crazy, Bella wanted him less and less. "Ooookay," she murmured, backing toward the mall entrance. Once she came out from behind the support, she already felt safer. This mall might not do the business that the new one would, but there *were* people around.

Decent people.

"Wait," called Denarri immediately. "I apologize. I was—startled."

"Everything seemed pretty normal to me," said Bella. *Until you started yelling at nothingness.*

Still, when he grinned in that confident way he seemed to have, she found herself hesitating.

"I don't understand," he murmured—a brilliant stroke of vulnerability. "It's not like *you're* . . ."

And then he stopped, stared at her boobs. "Ahhh."

Strangely, he didn't say it in an admiring way or an upset way. More as if he'd just noticed something.

"What?" Bella looked down at her own chest, at the stupid cartoon unicorn displayed on it—and suddenly she got the weirdest feeling, deep inside her. As if things that shouldn't make sense . . . did.

Oh, crap.

"It's not like I'm a virgin," she whispered, finishing his sentence.

"What I meant to say," corrected Denarri, "is that it's not like you or your boss are going to get ahead in a place like this. I'm sure *you* recognize that you'd all be happier, and earn more, at the supermall."

But she wasn't going to be so easily seduced a second time. As long as she'd thought it was mere, mutual lust—well, who would have a problem with that? Other than the Little Mary Sunshine types like Kori? But Denarri wanted something else from her, something more, and it had to do with unicorns.

Dyann's unicorns.

"Not interested," said Bella.

"You haven't even heard the offer," he countered, with a winning grin. "Why don't I take you out to eat tonight, and we can talk it over at our, mmm, leisure?"

This sort of man would buy her steak and lobster, and he probably had a maid service providing him with clean sheets. This sort of man would be fall-down *great* between those sheets.

But he wanted something *other* than her.

"*Not interested*, asshole," snarled Bella.

It took all her not-inconsiderable courage to keep from running all the way back to the shop.

Kori was helping a teenaged boy choose a necklace for his girlfriend when Bella stalked back in and demanded, "What the *hell* is going on here?"

The boy jumped, startled. Kori was startled, too—but more by the wild look in Bella's mascaraed eyes, the way her lipstick had been smeared.

"Bella? Are you all right?"

"*Dyann!*"

"Never mind," said the boy, who'd already seemed nervous that someone might see him making such a "wussy" purchase.

"*DYANN!*" screamed Bella, again, so loudly that people across the way glanced toward their shop.

"She's not here," insisted Kori. She took one of Bella's hands. "What *happened* to you?"

"I believe I did," rumbled the answer from the doorway, and both women looked up at Mr. Denarri, in all his leonine presence.

"You get the hell away from me," warned Bella.

"It wasn't you I wanted in the first place," he purred pleasantly. "I'm afraid you were just a means to an end."

Again, Kori felt more was going on, in undercurrents and eddies, than she could wholly grasp. "What end?"

In answer, Denarri simply lifted a ceramic unicorn from its shelf, held it in front of his glittering green eyes, and dropped it to shatter on the floor.

Like broken shards of . . . hope.

"You broke it," noted Bella, "you bought it."

"If you would be so good as to intercede for me, I meant to buy it all," he said. "I can make it worth your while."

"Eat shit and die," said Bella, stepping more surely between Kori and Denarri. It occurred to Kori that, little though she liked Bella, she felt increasingly safe around her.

Even better was when Dyann announced from behind him, "You should know by now that I recruit *very* carefully."

But best of all, in a way both strange and perfectly natural, was what Kori saw standing beside Dyann when Denarri turned to glare at her.

"Holy shit," muttered Bella—*Bella!*—in disbelief.

The size of a small Arabian horse, the unicorn wore the same silvery white coat and thick, silver-shot mane and tail that so many of the ceramic statuettes duplicated. His horn reflected fluorescent light like a pearly seashell, and his long-lashed eyes, dark and rich, focused on one thing.

The intruder.

"Perhaps you do recruit well," granted that intruder. "More carefully than I'd estimated. But believe me, Ms. Miro, there is no way you can continue peddling this kind of fantasy indefinitely. Sooner or later, my forces *will* take you over, buy you out, or shut you down."

"If it were a fantasy," said Dyann, "then it wouldn't threaten you, now would it? But I'm not selling fantasies, Denarri; I'm selling an *ideal*. And we both know just how powerful ideals can be, don't we?"

"You haven't seen the last of me," growled Denarri, just like a movie villain.

But somehow, in the presence of an honest-to-god unicorn, he didn't seem nearly as overwhelming as before.

"I'll send you a bill," promised Dyann drily.

As Denarri stalked out, the unicorn turned and bit him on the butt. He jumped, looking around him, and Kori realized he couldn't even see the unicorn. But she didn't feel crazy because she could.

She felt special.

Bella didn't get it. She just *didn't*. "I can buy the kid, here, seeing unicorns," she admitted to Dyann, watching Kori feeding the unicorn Cheetos. "I can even sort of understand *you* having some special power . . . but *you're* not a virgin, are you? Or are you gay? Does that count?"

"No comment," said Dyann, slowly standing as she stared out the display window.

"She doesn't divulge politics or religion, either," clarified Kori, as if she knew Dyann oh-so-as-much-better than Bella did. Then again, they were all seeing unicorns. . . . Who was to define weirdness?

When the door opened, and a hot, dark-haired

man ducked in with a called "knock-knock," Dyann sure didn't greet him as a lesbian would. She walked right up to him, crumpled his shirt at each shoulder into two fists, and said, "You were supposed to be here *hours* ago."

"The plane got delayed," he admitted, an apology in his deep voice. "By the time we got to the airport, I figured it would be almost as fast to surprise you as to call. I'm sorry."

"You'd better be."

"Forgive me?"

And Bella guessed she did, because Dyann kissed him. But the *way* they kissed—

They started by simply savoring each other's gazes, each other's faces. Dyann continued gripping his shirt, and he looped his arms loosely around her, by no means groping—rather, cherishing. As if drawn, they leaned tentatively, intimately nearer. He ducked his head slightly, as if relishing the very nearness of her face against his. Her lips parted, only a breath, more as if to taste his scent and presence than for the kiss itself.

By time their lips touched, no matter how lightly, Bella thought she was going to melt.

"Doug," said Dyann afterward, her voice husky with satisfaction, "these are Bella and Kori. I've written you about them."

"Hello, ladies," he greeted, with a charming grin that worked its own kind of magic. Then, without actually looking at the unicorn, he said, "Hey, Spike, wherever-you-are."

The unicorn—*Spike?*—tossed his head up and down, as if in return greeting.

"Can you two close for me?" asked Dyann. "Doug and I have some catching up to do."

"Sure thing," said Kori. With a wave, Dyann and her lover headed out.

Bella just wasn't sure, for once in her life, whether they were lovers in bed . . . or something else. Maybe even something more, whatever that might be. *She* couldn't imagine not sleeping with a guy who kissed her like that.

Like she'd never dreamed of being kissed in her life.

But, for maybe the first time, it struck her that there might exist relationships so powerful as to render even the most mind-blowing sex a mere accessory.

Wow.

"I don't get it," she repeated, finally, after watching Kori start to run the closing tape. "I'm not supposed to be able to see any of this, much less be protected by it. Could the T-shirt make that big a difference?"

"Maybe," marveled Kori, looking around her at the tapestries, the figurines, the jewelry, the calendars. Unicorns upon unicorns upon unicorns. "Maybe it worked as a talisman, to remind people of the ideal—what unicorns can really mean."

Bella repeated one of Dyann's words. "The ideal."

"Yes, the ideal. Like . . . Santa Claus."

"Except this ideal is standing in front of us, swishing his tail and going by the name of Spike."

Spike bobbed his head in that lopey, springy nod horses have. His heavy forelock slid over one eye, making him look like an old-time movie actress.

"I guess he's okay with us seeing him now," decided Kori.

"Newsflash, Kori. I'm not a virgin."

Kori thought about that, long and hard. "I think we both have the potential to be."

Which didn't make sense, either. Except . . . Spike gave Bella a look that somehow made her glad to be just herself, by herself. For a change.

"If I call my boyfriend and break up with him, will you give me a ride home?" Kori asked: "I'll tell you what Dyann told me."

"Sure," agreed Bella. Maybe, just maybe, the kid might have something worthwhile to say.

"I think I'll buy a unicorn necklace before we go, though," added Kori quickly.

"Good idea."

"You never know."

But Bella wasn't sure she had to. "Buy two," she suggested.

Spike—he'd always liked Doug, and so liked the nickname—followed the maidens out of the closed shop, to make sure they got to Bella's car safely. They'd won today's battle, certainly.

But when one was an ideal, one remained vulnerable enough to merit constant vigilance. Ideals, like unicorns and dragons, existed on the higher end of the vibrational spectrum. It took a certain amount of effort from both observer and observee to remain evident.

That's why sanctuaries like Dyann's meant so much, with her sale of talismans for the best and strongest kinds of innocence. There could never be too many reminders of the ideal.

Although, trailing the maidens into the covered parking, Spike snorted his amusement at Bella's T-shirt talisman. The front, true, showed a big-eyed, cartoon unicorn, standard to the point of cliché.

And the back of the shirt showed a fat, swirly tailed, cartoon unicorn butt.

THE LAST FLIGHT
by Michelle West

Michelle West is the author of several novels, including *The Sacred Hunter* duology and *The Sun Sword* series, both published by DAW Books. She reviews books for the on-line column *First Contacts* and, less frequently, for *The Magazine of Fantasy & Science Fiction*. Other short fiction by her appears in *Black Cats and Broken Mirrors*, *Elf Magic*, *Olympus*, and *Alien Abductions*.

The old man sat on the park bench at twilight. It was the last time he would sit on this bench, the last time he would gaze at the cultivated grass, the empty flowerbeds, the deserted bike paths.

He faced this knowledge with a certainty born of experience. Tonight, no matter what happened, this place would be lost to him.

This place, and the company he kept.

His granddaughter sat by his side, her face adorned by a thin stream of tears. She did not know that this was the last time she would sit by his side, and he did not choose to enlighten her. She was grieving, and although the grief was fresh and the wound shallow compared to wounds she would take later in life, he offered her the respect that such pain was due. He did not ask her what troubled her; she did not volunteer the information. But she reached for his hand and gripped it tightly.

No one passed them. The path by their feet might have been a private place, and although the sounds of barking and conversation occasionally reached their ears, no one found them.

This was his retreat, his special place, this tame, contemporary stretch of cultivated land. He shared it with no one but her, and although he had also shared it with his wife, they had come in the day, when the sun was high, and the colors of fall touched everything.

He had said his last good-byes to his wife a decade past and had had no desire to share those colors with anyone else; but he had, over time, forgiven the universe for her abrupt departure, enough so that he could once again open his world to her granddaughter.

She was his princess. She had been his princess since the moment of her birth, although he had not been given permission to attend her laboring mother and had not in fact met her until hours later when, swaddled tightly in hospital towels the color of a wan sea, she had been placed in his arms. By her father.

Her father.

Her skin had been red, her hair a shock of black, her eyes the blue that only infants possess. Her fingers and toes had been tiny miracles of perfection. She had weighed so little, he could carry her in the palms of both his hands.

He had kissed her forehead. She had fallen asleep.

He could remember her as clearly in that minute as he could remember anything that had happened in his long life; photographs were less likely to hold a true image.

But it was not just images that he carried; he carried

the sound of her voice. She had learned to speak slowly, and most of her words in the first two years were carried by song. Her steps were a one-two dance, a drunken gaiety of motion that had gradually become as graceful as her exuberance allowed. He missed the awkwardness, the spontaneity, of that toddler. She had torn the curtain sheers twice in her attempt to gain balance and had broken many of his possessions: two picture frames, his favorite pipe, the pocket watch his dead wife had left him as a precious, lasting gift.

He carried it with him now although it no longer told time; its value was not in the time it told but in the time it told him of. After all, nothing was completely lost if he remembered.

He did not call her princess, of course; she had passed the age where such a name meant anything but childhood, and childhood, in the territory of her adolescence, was a thing to be shunned. The only way she might acknowledge the lure of that foreign country was this: she would reach for his hand, and he would, wordlessly, accept the request for what it was. He offered no comment, passed no judgment, offered no advice.

But he looked up at the stars, thinking that they had changed little over time but that they *had* changed.

The tears on the cheeks of his princess had not dried; every time they were almost gone, her eyes grew moist again. Her memories were not as muted as his, not as long; her longings were more visceral. She had entered the territory not of the very young but of youth, and she found that the landscape had unexpected chasms, painful bumps, small pockets of wasteland that seemed, while she crossed them, endless and unendurable.

His own youth had been scarred by such experiences too, but it was thankfully distant, and he had no desire to visit it again.

She did not apologize for her tears because he did not judge them. She could not imagine that they would hurt him because when he was with her, his own life existed, in her mind, as a union of their time together; it revolved around her, existed for her. And that was true.

But she had come, this evening, because he had called. He had phoned his son, to plead with him. To ask for his help in making an end to a very long, and very tired, life. Instead of the son—who he suspected was sitting rigid by the phone gazing at the displayed number—his granddaughter answered. She spared few words, but he knew the tone of her voice, and when he told her that he was feeling like a quiet walk and a think in the park, he knew she would come with him. If he asked.

She was young, and if the young could be cruel, they could also be generous in a way that involved the whole of their being; nothing was done in that vague realm of half-measures that was adult life.

Her father, he knew, was still waiting.

His son.

He lifted his hat off the bench and placed it firmly on her head. She pulled its faded rim down and slouched into wooden slats, understanding what he did not put into words: it was time to go. It was late.

He waited until she rose; the moon had moved across the sky before she angrily wiped her eyes with her long, pale sleeves. The night had a color scheme of its own, and the angry, brilliant shades of the day gave way to its imperative. Things were dim and quiet.

And he found that he liked the quiet; it contained

the companionable sounds of two sets of steps, both heavier than they usually were. She did not let go of his hand; he did not withdraw.

But he began to speak, in his rambling way.

"Do you see those trees?" He asked her quietly. They were distant now, but tall and slender, and as he followed the path that led past them, the moon shone through their naked branches as if they were a spinner's web.

"Home's the other way," she said, speaking for the first time in an hour.

He smiled. "True. But if you follow this path, it will lead you home as well. It takes longer, but it passes beneath the trees. I met your grandmother here."

She hesitated and then lowered her face so that he had a good view of the hat's brim. "How old were you when you met Nana?"

"I don't remember." He lied, of course; he did remember. "I'm not very good at remembering numbers or dates. Your grandmother was the one who always remembered the important ones."

"You're just like my dad."

He chuckled. "Maybe."

"Were you older than me?"

"I was much older than you. I think I've always been older than you."

He couldn't see her eyes; he knew she was rolling them. He wondered if he'd scared—or annoyed—her off speech, but after a moment she gamely continued. "Were you as old as my dad?"

He did not choose to answer. After a while, she shrugged and asked a different question. "Did you love her the first time you saw her?"

"I don't know."

"How can you *not* know?"

"Well . . . memory plays trick on people as old as I am."

"What do you mean?" Suspicious little question.

He smiled. "I mean that I have always remembered falling in love with her the moment I saw her, but because we ended up spending our lives together, it's almost natural that I would remember it that way. When two people are in love—and they're young—they can spend an awful lot of time talking about the first time they saw each other, and the first thing they thought, and the story probably changes a little each time they tell it.

"But the truth? As I said, I don't know. She was a sad little thing. It was raining, and she'd run all the way here from work."

"She worked?"

"It's not a crime."

"Well, no—I mean, *I'm* going to. But that was a long time ago. I thought women weren't allowed to work back then."

"Women have always been allowed to work if they had to. But most of those didn't get paid all that well. Your grandmother was from a poor family. Her father had been crippled in the war, and her mother had so many children at home—none of them died, not one, and back then, that was rare—that the oldest of the kids had to quit school to work so that the family could eat."

"That must have been a *long* time ago."

"It was a long time ago. But she came here, and no one came here, so I was naturally curious."

"What did you do?"

"Well, I was up in the tree at the time. I'd climbed it to get away from people."

She laughed because she didn't understand how true the words were. "You climbed a tree when you were an *adult*?"

"I was younger then, even if I was older than you are now. I'm good at hiding. I've always been good at hiding. But some people are better at finding things than others, and your grandmother, Prin—" He caught the offending word before it slid out. "Your grandmother was better at finding things than anyone I had ever met."

"Was she pretty?"

He knew that her image of his wife—bowed by age, hair a white shock of cropped salon curls, skin delicately lined and colored with liver spots—was hardly the one he held in his heart. But he said, "She was the most beautiful woman I think I have ever seen."

"Oh." The hat rim cocked to the side; he could see a hint of cheek and chin. "You must have fallen in love, then." It satisfied her; in love, as in all things, she was terribly extreme. That would change, given time, although the pain it took to change that would no doubt stay with her for a decade.

"She coaxed me out of the tree. It took her a long time."

"How long?"

"I don't remember."

Her snort was musical, which should have been impossible. They were almost there. He felt his age now, a great, terrible weight. He had never felt age so strongly before, and it was frightening.

Frightening and exhilarating. Only a few hours, a few more hours. Only that much time.

But his son, his son would know. His son would come.

He let himself shed tears, although he had made it a habit never to cry in front of his princess. Old, he could be—but weak?

To his great surprise, she squeezed his hands. He knew, by the way hers trembled that she was crying, too.

"It's very hard to be here," he told her quietly, "without your Nana. I loved her very, very much."

His granddaughter only barely believed in heaven, and her belief was such a secular, diffuse notion that it almost could not be called belief so much as desire.

He felt a pang of terrible guilt, followed by anger. He was not lying to her, and if he attempted to use her, to invoke a sense of fellowship, was that so wrong? He was tired.

"I know you don't really believe in religion," he said quietly, avoiding a question that might send her down the road of early teenage rationalism. "But creation is so vast and so incomprehensible that I believe that God *must* exist, and since he does, he must have taken my wife as quickly as he could, to be with him in heaven.

"And I hated him for it for a long, long time. But now, I think I'm grateful."

"Because you get to be together again."

"Because I get to see her again, yes."

She was very quiet. He thought she would lapse into her own pain and misery, for he knew that she cradled a broken heart in her small chest. But after a pause, she said, "Did you ever love anyone else?"

"You."

"Not *that* kind of love."

He chuckled again. "All love is good."

"But—that kind of love isn't nearly as important, don't you think? Not as important as finding the one person who'll be a part of your soul."

He did not point out that, as she didn't believe in God, the concept of a soul was pointless. Instead, he said, "One day, when you hold your first child in your arms, or your second, or your third—"

"I get it."

"One day, you'll know that it's just as important. But . . ." He lifted his head as the branches above them both shifted in the wind, bare of leaves, and waiting impatiently. For him. "But yes, little one, you are right. It is a different love. It is very, very strong. Look at me. Do you think I want to die?"

It had never occurred to her to ask the question; he could see that in her response. But after a while she said, "No."

"No?"

"No one wants to die."

"Do you think I wanted to get old?"

"No." That one took no time.

He smiled. "But I know that if I never aged, my children would never age; they would never grow. And I know that if I never died—" His voice broke for a moment. "Let me try this again. Your father, when he was a child, was terrified that Nana would die, or that I would, or that we both would, that we would die and leave him all alone.

"But when you were born, you became the most important person in his life, and although he still loved us, he understood that as you grew, we would grow older. The thought that anything would happen to you became much, much more terrifying for him

than the thought that anything would happen to us.
And he told us that. That he understood that losing
a child—any child—was the most terrible thing that
could happen to a parent. He was adult, but he knew
he was *our* baby, even if he'd gone and had one of
his own. So he promised us that he'd let us die before
he did, so we'd never have to suffer that loss."

He must have frowned, then, because her own expression changed. "Something happened. What?"

"Then your Nana pulled your father to one side, and
she told him a terrible story, my dear. In all the years
we lived together, your Nana was a brave and decent
woman. But she wasn't perfect, and she broke her
word that night. Just once, but that once was enough."

"What do you mean?"

"She told him our secret," he said sadly. They
were close enough to the tree that he could reach out
and touch its bark, but he hesitated a little longer.

"What secret?"

"It wouldn't be much of a secret if I told everyone,
would it now?"

"But she told Dad, right? So you could tell me."

"You're going to be a lawyer."

"Grandpa!"

"Why don't I finish the other story first?"

"You mean, about when you met?"

"Yes, that one. You asked me if I had ever loved
anyone else."

"Did you?" Her voice had gone quiet.

"Yes. Yes, before I met your grandmother."

"Oh."

He knew she was disappointed, because she
wanted some affirmation that love was a single,

thunderous strike that echoed forever in a life. "And before I met that woman, there was another."

"How many women were there?"

"Many, many women."

"*How* many?"

"I don't remember."

"*Grandfather!*"

"Hush."

"But—you couldn't have loved them all, could you? I mean, you must have loved Nana best."

"I loved them all."

He could feel the narrowing of her eyes in the chiselled sharpness of her words. "What about after Nana?"

"After Nana? No one but you."

"So she was finally the real thing." She put her foot between the exposed roots of the tree and wedged her shoe beneath a twisted, hard knot, balancing there. "What happened to the others?"

"They died," he told her quietly.

"I mean, why did you leave them?"

"They died."

"*All* of them?"

"Every single one. You must forgive me, but I am feeling sentimental, and I think I would like to climb this tree."

"What—right now?"

"Right now."

"I don't want to climb a tree."

"I didn't say I wanted you to climb it; I merely said that I would. This is where I met her. This is where my life started again."

The tree was old; he was old; he felt bark give way, like a crumbling tenement, in his hands. Almost nothing lived here. A bolt of lightning would destroy it utterly, if it knew where to hit.

"Grandpa," she said, her voice quivering slightly, "is this a good idea? That tree looks like it could fall down any time now."

"It could. But it won't."

"All right . . ."

"Your grandmother was a very practical woman, so I was a shock to her. She wasn't young—not nearly as young as you are now—and she wasn't, in her own mind, beautiful. Her sisters had all married, and so had all but one of her brothers, and she had consigned herself to the fate of a spinster."

"A spinster?"

"It's a useless old word. It just means that she realized that she would never find a husband or raise a family."

"Oh. You mean like me."

"Yes, a little like you feel now."

The branch he clutched groaned with his weight; he was heavy, inordinately heavy. He had forgotten how to fly.

He did not want to remember.

My son. . . .

"What happened?"

"She was standing beneath the tree, crying and swearing so loudly I couldn't sleep—and I had slept a long, long time."

"You slept in the *tree*?"

"Yes. In the tree."

"Why?"

"I was smaller then, and it was comfortable. Don't interrupt me; your father will be here soon, and I have to finish the story, because I want you to understand why you must stop him."

She was now confused.

She would not, of course, admit it—not yet.

"Finally, when I realized that she was somehow beneath my tree and that she would not stop, I told her to shut up and go some place else."

"*Grandpa!* You said—"

"I said that she was very beautiful when I first saw her, and she was—but I hadn't see her then. I heard her, and I did not want to wake. I wanted to sleep and forget."

"Forget what?"

"Forget my previous wife, my previous child."

"You had other children?"

"Yes. I'm sorry, Princess—" he paused to leave space for her usual response to the word, but she didn't offer it. "But it didn't seem important."

"Does—does Daddy know he has a brother or a sister?"

"Yes."

"Great. Why doesn't anyone ever tell *me* anything?"

"Because," he said, although his tone was so affectionate he hoped she would take no sting from the words, "you interrupt too often. Your grandmother heard me, because I was rude, and she looked up into the tree, and she saw me sitting in the branches."

"What did she say?"

"She was very, very surprised to see me there. She didn't say anything for a long time. An hour, maybe. She just stared."

"Why?"

"Because I looked very different, in the tree's branches. She asked me, after an hour, if I had spoken and if I had spoken to her, and I looked down at her and met her eyes, and although I was very, very tired, I nodded."

"What did she do?"

"She cried."

"Why?"

"Because she thought *I* was very beautiful."

The wrinkled nose was an artifact from the childhood he so missed.

"She came every day. She would not leave me be. There were leaves on this tree, back then. They were faded and dry, but they were still beautiful, and she loved them. We used to come here often, while she was still alive, just to look at this tree, and to remember the early days."

"But—but what happened?"

"She coaxed me out of the tree, and I came. I was tired, Princess. I was tired, and although she was beautiful, I did not love her for her beauty; I hated and feared her for it."

"I—I don't understand."

"No, I know. But . . . sometimes if you know, for certain, that you are going to lose something, you try very hard not to become attached to it, because you believe the pain will be less. I did not want to be with your grandmother, and I told her so, but she would not leave me alone, and in the end, because I was already tired at that point, she wore me down." He smiled, although he knew his granddaughter could no longer see his face. "I found happiness with her, and with our child, and our child's child. I am happy now, Princess. I am as happy as a man can be when his wife is dead, and his son is healthy, and his granddaughter is healthier yet."

The branches held him. He felt their creaking as a shudder of anticipation. *Old friend,* he thought, but he did not speak the words aloud; there was no need. *Maybe. Maybe this time.*

"I went home with your grandmother, and she taught me about her life, and she taught me all the rules she thought I needed to know—"

"What do you mean, she taught you the rules?"

"It is very easy to forget how to live with people," he said quietly. "If you hide from them for years. Now stop interrupting me—"

"I wouldn't, if you made more sense."

"—and in the end, when she asked me if I would stay with her, I said I would. But I made her promise that she would tell no one of where she had first met me, and of what—of what I had been."

"What do you mean?"

"So she agreed. And I changed, and I went with her to her father, and I asked for her hand in marriage. Her father did not like the look of me—I was awkward then—but he also knew that no one else had asked for this daughter and that maybe she would be happy. So he said yes, but he made us wait a full year before the wedding. He wanted his daughter to have to time to get to know my character, and if she discovered all the dark secrets of my past in that time, she could break the engagement and send me away with his blessing.

"So we waited a year, and then we married. I found a job, and I worked long hours, and three years after our marriage, your father was born. He was our only child."

He bent his head, grazed his forehead with the roughness of bark. The tree knew him, although it did not understand his shape. It arranged its multiple branches in layers, building a familiar nest: his resting place. The wood was pungent, sweet, the scent of it sharper than he remembered.

"Tonight," he told his granddaughter quietly, as he tried to arrange two legs and two arms into the folded wings that he remembered, "you were very, very sad."

She didn't answer.

"And I understand that sadness; you wept for the loss of love. Imagine, Princess, a life in which every person you love leaves you. Every single one. The first time it happens, it's terrible; you want to die from it just to stop the pain. But you have others who love you and others who depend on you, and you live because you must. You meet someone, years later, who touches you, who reminds you of the dead, and you fall in love again—

"And that person also dies."

It was terribly cold now; the moon in the trees was harsh and unforgiving.

He heard his granddaughter gasp as he sank into the curved walls of dry wood.

"Imagine that you have to live, over and over again, while everything you've ever loved passes away."

"G–grandpa?"

"I don't remember my childhood, Princess. Not my first childhood." His voice was thinner, higher. He folded his arms at the elbows as the elbows became pinions, spread his fingers wide as they blended in twilight and became smooth, hard flight feathers.

He knew that in the darkness he had none of his color, none of the reds and golds, none of the oranges, that were his by birth and nature, and he was happy for their absence.

"But I remember my first rebirth."

She was staring now. He stretched his long, slender neck and peered over the nest's wall, between the branches of the great tree, much as he'd peered first at his wife.

"I was happy to be young again. I was happy to be strong. I was happy to fly, and to feel no ache or pain when I took to the thermals. I loved the touch of fire, of flame, I loved the way it leaped across my skin, burning away the old and the decrepit, leaving just youth, only youth, behind."

"Grandpa—what are you?"

"I am," he told her softly, "Benu. I am Fenix. I am the firebird of old."

"Phoenix?"

"Yes, Princess."

"But—"

"Yes?"

"If you're—old—"

"Yes. This is my tree. If it is set on fire, it will burn, and I will burn with it, and age will be ashes and dust; out of the fire I will fly, and in my claws I will clench a sapling that the fire cannot burn, and I will plant it, and begin again."

"You'll be young again?"

"Yes."

She was a teenager; she wore a face that was not quite a child's face, but as that façade cracked, some sudden, sharp glimpse of wisdom and understanding could peer through, unfettered by experience.

"You remember all your wives."

"Yes, Princess. I'm sorry, but yes."

"And all you children?"

"Yes."

"And all your . . . all your grandchildren, too?"

"Yes."

"Did they all die?"

"Yes. Every one. Some quickly, some slowly. Some had forgotten me in their dwindling, but some remembered, and they hated me because they thought that it would be so wonderful to be young again, and I could give them nothing at all but the promise of death. There is only one phoenix."

"Are you dying?"

"Yes."

"And if I burn the tree, you'll live again?"

"Yes."

"You don't want me to burn the tree."

He wept. "No, child, I do not want you to burn the tree. I want you to remember me as I am. I want you to remember me as your Nana's husband, as your grandfather. Can you do that?"

"But you'll die!"

"Yes."

"And hope will die with you."

He wept again. Because he recognized the man his son had become. His wife's son.

His granddaughter turned, startled at the intrusion. She saw what he saw: her father, burdened by two large, metallic containers, one in either hand.

"Diana," his son said quietly, "it's time for you to go home." He walked to where she stood, and in the clear, full light of the silver moon, his face was cold as the stone that bore his mother's name.

"Daddy—"

"No. You listen to me, and you go home now."

"I don't want to go home."

"I don't have the time to argue with you."

"'Daddy—'"

"Son," the bird said, still weeping. The weariness was unbearable. He could not lift his head. "Do not do this."

His son flinched. His son, whose voice had once been so high and sweet, whose tears had been so precious. There was almost nothing of that child in his face. "I promised my mother that I would set you free."

"I desire freedom."

"You desire death. This is suicide. When the fires return you—"

"I will be young, yes, and you will be as you are, and I will watch you age and wither, I will watch you die. And I will watch my princess age, and wither, and I will watch her die."

"Can you not just wait? Can you not see that science has reached a point where *we* might catch up with you, where we might live forever by your side?"

"I have waited and waited and waited; I have built my pyre; I have fanned the flames. I have lived, and I have seen the rise and fall of gods. There is no altar upon which to lay my ashes. The halls of the dead are silent and empty, and no one waits within.

"Your mother promised me—"

"My mother loved you. She loved what you *are*."

"And I loved her. I loved her enough that I would never have forced her to bury you. I would never have forced your mother to bury your child. Burn the tree, and you will do that to me for half a millennium." He turned to his granddaughter. "She is waiting for me. Your Nana. She is waiting, and she will open her arms to catch me in flight when I ascend to her heaven.

"Will you keep us apart for eternity?"

He could see that she was crying again, and he knew that he had caused those tears. He almost stopped speaking because he had never been able to deny her anything she desired when she cried; that had been her mother's job, and her father's.

His son's.

"I don't want you to leave me," she whispered.

He closed his eyes.

Let his heavy head sink into the stale fragrance of an ancient tree.

He heard the scrape and creak of metal against metal; his son was struggling with the caps of the gas cans. He could not hear his granddaughter's voice at all.

"Diana, *go home*."

He waited for an argument to ensue; Diana was of an age where obedience came one step behind defiance—but she had to have that act of defiance as her opening move in any sequence of events.

But she did not argue. He heard her footsteps as she moved away from the tree. "Dad—"

"Are you crying?"

She didn't answer, or rather, she didn't answer in words he could hear. But he heard his son's breath stop for just a minute, and when it came again, it was on a heavy exhale. "He shouldn't have called tonight. I *told* you, honey, that he was really too tired for company."

Again, he expected sarcasm, something sharp and angry, from Diana's lips. But, again, she disappointed him.

"Why does he want to die?" She asked her father, as if his own explanation wasn't enough. "Daddy?"

Cloth rubbed against cloth; he thought that his son was hugging his granddaughter. His words were muffled. "Because he's selfish."

She was silent for a long time; too long. His son said, "Diana, if you won't leave, you won't leave. But we *don't* have much time left."

"But—if he lives forever why do we have to do this?"

"I don't know. Your Nana wasn't clear. She said— she said he was supposed to light the fire *himself*, at the appointed time. That's what he's always done before. But that if he didn't . . ."

If I didn't, I would not be reborn. The flames would not find me. The pyres would never be lit. I would be taken not by wind and heat, but by sleep and oblivion.

Yes.

"Daddy," she said quietly, "Why do you want him to stay?"

Her father hesitated a long time. And then, as if the question were an accusation—and a wild hope flared in the bird whose limp wings were so awkwardly folded—he said, "Not *now*, Diana. Call me whatever you want, but later, all right? If we don't finish this tonight, my father will be dead. Not sick, not sleeping, just *dead*. And it's not his—it's not his time."

It is never my time.

"Okay. Okay, Dad, but I don't want to watch. I'll meet you at home."

I heard her steps. She came up to the bark of the tree; her voice was caught in its broken folds. "Grandpa," she said, "Thank you. For listening. For being there. I'll miss you. I'll miss you a lot. But if there's really a heaven, and if Nana is really waiting for you—"

His voice was the barest of whispers, and he did not think she could hear his quiet *yes*?

"Tell her you have to wait for *me*, okay?"

And then she was off at a run, a wild, crazy run, her feet faster than heartbeats, faster than the wings of a tired, old bird.

He might have followed her on one last flight, but he did not have the strength. He regretted the lack.

He heard his son curse. His wife would have been upset at the ferocity of the word, had she lived. Would have been ever more upset to hear it repeated, over and over. He could not open an eye, could not look to see what had so aggravated his son.

But he heard the metallic clink of zippers; pocket zippers, he thought, being undone one by one.

For a minute, that sound grew louder, more frenzied, and then his son shouted a single word. *"DIANA!"* And ran in the same direction that Diana had run, at least by the sound of his footsteps.

But his steps were heavy, where hers had been light and fleet, and they did not travel nearly as far. They came back; they carried him back.

He came to stand at the base of the tree, or at least the sound of his feet stopped there, and they were replaced by other sounds; the grunt of strenuous breath, the crack and snap of old, dead wood, his son's swearing.

And he felt, to his alarm, the tree shaking as his son struggled to climb it.

It was dangerous. He wanted to tell the boy to stay out of the tree, and he did, but even he could barely hear the words; they would not carry.

"Why—" his son's voice was close now, punctuated by grunts, "did you even come here at all? Why did you come back to *this* tree, if you didn't want us to light the fire and set you free?"

Why, he thought, *do men die at all?*

But he said, simply, and because it was also true, "Because this was where I first met your mother."

He knew his son had heard him because there was a moment of silence, of stillness.

"I might have to apologize to Diana. If I don't kill her first. If you see Mom, tell her I'm sorry for failing her."

And then he felt his son's hands, and they were warm in a way that fire could never be; he heard his son's voice, breaking against the surface of syllables, and gathering again around them. The words themselves were lost; but the contact was not.

He was lifted, in those hands, those warm, gentle hands, as if on the wings of the flame, and he felt as weightless, as light, as he had felt during any of his births, and for as long as it lasted, he marveled at this last flight.

DESTINY
by Kristine Kathryn Rusch

Kristine Kathryn Rusch is an award-winning fiction writer. Her novella, *The Gallery of His Dreams,* won the *Locus Award* for best short fiction. Her body of fiction work won the 1991 John W. Campbell Award. She has been nominated for several dozen fiction awards, and her short work has been reprinted in six *Year's Best* collections. She has published twenty novels under her own name and has sold forty-one total, including pseudonymous books. Her novels have been published in seven languages and have spent several weeks on the *USA Today* and *The Wall Street Journal* bestseller lists. She has written a number of Star Trek novels with her husband, Dean Wesley Smith, including a book in this summer's crossover series called *New Earth*. She is the former editor of prestigious *The Magazine of Fantasy and Science Fiction,* wining a Hugo for her work there. Before that, she and Dean Wesley Smith started and ran Pulphouse Publishing, a science fiction and mystery press. She lives and works on the Oregon Coast. The main character of this story, Solanda, also appears in the five *Fey* novels: *Sacrifice, Changeling, Rival, Resistance, Victory.*

Solanda walked the cobblestone streets of Nir, the capital city of Nye, her tail up. She had a meeting with Rugar, the son of the Black King. He had sent a Wisp to find her, and it had taken the little creature nearly a day to do so.

Solanda was in her cat form, as she had been since the Fey captured this repressed country—and was thus very difficult to find. The Nyeians had many faults— they were prissy, overdressed, and pasty faced, not to mention abominably poor soldiers—but they did treat their animals well. She had found a family who fed her to excess, allowed her to roam outside, and pampered her as no cat should be pampered.

How appalled they would be if they ever discovered that the golden cat their daughter had adopted was really a Fey Shapeshifter.

Solanda's tail twitched once in amusement Every day she imagined eating her lovely tuna dinner in the glass plate that the family gave her and then Shifting into her Fey form just to say thank you.

She didn't know what would appall the Nyeians the most: the fact that she was Fey or the fact that she would be naked. She doubted any of them had seen a naked woman before: The wife managed to change her clothing one piece at a time, without ever taking it all off at once, and the husband didn't seem to think this unusual. He would probably be more shocked than his wife at the appearance of a naked Fey woman in his house. He would probably fall over in a dead faint.

Only the daughter, a girl of five, was redeemable. Esmerelda was a good child. She had to be. She was raised Neyian. Her mother trussed her in layers upon frothy layers of clothing, making movement nearly impossible, and then yelled at the poor child whenever she did something natural, like running.

Sometimes Solanda thought she went back to that

household at night because she felt sorry for the child. But in truth, she stayed there because they gave her fish properly deboned, and they brushed her, and they put a warm cedar bed in Esmerelda's room. Esmerelda, good child that she was, never confessed to her parents that she often picked up the cat and carried her to bed, cuddling with her long into the night.

And Solanda would never tell anyone—Fey or Nyeian—that sometimes she purred when she slept, pressed against the little girl's back.

Shifters were supposed to be the coldest of the Fey, the most fickle members of a warrior people, incapable of real emotion, flighty, restless and completely self-absorbed. They also were supposed to take on the characteristics of the animal they had chosen to Shift into, so Solanda's fickleness—theoretically—was doubly compounded by the fact that she had chosen the cat as her alternate Shape.

Of course, it didn't matter how many times she had proven herself trustworthy. In the war against Nye, such as it was, she had done intelligence for the Black King. She had worn her cat form and slinked into Nyeian villages, soldiers' camps, and mess halls, keeping her ears open and learning more than she should have.

Most countries that the Fey had fought had banned strange animals from military compounds. Solanda had heard that the Co had gone so far as to slaughter any strays, thinking they might be Fey reconnaissance. But the Nyeians had a fondness for cats, and while they kept stray dogs out of their camps, they fed cats on the side.

Solanda had spent most of the war as the pampered resident of a Nyeian general's tent. He used to feed her bits of meat off his own plate while telling his staff his battle plans for the next day.

And then when he fell into his snoring sleep, she would go to the nearest Shadowlands and inform the Fey general of all she had heard. Toward the end of the war, she reported directly to the Black King, who shook his head at the stupidity of the Nyeians.

Conquering Nye was the first step toward world dominion. The Black King didn't say that, but Solanda knew that was his goal. The Fey were a great warrior people, but they only owned half the world right now. The Black King—and the Black Throne—wanted all of it.

Solanda entered the merchant sector of Nir and silently cursed to herself. The merchants often shooed cats out of this area. Her presence here was suddenly noticeable, and she didn't dare Shift. She'd shock an entire community of Nyeians—which would probably be good for them.

Scents from the nearby vendor stalls caught her nose. Fried beef, more fish, some sort of vegetable something which turned her feline stomach. The fish was enticing. It almost made her forget that she was here because she had been summoned by the Black King's son.

Rugar had been her commander for part of the Nye campaign. He was an able warrior, frustrated under his father's tight leash. The problem with Rugar was that he believed himself to be the equal of his father, and he was not.

Solanda would rather work with the Black King, ruthless as he was, than with his less talented son.

The tall stone buildings prevented the sun from getting to the cobblestone. The stone was wet beneath her paws from the morning rain. The air was thick and muggy, making the six layers of clothes the Nyeians wore look even more uncomfortable.

The handful of Fey who were on the street wore their traditional uniform, a leather jerkin and pants. The Fey were so much taller than the Nyeians that even if they didn't dress differently, they would be noticeable.

She ducked under some clothing stalls, past the buildings that housed the year-round indoor merchants, and turned on the street that led to the Bank of Nye. The Black King had taken over the building. It was four stories of gray stone, towering over the buildings around it—as close to a palace as there was in Nye.

She sighed heavily and crossed the street, climbing up the stone steps and staring at the large stone door. She'd have to Shift just to get into the place.

Then she saw a nearby window ledge. The window was open. She leaped onto the ledge and jumped to the stone floor inside. She thought this building unusually cold for a Nyeian structure. The house where she was pampered was made of wood and had thick rugs on its floors. Every surface was soft, and the air was perfumed.

Here the air smelled like chalk, and the stone was chilly despite the heat. There were no guards in this room, although there should have been. It looked like someone's office—a desk in the center, chairs on the side for supplicants.

The door was open and led into a cavernous hallway. She heard voices and followed them. Several Fey guards huddled in an alcove. They were Infantry and young, tall even though they hadn't come into their magic yet. Their dark skin and black hair was a welcome sight. She'd gotten tired of looking at the pasty-faced Nyeians and hadn't realized how much she missed her own kind.

". . . fool's errand, don't you think?" One of the young men said.

"If it's so important, why doesn't the Black King go?" another asked.

"Blue Isle is important," said a young woman. "It's the only stop between here and Leut."

Leut was the continent on the other side of the Infrin Sea. The Black King wanted to go there more than anything. He wanted to conquer as much of the world as he could before he died.

"If we are going to conquer the world," the girl was saying, "we have to go through Blue Isle first."

"Then it doesn't make sense," the first man said. "Why send Rugar? He's not as good a commander as his father."

"Maybe," Solanda said in her most authoritative voice, "the best commander in the world has a plan that's too sophisticated for you to understand."

They all turned. They had similar upswept features, narrow faces, and pointed ears. Solanda had often thought that her people looked like foxes—most of them, anyway. Shifters, like her, often took some of the characteristics of their animals. Her hair and skin were more golden than dark, and she had the Shifter's mark on her chin—a birthmark that established who and what she was when she was in her Fey form.

But they couldn't tell now. All they could tell was that a cat had spoken to them.

"Well," she said, sitting on her haunches and wrapping her tail around her paws. "Where do I start? Do I reprimand you for gossiping in the middle of the day? Do I tell you that I got into the building through a window that some careless fool left open and, if I had been some young Nyeian bent on assassination, I could have walked right past you and you wouldn't have noticed? Or do I ask that one of you poor, magickless fools get me a robe so that I can have my meeting with Rugar?"

They didn't answer her. She raised her chin slightly. Amazing how she could intimidate them, even though she was so very small.

"By the Powers," she snapped. "Get me a robe. And put a guard on the window."

She nodded her head toward the room she had just come out of.

Two of the young men ran off toward the room. The third young man hurried off, presumably to get her a robe. That left the young woman.

"I really should report this," Solanda said. "Technically, you put the Black King's life in danger."

"From the Nyeians?" the young woman snorted. "You snarl at them and they run. They couldn't fight us in the war, and once they found out that they'd remain in charge of their businesses, they really didn't care that we took them over. Why would one of them try to get in here?"

"Revenge?" Solanda said. "We did, after all, slaughter half their army. Those young men were all related to someone."

"Then that should take away half the threat, shouldn't it?" the young woman said. "After all, the Nyeians believe that only men are capable of fighting."

Solanda felt amused. "I have a hunch that belief has changed since they were defeated by us. What's your name?"

"Licia," the girl said.

"You haven't come into your magic yet, have you?"

The girl straightened her shoulder. Magic was always a touchy subject with Infantry. They were tall enough to show that they would get magic, but chances were if they neared adulthood and still hadn't come into their magic, their abilities would be slight.

"No," she said.

"You showed a tactician's mind. Why do you waste it gossiping with people who aren't worthy of you?"

The girl straightened her shoulders. "I don't normally guard. I am usually in the field."

"But there's no field at the moment, is there?" Solanda said. "What are you doing here?"

"Rugar asked me to come. He says his daughter needs more swordfighting training."

Solanda narrowed her eyes. Jewel, Rugar's middle child, was the most promising of all his raggedy offspring. She hadn't come into her magic yet either, but her height and her heritage suggested when her magic came, it would be powerful. She was a good swordswoman now; Solanda had seen her fight in the last of the Nye campaign.

"Why would she need more training?"

Licia shrugged. "I suspect it has something to do with the fight Rugar had with his father this morning."

Solanda tilted her head to show her interest.

"They had left that room you came through. They were screaming at each other all morning long."

"About what?" Solanda asked, realizing that she was now gossiping. But she didn't want to go into a meeting with Rugar with less knowledge than he had.

"About going to Blue Isle. Rugar says he won't go without his daughter."

"Not his other children?"

"He didn't mention them." Then Licia smiled. "At least not at the top of his voice."

Solanda suppressed a sigh. The Black King favored Jewel. He felt that her brothers were idiots—and he was right. Their magic was slight, like their mother's had been. Rugar's entire life had been about defying his father. Rugar should have married a woman who had great magic. Instead, he had chosen someone he could control.

The young man returned with a flowing golden robe that was clearly of Nyeian origin. Solanda didn't ask where he had gotten it. She didn't thank him. Instead, she said, "Place it over me."

He did, blotting out the light. The robe smelled faintly of perfume and perspiration, but it clearly hadn't been worn in some time. The fabric was heavy satin—too heavy for a humid day like this—but she wasn't in a position to be choosy. If Rugar was planning something stupid, she wanted to meet him Fey to Fey. Psychologically, it gave her an advantage.

She Shifted, feeling her body slid into its familiar Fey form. Her body stretched and grew. Her tail and whiskers slid into her skin, her hair flowed down her back, her front paws became hands. She ended up in a sitting position, her knees drawn to her chest, the robe draped over her like a tent. Inwardly she sighed, and wished that there were a more dignified way of Shifting into clothes.

Then she slid her arms through the sleeves and her head through the neck hole, letting the stiff fabric flow around her. It was a woman's garment, although she had no idea why someone would store one in a bank—or perhaps she did, and didn't want to think about illicit affairs among Nyeian bankers.

She lifted her long hair out of the garment's neck and let it fall down her back. Licia bit her lower lip, and the other Fey looked down. They hadn't realized they were talking to the best Shifter in the Black King's army—at least, not until now.

Fools. Shifters were rare. How many of them would come into the Black King's dwelling and order Infantry around?

"Licia," she said, "announce me to Rugar."

The girl's skin colored slightly, but she moved in front of Solanda and led her down the hall. It got stuffier the farther in they went. Solanda was grateful that her feet were bare. The cool stone was going to keep her from melting in this robe.

Licia led her up a flight of stairs into a rabbit's warren of what had once been offices. Solanda smiled. Rugar was hidden here, in an obviously less desirable area of the building. The Black King had a thousand ways of showing his displeasure.

Licia knocked on a door at the end of the hall. Solanda stood far enough back that she wasn't visible from inside. She heard Rugar's gruff voice and then Licia's response, announcing her.

The door opened, and Licia stepped aside.

"I guess that means you're supposed to go in," she said.

Solanda stopped and put a hand on the girl's shoulder. She spoke softly so that Rugar couldn't hear. "If Rugar and his father are fighting," she said, "side with the old man. Rugar is not the future of this race. You're better off remaining in Nye with the Black King than going to Blue Isle with Rugar."

Licia nodded, then glanced over her shoulder as if she were afraid of Rugar. Solanda walked past her and through the open door.

Rugar stood in the center of the small room. He was medium height for a Fey, and his features had a predatory, hawklike look to them. His almond-shaped eyes were the deep black that Solanda associated with the Black Family. It was as if the Throne echoed in their very essence. He had thin cruel lips and an expression of permanent unhappiness.

For man in his fifties with grown children, he looked startlingly like a petulant child.

"You sent for me," she said, not disguising her lack of respect for him.

He clasped his hands behind his back, his father's favorite stance. "I'm taking an army to Blue Isle. You will be part of it."

She snorted. "I serve your father, not you."

Rugar glared at her. "He gave me permission to chose whomever I wanted from the standing armies in Nye."

"You have no need for a Shifter," she said. "Blue Isle is a tiny place, filled with religious fanatics who have never seen war. You'll sail in with your troops, wave a few swords, and be able to claim victory over an entire country in the space of a day. I'll be useless to you."

He shook his head. "I'm taking you and a lot of Spies and Doppelgängers. I am to be military governor of Blue Isle. My father will launch an attack from there onto Leut."

Solanda narrowed her eyes and was glad she wasn't in cat form. She probably would have found an excuse to scratch Rugar, and that wouldn't have been good for either of them.

"Spies, Doppelgängers, and a Shifter," she said. "It sounds like an intelligence force. You won't need it if you conquer the country as quickly as you believe you will."

His gaze went flat. "I will need it."

She stared at him for a moment. He knew something, and he wasn't going to share it with her. Spies made sense, even in an easily conquered country. They would find the pockets of resistance. But Doppelgängers had no place there. They killed their hosts and then took over the body, including the memories. Except for the gold flecks in the eyes, no one could tell them from their victims. Doppelgängers had a sophisticated magic, one that the best commanders used sparingly. And certainly didn't waste on an already conquered country.

"You have no need for me," she repeated. "I stay with the Black King."

"You'll come with me."

"Your father said so?"

"No, but he will."

"Because he already acquiesced on Jewel?"

Rugar started. He hadn't expected her to know that. Solanda raised her eyebrows and allowed herself a small smile. "I am good at gathering intelligence."

"And," he said, "as you pointed out, there's no need for intelligence gathering in a conquered country."

She nodded. "I'll go to Leut with your father, when he's ready. Until then, I'll relax here."

"Solanda—"

"Rugar," she said, holding up a hand. "You and I have no great liking for each other. I have a hunch your father is sending you to Blue Isle to get you out of his sight. I'd rather not be associated with you in any way. Right now, I hold your father's respect. I'd rather not change that."

Rugar took a step toward her. She could feel the violence shimmering in him.

She grabbed the door knob. "Touch me," she said, "and I'll scratch out your eyes."

"You can't touch me. I'm a member of the Black Family."

She smiled. "I'm a Shifter. Unpredictable, irresponsible, flighty—remember? I'm sure the Powers would let this slide."

"But my father would not," Rugar said.

"Oh," Solanda said softly, "but I think he would."

She tried to see the Black King before she left the building, but he was nowhere to be found. His personal guards were gone as well. She decided she would find him in the morning, and she went back to her life as a pampered Nyeian cat.

The home that she had chosen was a large one on the outskirts of Nir. It had two stories filled with more clutter than any home she had ever seen. Books of poetry, musical instruments, incredibly ugly paintings, and furniture everywhere. The only saving grace was that the furniture was comfortable and the kitchen had a cat door that she could escape through when the wife decided it was time for music.

Solanda slipped through the cat door, past the kitchen hearth. One of the three Nyeian servants was cleaning the pots from the evening meal. The air smelled faintly of roast beef, and Solanda's stomach rumbled.

Still, she didn't beg from the servant. She knew

better. The idiot had kicked her "accidentally" once, and had the scars to prove it. But Solanda knew that if she attacked anyone in the house too many times, she would be thrown out, and she wasn't willing to lose her rich dinners and soft bed just yet.

She blended into the hideous yellow wallpaper as she hurried up the stairs to Esmerelda's room.

Esmerelda sat on the edge of the bed, fingering a rip in her dress. She had a forlorn expression on her small face. Her brown hair hung limply around her cheeks, and a streak of dirt covered the pantaloons beneath the skirt.

Solanda had never seen Esmerelda look dirty before, nor had she seen the girl's hair loose at any time except bedtime.

"Oh, Goldie!" Esmerelda raised her voice in relief. She was speaking Nye, which was a language that Solanda hadn't known well when she moved into this house. Here her Nye had improved greatly, but she wanted to be fluent in it by the time she left.

The little girl launched herself off the bed and grabbed Solanda before Solanda could jump out of the way. Esmerelda wrapped her arms around Solanda and held tightly. Esmerelda had never done that before. If she had been a grabby little girl, Solanda would have been gone a long time ago.

So this meant, quite simply, that something was wrong.

Solanda let herself be held for a moment, then she turned her head toward the door and flattened her ears. Esmeralda, smart child that she was, understood both signals. She pushed the door closed, and then let Solanda go.

Solanda jumped on the windowsill. Esmerelda followed her, but didn't open the window like she usually did.

The room was hot and sticky. Solanda wouldn't be able to stay here too long if that window wasn't opened.

"I don't dare," Esmerelda said softly. "Mommy's really mad at me. She didn't even let me have dinner."

Now Solanda was interested, but she didn't want the story, not yet. She bumped her head against the window's bubbled glass.

Esmerelda bit her lower lip and shook her head.

Solanda placed a paw on the glass and meowed softly.

"Okay," Esmerelda whispered. "But if anyone comes, I'll have to close it."

Solanda almost nodded, then caught herself. When Esmerelda came close, Solanda bumped her affectionately with her head, and then watched as the little girl pulled the window open.

A cool breeze made its way inside. That was the other nice thing about this house. Esmerelda's room opened onto a large undeveloped area, so the smells of the outdoors came in strong. Breezes were unencumbered. Esmerelda's mother hated this, and often wished for close neighbors, but Solanda saw it for the blessing it was.

Esmerelda knelt down beside the window and put her elbows on the sill. She didn't touch Solanda, but she was still a bit too close. Her body heat was ruining the breeze.

"I been so bad," she said, "I won't get to go outside ever again."

Solanda watched her. The little girl had never been

able to resist a cat's gaze. Solanda had never been a child who was so very lonely. Esmerelda wasn't allowed to play—except with dolls with clothes as frilly as the stuff she was trussed in—nor was she allowed to associate with the neighboring children who were, in her parents' mind, beneath her. She had lessons in poetry and music, art and dancing, but she liked none of it. What she really wanted to do was run as far as she could, and climb trees, and learn how to swim.

She'd probably never get to achieve those goals.

"I was running this afternoon," Esmerelda said. Her face was wistful. She leaned her forehead against the glass. "Mommy was looking at fruit, and I thought I could just go around the block, but she saw me. I guess she followed me."

Esmerelda had done this before, and it hadn't gotten her sent to bed with no supper. Solanda suspected the problem had something to do with the rip in the dress. Clothing was sacred, at least to this family. Solanda wanted to tear every piece so that this little girl could be free.

"She saw me fall." Esmerelda said, fingering her skirt. "She saw me hit a Fey."

Solanda stiffened. She almost asked who, and caught herself. Two near lapses in one conversation. She was getting much too relaxed with this child.

Esmerelda ran a soft hand over Solanda's head. Her touch was gentle again, as it had always been before.

"She said she was the Black King's granddaughter, and she yelled at Mommy for dressing me the way she did. And Mommy yelled back. The lady said yelling at her was like yelling at all the Fey all at once."

Only one Fey woman could make that claim. Jewel. No wonder Esmerelda's mother was upset.

"And then Mommy told Daddy, and he said that the Fey might hurt us. Because I ran." A tear coursed down Esmerelda's cheek.

And those fools were blaming the child for being a child. Solanda pushed against the girl's hand, and Esmerelda sniffled.

"I didn't mean to run. I just can't stay still sometimes."

Solanda understood that. She could never stay still. It was a curse of being a Shifter. It was the reason Fey wisdom said that Shifters were the most heartless of the Fey. Most Shifters did not have children, and most rarely stayed anywhere long enough to form a real relationship.

Esmerelda sighed. "I wish I was like you. I could do what I want. Or like that Fey lady. She was nice to me. She didn't like Mommy, though."

Neither did Solanda.

"She said children shouldn't be dressed like me. She said I ran into her because my clothes didn't let me run properly."

Probably true, Solanda thought.

"And that made Mommy really mad."

Esmerelda let her hand slide off Solanda's neck. She bunched her hands into fists and rested her chin on them, looking fierce and strong. Solanda felt her whiskers twitch in amusement. One day, Esmerelda's parents would no longer be able to control this child. If she was this strong, articulate, and intelligent at five, she would be impossible to control at fifteen.

Especially with all of the Fey influence around her.

"I wish I had magic," the little girl said. "Just a little

bit. Then I could run and no one would know. I'd make myself invisible, and no one would see me."

Solanda looked out the window, knowing her expression was too sympathetic for a cat. There was a ring of oaks at the edge of the lawn. They were blowing in the breeze. Maybe there would be another storm. Maybe this storm would finally cool the place off, although she doubted it. Nye's hot season was the worst she had encountered in any country she had ever been in.

'Esmerelda!" her mother's voice echoed from the hallway. "Why is your door closed?"

Esmerelda gasped and pulled down the window so quickly she almost caught Solanda's tail in it. Then she leaped onto the bed, stretching out. Solanda jumped beside her and curled up at her feet just as Esmerelda's mother opened the door.

The woman's face was flushed. She looked like a tomato about to burst. She was so tightly corseted that her body looked flat, and Solanda wondered how the woman could even breathe. She wore an evening dress of white satin that accented the redness of her face. The sides were lined with sweat.

"What are you doing?" she asked. Then she frowned. "How did that mangy cat get in here?"

Solanda growled softly in the back of her throat. She was not mangy. And the woman had never called her that before.

"I told you that you were supposed to be in here by yourself to think about what you did today. Things could have been much worse. Fortunately, she was in good mood. You know what those people can do? Why, it's said they can cut the skin off a person with the flick of—"

Solanda yowled, and the woman stepped back, a hand over her heart. Esmerelda sat up, worry on her small face.

"Are you okay, Goldie?"

Solanda kicked her right paw as if she had twisted it. She was not going to let that woman tell this little girl about Fey atrocities—even if they were true.

"Come on, Goldie," Esmerelda's mother said. "There's some beef for you in the kitchen."

Usually that would have gotten Solanda off the bed. But she could sneak down after everyone was asleep and take what she needed. Right now, she wanted to stay beside Esmerelda.

"Goldie," the woman said.

Esmerelda, good child that she was, bit her lower lip and said nothing. She didn't beg for the company that she obviously wanted.

"Goldie!" her mother sounded exasperated now. Then she shook her head. "Why do we put up with this animal?"

Neither Solanda nor Esmerelda answered.

Finally Esmerelda's mother sighed. "All right, she can stay. But I do expect you to sleep in that dress tonight and to think about how you could have hurt us all. That rip should be a reminder of the danger your misbehavior put us in. Nye isn't the place it used to be, child. Do something wrong, and those Fey will harm all of us."

Then she pulled the door closed, and Solanda heard the boards creak as the woman made her way down the stairs.

Esmerelda's fingers played with the rip. Solanda looked at it, then crossed the bed, took the skirt in her teeth and pulled. The rip grew. Esmerelda giggled, then covered her mouth. Solanda pulled harder. If the little girl had to sleep in these clothes, she might as well be comfortable.

Esmerelda ripped the pantaloons too, along the dirt line, giggling as she did so. "Mommy will think I did it when I was running," she said. "You're so smart, Goldie."

Of course she was. Solanda preened and allowed herself to be petted one more time.

Then Esmerelda looked at the door, her smile fading. "Sometimes I think Mommy doesn't want me. She wants somebody else. Somebody perfect."

Too bad she didn't realize that the child she had was better than perfect. Solanda sighed softly. Some people had more than they deserved.

The idea came to her in the middle of the night, in that hot and stuffy room. She could take Esmerelda away, and Esmerelda's parents wouldn't even know it had happened. But it would take the cooperation of the Fey Domestics.

Fey magic was divided into two parts: warrior and domestic. Warrior magic was designed for warfare. Some Fey magic turned its practitioner into a weapon, like the Foot Soldiers who had fingernails that could slice better than a blade. Domestic magic could not be used to fight any war. Domestics lost their magic if they killed. Their magics were healing magics or home-bound magics, such as spells that made chairs more inviting or fires warmer.

The next morning, after making certain that Esmerelda got breakfast, Solanda slipped out the cat door. She went to the Domicile that the Fey Domestics had set up just outside of town. The Domicile had been built especially for the Domestics, and covered with various protection and healing spells. It was a traditional U shaped building, with hearth and home magics on one length of the U, the healing wards in the other, and the middle section as a meeting place in between.

Solanda usually didn't seek out the Domestics. They always wanted to experiment with her—have her try on a new cloak covered with some sort of rain protection or have her taste a new food to see if it had an effect on her Shifting. The last time she had been in a Domicile had been when she had broken a paw jumping from a tree in one of the last Nye battles. The Domestics had mended the bone and had given her a smelly ointment she had to apply in cat form. She had thought the stench alone would kill her.

As she mounted the steps to the center part of the building, she shook off her paws. Here she would not Shift to Fey form. The Domestics weren't as obsessed with power as Rugar was, so she didn't have to use her height as a reminder of the strength of her magic.

She pushed open the door and stepped inside.

The air was cool and welcoming. It smelled of a sea breeze. Bits of magic floated in the air. Spinner's magic. They were working on their looms. She could hear the hum just down the corridor.

A Baker entered, his fingers dusted with flour. They glowed. And she knew he had spelled the bread he'd been baking to remain fresh for as long as possible. It was a traveling spell, one most often used when troops were heading off to battle. She wondered if someone had requested it.

"I'm here to see Chadn."

The Baker nodded, then slipped through a door that led to the Healing part of the Domicile. Solanda hopped onto a chair. Her mood rose and she cursed, jumping down. She didn't need to be spelled to wait, happy and contented, on a chair dusted with Domestic magic. Instead she paced the cool floor and wondered why she couldn't smell the baking bread.

Finally Chadn entered the room. She was a young Shaman, although the toll of her power had already turned her hair white. Her face was wizened, her mouth a small oval amid wrinkles. Only her eyes were bright—sparkling black circles of light in a ruined face.

She had been assigned to stay with Rugar during the war, and she was happy to be free of him. Shaman were the most independent Fey: their Vision as strong as those of the Leaders, but their magic Domestic so they could not rule a warrior people. They were the wise ones, the advisors, supposedly the strength behind the Black Throne. The Black King required his son to have a Shaman, but he did not use one himself. He had dismissed his own Shaman, years ago, for disobeying him. It was one of many areas where the Black King broke with tradition.

"Solanda," Chadn said. "I had hoped to see you."

Solanda jumped on an end table and was relieved that her mood did not change. She sat on her haunches and looked into Chadn's face.

"I have a request," she said. "It's for a Nyeian child."

"A child?" Chadn sounded surprised. "And not a Fey child?"

Solanda shook her head.

"I had Seen you with a Fey child."

The Shamans' Visions—and the Vision that leaders like the Black King had—allowed them glimpses into the future. Some said that the glimpses allowed the Visionary to change the future. Others believed that the glimpses led the visionary to that future.

Solanda's eyes narrowed. "I have not been with a Fey child."

Chadn nodded. "It was on Blue Isle. The child was a Shifter, and you kept her from death."

Solanda's whiskers twitched. "I told Rugar I would not go to Blue Isle with him."

"The future of our people lies with you, Solanda."

"And a child?" Solanda raised her chin. "Are you sure it was a Fey child?"

"Not entirely," Chadn said. "The child had blue eyes."

Solanda gave a soft grunt of surprise. She had heard of blue-eyed people, but she had never seen one. "The child couldn't be Nyeian?"

"She was Fey, and newborn. She had a birthmark on her chin. Only her eyes were strange, and perhaps that was because of the Shifting. I Saw you put your hands on her lips and swear to protect her, raise her, and make her strong. Then I Saw her full grown, saying you had been the closest thing she had to a mother."

Solanda laughed, although inside she felt cold. A Shifter only sore to protect a child who he'd the future of the Empire. A blue-eyed child that Shifted? The center of the Empire?

"Visions can be altered," Solanda said. "I am not leaving Nye."

"You may have no choice."

"I'll always have a choice," Solanda said.

Chadn inclined her head toward Solanda as if giving in on that point. "What does the Nyeian child need?"

Solanda took a deep breath. "She is different from any other Nyeian I've seen. Strong, independent. She met Jewel yesterday and is being punished for it. I would like to remove the child from her family and bring her here, to be raised among us. She will be useful when she's grown. She will be part of the second generation, the Nyeians that rule Nye for the Fey."

Chadn stared at her for a moment. "So take her. Shifters steal children."

"This one's mother will raise a fuss if she's gone."

"What mother wouldn't?"

"She'll come to us."

"And you can't prove to the black King that we must keep the child."

"Not yet, anyway," Solanda said.

Chadn folded her hands over her stomach. "You want a Changeling."

"Yes," Solanda said.

"How old is the child?"

"Five."

Chadn sighed. "Have you asked the child if she's willing to leave?"

"Not yet. I wanted to know if I have help first."

"You will keep the child at your side?"

Solanda frowned. That wasn't a normal request. Shifters rarely kept children. They usually brought them to Domestics to raise. "Must I?"

"At five, it will be you she trusts."

Solanda shrugged. "Then she shall stay with me."

"And you will stay away from Blue Isle." Chadn said that not as a question, but as a statement.

"Rugar will not let a Nyeian child in his war party."

"So the child serves two purposes." Chadn's eyes narrowed. "Has she magic?"

"Of course not." Solanda laughed. "There is not magic outside the Fey."

Chadn frowned. "I am no longer certain of that."

"Because you Saw a blue-eyed Shifter?"

"Because I Saw a great war, coming when we least expect it."

"War is part of Fey life." Solanda jumped off the table and headed for the door. "I'll bring you news of the child tomorrow."

"I'll have Changeling stone ready," Chadn said. "But realize before you act, that this is for life."

"I already know that," Solanda said. "I have chosen well."

"I hope so," Chadn said.

Solanda went to the docks and sat on a fence. She loved it here. The Infrin Sea formed the most natural harbor on Galinas, and there was always some sort of activity. Toward the north end of the harbor, the Nyeian builders made the great ships. Those ships traveled all over the known world, and now Fey Domestics helped unload cargo that would go all over the Empire.

Ships from Blue Isle had stopped coming to Nye when news reached them of the Fey takeover. She would never see an Islander, never learn more about them than she already had.

And that would be all right.

For there were some things she couldn't discuss with Rugar's Shaman. Like the prophecies that had been made by another shaman at Solanda's birth, prophecies that claimed her legacy would be in the children she saved.

Children—not child, like Chadn had seen. Solanda would influence the life of more than one.

The breeze was cooler here, carrying with it the smell of salt and a tinge of dead fish. That smell made her stomach rumble. She tried not to think of the things she ate in her cat form, things she would find disgusting when she was in Fey form. Right now, raw dead fish sounded extremely appetizing.

But she didn't to in search of the source of the smell. She had some thinking to do. Prophecies and Visions made her nervous. She had no idea what to do with the information Chadn had given her. Because, at various points in her life, Solanda had been told by Visionaries that her future held contradictory things.

One Shaman had told her she had to avoid the Black Family for she would kill a Black Heir. Another Shaman had told her she would raise a Black Heir. And now Chadn had Seen her swear to protect a blue-eyed Shifter, a newborn who couldn't survive on her own.

Solanda bowed her head. The prophecy she never mentioned, the one her parents had kept silent, had come the day of her birth and she had never forgotten it. The prophecy was a cold one: she would die before her time, far from home, for a crime she did not regret.

The Fey did not believe in crime. They were constantly at war, so the crimes that plagued other races—murder, theft—were absorbed into the wars themselves. The Fey only punished two crimes: treason and failure. Both of those crimes were considered crimes against the Empire. Failure was a large crime, encompassing the failure to follow an order or the failure to defeat an enemy in a prolonged battle.

Treason was any crime against the Black Family and was such a heresy that it wasn't even discussed among rational Fey.

Both crimes bore the penalty of death.

It seemed to her that she would never commit crimes like that, that the prophecies had come because she was a Shifter, not because of her character. She wasn't as flighty or as difficult as anyone said she was.

And besides, she had to take care of Esmerelda.

She wished she could be there the morning that Esmerelda's parents discovered the Changeling. It would look like Esmerelda, even act like her—if stone could act like a living breathing creature. But it would only last a few days, and then it would cease to exist. They would think Esmerelda dead, when, in actuality, she was only gone.

Then, perhaps, that wretch of a mother would regret how she treated her daughter.

Esmerelda would live a life she couldn't even imagine now. She wouldn't have to wear six layers of clothes on the hottest day of the year, and she would learn how to live life to its fullest instead of remaining indoors and studying all the time.

Esmerelda would be the closest thing to Fey that a Nyeian could be, and for the first time in her young life, she would be happy. Solanda would see to that.

They would both be very happy.

* * *

Solanda returned to the house after dinner. Ultimately, she found she couldn't resist the dead fish that were piled near one of the docks. She had eaten herself sick and then had to clean every inch of her fur before she even attempted the walk home.

Not that the house was home. In some ways, Esmerelda was.

Solanda used the cat door. Esmerelda's parents were talking softly in the parlor.

"Perhaps boarding school," the mother was saying. "If she is this incorrigible now, imagine what she'll be like when she gets older."

"Give it time, darling," the husband said. "She's still a child. She will learn, as we all did."

"It's just I despair of ever teaching her manners. You didn't see her with that Fey. . . ."

Solanda had hard enough. She hurried up the stairs. She would talk to Esmerelda tonight. Tomorrow the Wisps would come, carrying a bit of stone in their tiny fingers. They'd fly in the open window, leave the stone on the bed and it would mold itself into a replica of Esmerelda while Solanda was leading the real Esmerelda out of the house.

Quick, neat, and completely perfect. The parents wouldn't have to worry about manners or boarding school. Esmerelda would get her heart's desire. And Solanda would have her reason for staying in Nye.

The door to Esmerelda's room was open. Esmerelda sat beneath a lamp, a long skirt over her lap. The air was stuffier than usual, and Solanda saw that the window was closed.

It had probably been closed all day. Sunlight had

poured in, and the poor child had had to sit in the heat, working on some task her mother assigned her.

When Solanda got close, she saw what it was. The child was attempting to mend her own ripped dress.

The stitches were uneven, and Esmerelda had stitched the bottom layer of fabric onto the top. That would make her mother even angrier. Esmerelda's eyelashes were stuck together, her nose was red, and there were tearstains along her cheeks.

"Goldie!" she said, and let the dress topple to the floor. She was wearing another dress, equally inappropriate to the hot weather. She reached for Solanda, but Solanda jumped onto the window sill.

She was not going to be hugged by a hot sweaty child—not, at least, until the window was open and the fresh air came inside.

Esmerelda glanced toward the door. She put a finger to her lips, as if she thought Solanda were going to give her away, and then called, "Mommy! Can I go to sleep now?"

Solanda froze in her spot. She didn't want to be seen in here, not tonight. She wanted to have her conversation with Esmerelda in private.

"Are you done with your dress, darling?"

"Yes."

Solanda looked at it. The dress was ruined. The poor girl would have an even more difficult day than usual tomorrow.

"Then blow out the lamp. Good night."

"Good night." Esmerelda pushed the door closed. Then she went over to the window and opened it.

A strong breeze came in, and on it, Solanda smelled rain. Maybe, after she spoke to Esmerelda, she would go outside. By then it would be raining, and she would be able to cool down.

Esmerelda put her hand over the lamp's chimney and blew. The flame inside the glass went out. Solanda blinked in the darkness, letting her eyes adjust. It only took a moment. There were clouds over the moon this night, and it was very dark.

Esmerelda went back to her chair. "I wish you knew how to sew, Goldie."

"I don't," Solanda said. "But I know someone who does."

Esmerelda let out a small yelp, and put her hands over her mouth. She peered around the room as if looking for the source of the voice.

Solanda had to go slowly with this. The child wasn't used to magic, not like fey children were.

"I could take the dress to her tonight," Solanda said, "and by morning, you wouldn't even know there had been a rip in it."

Esmerelda's eyes were wide. She finally turned in Solanda's direction. "You can talk, Goldie?"

"As well as I can listen." Solanda jumped from the windowsill to the bed. The room had cooled down. The fresh air felt marvelous. "What would you think, Esmerelda, if I took you to a place where you could wear comfortable clothes, play with children your own age, run and jump and swim to your heart's content? What if I told you that you would never have to sew another stitch, have another music lesson, or sit in a corner when you've done something that your mother didn't like?"

Esmerelda looked for her, but clearly didn't see her. Cat's eyes were far superior in the dark. Solanda watched the child lick her lips, rub her hand over her knees, and then sigh.

"How long would I stay?" Esmerelda asked.

"Forever," Solanda said.

"Would I have to be a cat?"

Solanda laughed. For all her verbal sophistication, Esmerelda was still a child at heart. "No," Solanda said. "You'll stay just as you are."

"Would Mommy come?"

"No."

"Daddy?"

"No."

Esmerelda's shoulders stiffened. Her little body looked rigid. "Who would love me then?"

Solanda started. She hadn't expected that question. "I would be with you," she said.

Esmerelda was silent, as if she were thinking this over. "Where would you take me?"

"To my people," Solanda said.

"I'd live with cats?"

"No," she said gently. "With the Fey."

Esmerelda gasped. She held onto her chair as if she expected to be dragged from it.

Solanda wondered if she should have said that, but she had never taken a child before. Certainly she knew of no one who had ever taken a child of this age.

But Chadn had said she had had to speak with the child, and the choice to come had to be the child's. There was sense in that. Esmerelda, at age five, would always have a memory of living with her parents. She needed a memory of her choice to leave them.

"Esmerelda," Solanda said. "I—"

"No!" Esmerelda screamed. "No!"

She launched herself out of her chair as if her voice had given the ability to move again.

"Help! Mommy! Help!"

Solanda's ears went back. She hadn't expected this from Esmerelda, not her sane, different child.

"Esmerelda, I only want to give you a better life—"

"Mommy! Daddy! Help!"

Finally Esmerelda pulled the door open and blundered into the hallway. Solanda followed, tail between her legs, ears still back. The little girl's screams echoed down the stairs. Her parents had reached her, and they both put their arms around her. Esmerelda was too terrified to be coherent.

Then the mother looked up the stairs. She saw Solanda, her gaze flat.

And Solanda realized she had no choice.

She shifted, her body lengthening, her tail disappearing, her fur becoming skin.

Then she walked, naked, to the floor below.

Esmerelda's mother gathered her child in her arms and backed away. The father placed himself in front of his small family, arms out.

"You came from the Black King, didn't you?" the woman said. "To punish us by stealing our child."

"It's not about you," Solanda said.

Esmerelda peeked around her father, eyes wide. Solanda had never, in her entire life, been so conscious of her nakedness.

"Wh–what do you want?" The father asked. He was trying to sound brave. Like most Nyeians, he was failing.

"I had hoped to take your daughter, but it seems

that she prefers this place, even though you treat her as less than a housepet. It seems, for reasons I cannot understand, that she loves you."

"Of course she does," the woman said. "We're her parents."

"As if that's a divine right." Solanda stopped on the middle stair.

The family cringed below her as if they expected her to strike them with a lightning bolt. She didn't have that kind of magic. They had seen the extent of her powers, but apparently they didn't know that.

"She is a child," Solanda said. "She is to run and play. She is to have friends of her own age. She is to have comfortable clothing so that she can move without tripping. She is supposed to get dirty, to rip her skirts, and fall on her behind. She is to have some joy in her life. Do you understand?"

"I thought you Fey were supposed to leave us alone," the mother said. "I thought—"

"Be quiet," the father said.

Esmerelda clung to her father, her curiosity moving her closer.

"You will give her those things," Solanda said, "or I will take her from you. Do you understand?"

"Yes," the father said.

"You can't do this," the mother said. "You can't change our customs. The Black King promised you wouldn't."

"A promise made to a conquered people is worth nothing," Solanda snapped. "You will do what I say, or the child is mine."

"Mommy." Esmerelda reached for her mother. Solanda's eyes narrowed. Couldn't she see that her mother saw her only as a thing to be trained, to be forced into the right and proper life?

Probably not. It was too sophisticated a concept for her. The same innocence that allowed Esmerelda to accept a cat's speech, allowed her to believe that she was loved.

"Do I take her now?" Solanda asked.

"No," the father said. "We'll do as you say."

"But our friends—"

"Shut up," the father snapped. "Do you want to lose her?"

For a moment, the mother's gaze met Solanda's and in it, Solanda saw something she recognized, a coolness perhaps, a calculation. How would that woman have answered if she had been asked *who would love me then?* Would she have dodged the answer like Solanda had? Or would she have heard it at all?

"She will stay with us," the woman said. She sounded resigned.

Solanda felt a hope she hadn't even known she had die inside her. "Then I'll watch. You will treat that child as if she is more precious than gold. And if you fail, even once, she's mine. Is that clear?"

"Yes," the father said.

But Solanda did not take her gaze from the mother.

"Yes," the woman said.

Esmerelda had stepped to her father's side. She was still holding his leg. "Are you Goldie?" she asked.

Solanda gave her a small, private smile. "Only for you."

The little girl slipped behind her father again. Her

answer was clear, too. She would stay, no matter what. And Solanda had done all she could.

So she Shifted back to her cat form. For a moment, she watched them all, tail twitching, then she ran up the stairs and into Esmerelda's room. She stopped for only a moment, knowing she would never return.

She leaped onto the window sill and sighed. She had just lost her excuse for staying on Nye. She was bound to the Black Family. She had to do as they wished.

Rugar wanted her to go to Blue Isle.

Where a Shifter awaited her care. A newborn child with blue eyes. A child who would think her the closest thing she'd ever had to a mother.

Solanda looked over her shoulder. She heard Esmerelda's voice, high, piping, excited; the soft answers of her parents. Solanda had lied to them. She would not be able to watch.

She hoped they would take good care of her little girl.

Then she jumped out the window and climbed along a tree branch. Maybe her future had been preordained. Maybe she had no choice. She would raise a Black Heir, maybe kill one, and influence children.

How different would tonight have been if she had told the child that she would love her?

She would never know. Perhaps that was the moment in which everything could have changed. Maybe she had just missed her only chance to save herself.

She moved off, alone, into the night.

NOTHIN' BUT A HOUND DOG
by Josepha Sherman

Josepha Sherman is a fantasy novelist and folklorist, whose latest titles include: *Son of Darkness; The Captive Soul; Xena: All I Need to Know I Learned from the Warrior Princess;* by Gabrielle, as Translated by Josepha Sherman; the folklore title *Merlin's Kin;* and, together with Susan Shwartz, two Star Trek novels, *Vulcan's Forge* and *Vulcan's Heart.* She is a fan of the New York Mets, horses, aviation, and space science. Visit her at www.sff.net/people/Josepha.Sherman.

It followed me home.

And no, this isn't going to be one of those cutesy "Can I keep it, Ma?" stories. I'm an adult New Yorker, not a kid, and even though I'm a woman writer and storyteller, that doesn't mean I like cute or believe in the fantastic. I also have my full share of the average New York woman's wariness about being followed by anyone. Anything.

Not that the critter standing behind me on the crowded Manhattan sidewalk, people parting about it as though it were a rock, looked particularly dangerous. It—he—was just a shaggy gray mutt, medium size, floppy eared, possibly some sort of hound mix. He didn't seem to have anything rabid or Pit

Bullish about him. Barely out of puppyhood, I guessed from the gawky body and too-big paws, just past the point of furry charm—or any sort of charm, since there was a *lot* of dirt and gunk plastering down his fur. The tip of his tail wagged hopefully at me, but a strong aroma of DOG wafted to me.

Ugh. I liked dogs, but there were limits. "Go home," I said. Useless command, since the mutt didn't have a collar or, presumably, an owner. "Shoo."

Turning my back, I stalked away. It was already nearly six o'clock, and the night was coming on and, with it, the streetlights, casting that orangey glare that's supposed to be as good as daylight. The wind was rising, damp and chilly, and a quick glance skyward showed ever-thickening clouds. Oh, joy. I quickened my pace, doing the New York Broken Field Scurry. The streets were still crowded with Manhattan traffic, and sidewalks and crosswalks were jammed with frantic homeward-bound pedestrians, all trying to beat the promised rain.

Yes, and I had my own reason to rush now that I remembered it. I had a magazine deadline waiting for me at home. The mutt would have to find himself some other soft touch. He would. Surely.

No, he wouldn't. When I impatiently stopped for a red light and waited for a herd of taxis to pass, there was a doggy sigh behind me. Sure enough, there he was, sitting back on his haunches, tail tip hesitantly wagging, and studying me with hopeful eyes that were the most uncanny shade of . . . green?

Dogs didn't have green eyes. At least I didn't think that they did. For no real reason, a sudden little shiver raced through me. "Shoo," I said again, helplessly. The light changed, and I resolutely headed on, telling myself not to be an idiot. Dogs *didn't* have green eyes, but canine eyes could and did reflect light. Such as the green of that traffic light.

I live on the second floor of a brownstone, a walk-up of course, but a nice, secure building in a Good Location. A pant and a gust of warm breath on my leg, plus an aroma of DOG, warned me that the dog was close behind me, and I hurried up the stone steps to the outer door. Kicking back to give myself more room, ignoring the insulted doggy yelp, I quickly unlocked the outer door, managed to all but slam the door in the dog's face before he could slip through, and hastily relocked the door. Enough of this "followed me home," I thought. Time to call the ASPCA to pick up a stray. Climbing the stairway to my apartment, I unlocked the door—

An unmistakable aroma of dog greeted me. Sure enough, the mutt was sitting in my front room, staring at me.

"How the *hell* did you—"

Fire escape. Some dogs could jump pretty high, and climb, and—

And that window was still gated and locked.

I sat down with a thump, fortunately on a chair and not the floor. "No. Oh, no. I tell stories. That doesn't mean I believe them."

"Wurff?"

"Wurff yourself. Who—what are you?"

If he answered . . .

Of course he didn't. The dog simply shook himself like any other dog, sending a cloud of gunk all over my carpet. He got to his feet, sniffing what he'd shook off, then looked up at me, tail wagging. Again, just like any other dog. Well . . . maybe he really was nothing more than some really clever stray. Someone's lost pet, judging from what seemed to be his gentle nature. Long-lost, judging from the dirt. Or abandoned, maybe, when his owners got bored. Some people did that, threw their pets away like disposable toys.

Damn. I was babbling to myself. To stop it, I grabbed the telephone, ignoring the dog watching me with his head cocked so cutely to one side. The ASPCA? No luck there. They were full up, as were the handful of other animal shelters I could find in New York City.

Assuming that this really was an animal . . ."

Oh, come on now!

Cats could slip unseen into rooms, right past people, so maybe this dog could, too. And that's all he was, blast it: a dog!

With a sudden rush of water like a gigantic faucet opening outside, the rain poured down. I glared at the dog as though he'd planned it and got a pathetic little whine in return, those odd green eyes downright puppy-pleading. His tail wagged a little harder.

A dog. Green eyes or no, only a dog.

I threw up my arms in disgust. "You win. As the saying goes, I wouldn't put a dog out on a night like this."

It would have been different if he'd looked sick, or mangy, or downright rabid. No, this dog looked a little thin but otherwise perfectly healthy underneath all that grime. Until I could get him to a vet, I would just have to pray he didn't have vermin or worms or anything else disgusting.

"First," I told my canine "guest," who was contin-

uing to wag his matted tail at me like a matted met-
ronome, "a bath."

Maybe he really had been someone's pet, because
he hopped neatly into the tub on his own. Lacking
doggie shampoo, I used my own on him, and to my
relief, he seemed to really enjoy the soaping up,
scrubbing, and rinsing off, several times over. Clean
at last, he leaped out onto the newspaper I'd spread
on the floor, and I ducked as he shook himself vigor-
ously. Shedding, I thought, nice wet hair all over my
clean walls.

Shedding like mad. Shedding like, I don't really
need this winter fur anymore, so here it goes. Okay.
I started to work on his coat with a hairbrush I'd
been meaning to toss anyhow.

The hair flew. Oh, did the hair fly! I began to think
of that old joke about being able to knit a second
dog out of the sheddings.

Then I saw what had been hiding under all that
hair.

"Oh. Oh, hell."

Once I'd gotten most of the loose hair off him, the
dog turned out to be white, almost a blazing white,
from nose to the tip of his tail, save for those floppy
ears, which were a startling blood-red.

Faerie dogs are white. With red ears. All the stories
claim it.

I swore at myself. Stories. Right. Fiction. Fantasy.
"I'm being an idiot," I told the dog. "No reason a
perfectly ordinary canine can't have your coloring.
Piebald, I think they call it, or something like that.
Probably the inspiration for all those stories, anyhow.
And no insult to you, but you just don't look, um,
elegant enough to be a—"

I was babbling again. The dog put a stop to that by pushing a muzzle into my hand, his nose reassuringly cold, then gave my fingers a quick, friendly swipe with a warm tongue, and—

All right, I admit it, I melted. I do like dogs. The apartment *had* been getting awfully quiet lately. And there was nothing in my lease that forbade pets. Of course, he'd have to be walked, and I wasn't so thrilled with the thought of that Pooper Scooper Law. But other folks managed; I saw them and their happy-tailed dogs all the time.

So I petted my visitor, tentatively at first, then in earnest, ruffling his fur, and he whined and wagged his tail and tried to lick my face.

What do you know? I had myself a dog.

"I only hope you're housebroken," I said.

He was. He was also, according to the vet I found, perfectly healthy, as I'd hoped, save, of course, for being a bit underweight. That was no problem. Dog food wasn't all that cheap, but in the next few days, I found that Oisean, pronounced O-sheen (in a moment of whimsy I'd named him after a Celtic hero who'd married a Faerie woman), was worth the price. Affectionate and gentle: hey, he even "heeled" on command. And no, there wasn't the slightest trace of anything, well, supernatural about him. As he filled out, Oisean looked even less like the traditionally sleek Faerie dogs described in the tales, particularly not with those floppy ears. He looked like a stocky white and red hound dog, period.

Of course I had followed the rules. I had put a "Found Dog" ad in the papers and waited a little more nervously than I'd expected, but to my relief, no one replied.

Not to the ad, at any rate.

Not exactly.

But I'm getting ahead of my story a little. First I'll say that Oisean and I got along from that first day, as if I'd had him since he was a pup. We played together and had our peaceful moments together, his head resting contentedly on my lap as I tried out new stories on him. He seemed to enjoy them, too, or at least always wagged his tail as though in appreciation at the traditional "and they lived happily ever after."

Two happy beings, us. Even if, yes, he *did* need to be walked every day. Even that was fun, in a way, as long as the weather was reasonably warm and/or dry. Fun, that was, even though Oisean turned out to be a born explorer, not so much interested in the scents of the neighborhood but the sights, trying his best to lead me down new ways every time we went out, tugging enthusiastically on his leash and giving me an over the shoulder whine of encouragement. He managed to persuade me to follow him fairly often, since it really didn't matter to me which way we were going on our brief outings, though I refused to let him lead me into dark alleys—

"No matter how intriguing they smell to you, dog!"

I still hadn't gotten used to that necessary after-dark stroll—or to the fact that I wasn't unarmed. With Oisean along, I had some fangs at my disposal, Just In Case.

Like now. Catching me off-balance in the middle of a step, Oisean managed to drag me into the darkness of an alley. I braced my feet and pulled him around back towards the entrance.

"Dog, this isn't the time—oh. Hell."

We were suddenly facing, and I mean *suddenly*, without so much as a warning murmur, what looked like a gang of pseudo-Goths. Goth in that they were dressed, male and female, in sleek back leather pants, very chic, and eccentric tunics of floating black lace and silk, difficult to see in the darkness, but decidedly good stuff. Wealthy Goths. But I say "pseudo," because real Goth-types don't usually go in for street crime. Or carry what were definitely not-for-show knives.

Weirdest gang I ever saw.

They spread out soundlessly, blocking us from the safety of the well lit street. Instantly, Oisean was between me and them, ears flat back, teeth bared, and growling with very sincere hatred.

"I don't know if I can hold him," I said in my best noting-scares-me New York voice—hey, I *said* I was a storyteller. "Better let us pass."

One young man took one lazy half-step forward, tapping his knife thoughtfully on one black-gloved palm. *Was* he young, though? This was the most age-defying face I'd ever seen, downright beautiful in a narrow, sharp way and properly Goth-pale, framed by absolutely straight, jet black hair. "I think not," he purred. "Not yet. We have business to complete."

Musical voice, unidentifiable accent, cold beauty, all of them, men and women both, eyes greener than Oisean's and glinting like a cat's eyes in the darkness—*no, couldn't be, couldn't!*

As my mind jibbered at me, I snapped, "I don't *think* so! Oisean—"

"That is my dog."

"Oh, sure!" I struggled with Oisean, who was continuing to growl fiercely, trying to hang onto his leash. "That's why he's trying to take a piece out of you!"

He gave the most languid of shrugs, barely a motion. "He serves. How is it you are here, here where you did not think to be led?"

"Oh, come off it," I began—

And then realized I wasn't quite where I'd been. That decidedly mundane New York alley was still around me, but it was, well, on top of that reality was another, one with silky pale grass under a sky like the darkest velvet, a sky filled with glittering stars brighter than anything we see in the city. . . .

Than we see on Earth.

Aliens, these people, and I don't mean anything as relatively reasonable as extraterrestrials.

Looks like I was right about your coloring all along, I thought, but did not say, to Oisean. Because there behind the Faerie Goths were the traditional, just-as-the-stories-described-them, Faerie hounds. Gorgeous beasts, sleek and refined as greyhounds or those superstreamlined dogs you see in Art Deco sculptures. Blazing white coats, blazing red ears. Sharp, pricked-up ears.

No heroic First Contact words from me. I glanced at Oisean and burst out, "You can't tell me he's one of them."

Well, what do you know? I saw the faintest hint of—could that possibly be embarrassment crossing the man's cold face? He all but muttered, "His father was from your Realm."

I let out what could have been a suicidal whoop

of laughter. "A mongrel!" I ruffled Oiseen's fur. "You can't tell me you've come here to take back a— a half-breed, mortal *mutt!*"

A woman chuckled, low and musical, with a great deal of menace behind the music. "Perhaps we have come to take you instead."

"Me!" I exploded without thinking, then compounded my error with, "Don't be ridiculous!" They all stiffened as one, green eyes glinting alarmingly, and I added hastily, "I mean, this is the wrong era. It's the world of the Internet and the Space Age, and I—you—I—"

Wasn't getting through to them at all. These were, after all, not those sweet, elfy-welfy folk out of bad fantasy novels. These were the People with the really bad reputations, the ones who used to be placated ironically with words like "The Good People" or "The People of Peace" because they were neither.

"Why *me*?" I asked plaintively. "I have got to be one of the most ordinary human beings around. No magic, no—"

"You weave stories."

"Well, yes, but don't you . . ."

Whoa. *Did* they? Why was there that ballad of "Thomas the Rhymer," and all those other tales of human bards and poets carried off by the folk? Something was very wrong here, and I suddenly realized that they probably couldn't *invent* anything. Unchanging, eternal—yes, they could embellish what had been given to them, but they couldn't create anything really new.

Great.

Wait, wait, I had an idea . . . "What if I tell you a

story here and now," I wagered hastily, "one that you won't interrupt until the end."

"Interesting," a woman murmured. "She would trick us."

"No lies," I said. One thing that holds true in all the stories is that the People, good or ill, never lie. "Take it as it is. If I tell a story, and you interrupt me before the end, I win free, and my dog with me."

"Done," the first man said, so smoothly that I wondered with a quick pang of alarm what I might have failed to say, or had said wrong.

No way to find out now. Swallowing nervously, I told myself, *Showtime.*

"Once upon a time," I began, "there was a king who thought himself the cleverest of storytellers. He challenged any man to tell him a story he could not best. He who succeeded would wed his daughter. He who failed would lose his head. But his daughter already had a young man who loved her, and he came forward with a story. He began with the words 'But if you interrupt me before my story is ended, then I win.'"

And I continued with the tale within a tale, of the king from whom no man could steal. "He held all the grain in the land locked up in a great granary. But the cleverest of thieves was also friends with the ant people. An ant can slip into the most tightly guarded granary. That night, an ant entered, and took away a grain. Another ant entered and took away another grain . . ."

The full story, of course, has the king getting impatient and interrupting, losing to the young man. I kept up with the tale within a tale, figuring that it would wear down the patience of the People. Surely one of them would say something, or even cough, and interrupt me, and they'd have to let me and Oisean go.

Boy, was I being naive! They waited, still as so many eerie statues, not a muscle moving or wisp of fabric stirring. And me, I kept repeating like a robot, not daring to think about it or my tongue might trip on the words, "Another ant entered and took away another—"

Try that sometime, while your heart is pounding and there are People waiting to carry you off to who knew what slavery.

"Another ant entered and took away another—"

"It is ended," the man cut in with mockery in his voice.

"No!" I protested. "The story still—"

"The night," he said as though speaking to a child. "The night is ended."

"But I—"

"You said, 'If I tell a story, and you interrupt me before the end, I win free, and my dog with me.' You did not say which ending it must be. The night has ended."

Oh hell. *Hellhellhell.* Had time really passed so swiftly? Maybe so. Technically, it was still pretty dark around us, but there was, as the Moslems say, enough light to distinguish a dark thread from a light.

Hope springs eternal. If I could delay them a little longer, till the sun rose, they'd have to flee—

Right. And simply come back for us the next night.

As the man moved smoothly forward, I stepped back, dragging Oisean with me, and whipped out— *iron, cold iron, I had to have something iron on me and—*

There I stood like an idiot, bravely holding the People back with—

"*Keys?*" the man said with a laugh. "You would stop us with the mere keys to your house?"

"Hey, even a match can burn!"

"And be extinguished."

"I don't see you doing anything."

"There is no grace in this," a woman said sharply. "There must be a finer ending to this matter than . . . farce!"

Oisean took matters into his own, uh, paws, baying in a cold clear voice I'd never heard from him before, calling sharp challenge to the leader of the Faerie hounds. The People shouted angrily—but Faerie hound or not, the animal was still a dog, the alpha male in the pack. He answered challenge and lunged forward. I had just enough time to unclip the leash from Oisean's collar before he leaped to the battle.

"By Wind and Wave!" someone shouted, and something prickled along my nerves. Magic? "By Wind and Wave, let your champion fight for you!"

I could hardly yell a counterspell. But I could at least shout back, "By Cold Iron, let his ruling stand!"

The two hounds crashed together, whirling in a blur of white and red. The Faerie hound was swifter, graceful as the wind with nothing mortal about him, and Oisean fell back with a yelp, crimson trickling down one shoulder. I drew in my breath in horror, but he didn't seem to be more than scratched, because he charged, slamming into the Faerie hound, staggering him. Oisean's fangs snapped shut— But he missed, backing off, shaking his head and spitting out a few shining white hairs. God, he didn't have the grace or the uncanny speed of the Faerie hound, and he was going to die, because the Faerie hound was lunging, fangs bared to tear out Oisean's throat—

And Oisean simply sidestepped. He was no shining, elegant Faerie beast, he was a *mutt*, which is to say a survivor. His teeth closed with bulldog force on a sharp-pointed red ear. The Faerie hound yelped in startled pain and fought to free himself, but Oisean moved away, pulling inexorably backwards, and the Faerie hound had to follow, or lose his ear. While one of the People might sacrifice a digit or even a hand, this was, after all, only a beast. He didn't know about sacrifice; he knew only that 1) his ear hurt, and 2) he wanted to keep it.

As the People stood, bound by truthfulness not to interfere, but with their eyes glittering fiercely green with anger, Oisean dragged his captive, step by resisting step, out of the haze of magic and toward me. I glanced down at my feet, and shouted at the People, "Do you want him back? Do you? Or shall I slay him here and now?" *How*, my mind gibbered, *with a bunch of keys?*

Oisean growled thickly and tightened his grip on the hound's ear. The hound whined piteously, and suddenly the Faerie man cried coldly, "Release him."

"That's not enough! We all agree my champion would fight for me—" I wasn't going to make any mistakes in working this time—"and that we all would stand by his ruling!"

They might not have surrendered even so, but it really was getting lighter now, and that meant that the sun would eventually slip some rays between the city buildings—sunlight, deadly to such as these.

"So be it," the man said with a boneless shrug.

"There are other bards. Release the hound, and take your half-blood beast, and be free of us."

As though he'd understood, Oisean opened his mouth. The Faerie hound leaped free, dashing back to the haze of magic, tail not quite lowered in defeat. Everything, the People, the hounds, the haze of magic, was gone as suddenly as that, and Oisean was shaking his head anew, spitting out the taste of the hound's blood. His side was streaked with his own blood, and I winced. But his injuries didn't look to be anything more than a few scratches after all.

I hugged Oisean, and he whined and squirmed about to lick my face.

And then my champion and I went off, side my side, to face the new day. And maybe catch a little sleep.

TEA ROOM BEASTS
by P.N. Elrod

P.N. "Pat" Elrod has written over 16 novels, including the ongoing *Vampire Files* series, the *I, Strahd* novels, and the *Quincey Morris, Vampire* Dracula adventure. She has co-edited two anthologies with Martin H. Greenberg and is working on more toothy titles in the mystery and fantasy genres, including a third Richard Dun novel with Nigel Bennett.

Ellen stared in disbelief at yet another letter form her future ex-husband. She wanted to tear the thing to shreds and make its threat go away, but it would have to go into the growing legal folder she'd begun since he'd filed for divorce. When she was calm enough, Ellen called her lawyer. Marissa had gotten *her* copy of the letter that morning.

"I'm afraid there's nothing we can do," Marissa said in a cheerfully sympathetic, but ultimately unhelpful, tone. "His name's on the ownership papers, so he has rights to half your business. And then there's community property, you know."

"He doesn't *need* my tea room. This is pure greed and spite." Ten years ago it had been necessary to have her brand-new husband Randall in on the contract. The idea had been that if anything happened to her, he could inherit without any trouble. Ten years ago Ellen had been utterly besotted with him, quite blind to his faults. Everyone had faults, but nothing that enough love couldn't cure, and she had oceans of love for him.

Except that she'd finally, unbelievably, run out. He'd sucked her dry, then mocked the remaining husk. Gradually the abuses, mental and physical, the daily, sometimes hourly fights, had done it. She used to forgive, supplied him with excuses so he wouldn't leave her, and he was so sweet afterwards with his apologies. Each fight was always going to be their last, after all. Later, in therapy, she'd learned the ins and outs of things called "co-dependency," "enabling," and "battered wife syndrome" and could have kicked herself for being so naive, but that would have been self-destructive, which was also a no-no.

"But what can I do?" she demanded of Marissa. "He'll sell his half or insist I sell to him or the bank at a loss or something. He knows I don't have the money to fight him on this."

Marissa made comforting noises, but the papers, signed ten years ago in a fit of cupid-inspired sentiment, were ironclad.

Sick in heart, Ellen hung up and considered her options. Even if she burned the place down, he'd take half the insurance—after finding a way of proving arson and throwing her in jail. He had all the money; he had all the power. He had the whole town on his side, for God's sake.

Randall had apparently planned his divorce strategy long in advance. As a lawyer himself, he knew just how to do it. He'd hidden his own money very well and signed his major properties over to an old and trusted friend to hold for him until after the settlement. Community property laws would not benefit her, only him. He only wanted her little tea room to heap more insult onto injury.

She discovered he'd been spreading rumors about her through the small seaside town she had called home. Bit by bit, Ellen learned to her shock that she was a rapacious man-eater who had betrayed her marriage vows to poor, long-suffering Randall again and again. People she'd thought of as friends were now too busy to speak to her, though they were more than happy to gossip. Everyone was firmly on injured Randall's side, especially all his old cronies in the legal system. She suspected her own lawyer was on his side as well, with only the high fees keeping Marissa on the case.

Ellen quit her tiny office and went out front to look with new eyes on the little tea room she had made for herself. Randall couldn't want it for the money, for business wasn't that good. In fact, it was terribly marginal. She ran the place as a labor of love. It had always been her one joyful escape from her 'til-death-us-do-part tormentor.

She thought glumly of selling the fixtures and fittings, then lying about the amount of money she got for them, but those would not net her much of anything. Her cozy little refuge with its cucumber sandwiches, consignment souvenirs, and occasional antique sales was worth more open than closed. *Maybe I could paint a line down the middle and give him the less profitable half.*

"Maybe I could strangle him."

She hadn't meant to speak aloud. She'd wanted to scream it. Wonderfully violent images came to her:

Randall squirming on a roasting spit, Randall plummeting into a bottomless gorge, Randall being audited by the IRS . . .

But no, he'd get away with it. He'd stolen ten of her best years, would steal or control her tea room haven, and leave her scratching for pennies. He'd laugh his head off. Look at how he'd originally served her notice: the divorce papers had been in the gift box he'd presented to her on their tenth anniversary. How he'd hooted at the shattered look on her face as she ran screaming to the bedroom to weep over this last violation of trust.

How could she have ever fallen in love with such a cruel *bastard*?

The answer to that would have to wait. Well-to-do women, craving her shop's quaint, ladies-only charm, were beginning to wander in for lunch. They deliberated over what to eat and what to drink and debated hotly over the shortcomings of their neighbors. Ellen knew from the looks sometimes directed her way that she was one of the topics, but she endured with a brave smile and made sure everyone got free refills so they would keep coming back.

Thanks to Randall's propaganda campaign, Ellen had no one to whom she could truly confide her troubles. She felt the isolation keenly in the crowded room, yet almost savored it. This might be the last time she would ever be here. The thought of losing it made even the bitterness a precious thing.

She stared bleakly at the shop she'd built up. It wasn't much, but her devotion to its success shone from every corner. She had found the right location, had decorated it, made the gourmet delectables, and smiled at the customers with the sincerity of fulfillment.

Randall had visited it perhaps twice during their marriage and until now had dismissed all her work. It was
rightfully *hers*. How *dare* he take it away?

"Because he's a bastard."

Ellen jumped as though she'd gotten a static shock,
for someone had spoken her own answer aloud. She
found herself eye-to-eye with another fortyish,
slightly plump woman, a total stranger.

"I beg your pardon?" said Ellen.

The woman had large sad eyes. No . . . they were
more compassionate than sad. She possessed an air
of having seen a lot of life's sorrows, not unlike Ellen's therapist, but in less trendy clothes.

"My name is Phylis," said the woman. "I apologize for intruding, but your thoughts were so loud I
couldn't help but hear you."

"My thoughts?"

"About that man who's trying to take this sweet
place away from you—oh, there I go again. I'm sorry.
I'd like a pot of jasmine tea and one of those really
large chocolate eclairs, please."

The switch threw Ellen slightly off balance, but she
had the presence of mind to ring up the sale.

"Oh, that's awful what's he's doing to you," said
Phylis.

"What?"

Phylis grimaced. "Drat, did it again. I should shut
it off, but when I get low blood sugar, it takes more
concentration than I can spare. On the other hand,
maybe I'm supposed to be here and eavesdropping
on your mind. I'll be at that nice little corner booth.
I love the flower picture you have there."

Dazed, Ellen took the money and hurried to fill
the order. *The woman's a crazy, but she looks harmless.*

Phylis smiled benignly from the booth. Ellen wondered if there was a distance limit for telepathy. *Why am I even believing in this?* And inside she shrugged and answered, *Why not? You need the distraction. A little lunacy can't hurt.*

She delivered the tray herself, turning cash register duty over to her part-time helper.

"Are you a witch?" Ellen asked, half-jokingly. Her shop was near the local college, and some of the students there wore pentacles. Ellen had overheard things from them about spells and ceremonies, but she had fobbed it off as nothing more than youthful experimentation.

Phylis snickered. "Oh, no, that takes *years* of study, I don't have the discipline for it, I just dabble a little for myself. Nothing weighty."

"You're serious?"

"Hardly ever, if I can help it."

Ellen smiled in spite of herself.

"You need to talk, don't you?" Phylis motioned to the opposite side of the booth, inviting her to sit.

"I pay my therapist for that. No need to burden you with my problems."

"Oh, my dear, I'm a very good listener, I never judge, and I never repeat what I'm told."

Ellen found herself fighting tears. How she wanted to *talk* to someone, anyone. Even a stranger who would be gone as soon as she finished her meal.

"I'll stick around," Phylis promised. "I'm an artist, you know. I'm in town for a while to paint some of the sights and enjoy the quiet. You deal with this lunch rush, then we'll sit down like we're old friends, and you can tell me all about it."

Ellen did just that. While her part-timer cleaned

up, Ellen quietly poured her heart out to Phylis, who nodded and *tsked* as needed and handed over bushels of paper napkins for nose-blowing and tear-wiping.

"You have every right to be angry and afraid with *that* man," said Phylis, shaking her head. "I had one like him myself. Any little thing would set him off into screaming and hitting me, then he'd say he was sorry and make it up in some nice way to get me back. I finally wised up that I'd married a two-year-old. Divorce was the best thing that ever happened to me."

"Why does he hate me so?" It was the one question Ellen could not answer. She had been a *good* wife, always loving, always forgiving. Too much so, it seemed.

"Oh, it nothing to do with you, *he's* the one with the problem. He's a sadist and still trying to hurt you, but it's time to change things in your favor. I think I might be able to help you keep your shop, but the solution may be a bit Draconian."

Ellen's heart sank. "How much will it cost?"

Phylis blinked. "Cost?"

"Half my bank account or my immortal soul?"

Phylis giggled. "Sorry, I don't need either one. I'm helping you for my own selfish purposes. I *like* this place, it's got lovely energy. I don't want to see it shut down. If I can help you save it, I will."

"Is it some sort of witchcraft?" Ellen whispered the last word.

"Well, it does involve a spell, but that's pretty much like saying a prayer."

Ellen liked the sound of that. "What will you do?"

"It's what *we* will do. Nothing harmful to us, though. Have you a quiet place where we won't be disturbed?"

"I've a storage room in the back."

"Great. Let's start now while I'm still full of righteous anger."

In the back room Phylis lighted four of the shop's decorative candles, placing them on a small table. She linked hands with Ellen across the table. Phylis shut her eyes and hummed a bit to herself, then asked for help to be sent to restore Ellen's "balance." Ellen felt nothing happening, but she didn't know what to expect. Her experience with magic was limited to TV shows. No special effects took place for her.

What if . . . what if *Randall* had sent this woman? How awful, how humiliating. If some newspaper person with a camera burst in on them just now—

Ellen shook her hands free.

"I wish you hadn't done that," Phylis said, chagrined.

"I'm sorry, this is just—I mean, it's—"

"Silly? I think not." Phylis pointed.

In spite of her sudden flash of distrust Ellen turned to look and saw . . .

Them.

She stifled a shriek of abject horror and flung herself backwards, upsetting the table and candles.

"Oh, dear. You shouldn't have done that," said Phylis, ducking out of the way.

"Eeeee!" screamed Ellen. She fled to the broom closet and shut herself in.

"Now don't be like that, you'll hurt their feelings," chided Phylis.

"What. Are. Those. *Things?!?"* Ellen shoved a folding chair under the doorknob and hoped it would hold.

"I think they're elementals. I know they look a

little strange, but they can really be quite helpful if you give them half a chance."

"Strange?! They're awful! I can't stand them! Make them go away!"

"But you broke the circle I made. We're sort of stuck with them for the time being."

One of the creatures, the goat-sized, slimy one with a lower jaw better suited to a gorilla, appeared in the closet next to Ellen. Though it was pitch dark within, she could see its glowing blue eyes and skin. It showed a mouthful of needle teeth and reached for her with a web-fingered appendage.

Ellen screamed and clawed her way out, nearly running Phylis over. Phylis caught her and held her in place, showing surprising strength. "Calm down! They won't hurt you! They're here to *help* you."

Ellen gulped back her panic. The slimy one ambled from the closet, walking *through* a stack of plastic crates, and rejoined its companions. It sat on its haunches and began licking its front paws just like a cat. The others, both bipedal in contrast, squatted down and stared at her. She hoped they weren't hungry.

"Not for food as you know it," said Phylis, picking up the thought. "They live off energy. You're giving them a feast with all the fear you're projecting. That's why Water went after you. Like a pet begging for scraps at the table."

"W–w–water?"

"Yes, it looks like you are in *real* need; we've got a fine assortment; Water, Earth, and Fire. Wonder what happened to Air?"

One of the plastic crates jumped from the stack and crashed to the floor. Ellen jumped. She heard the whoosh of a strong gust of wind, but felt nothing.

Phylis clapped her hands. "Good, there you are. Would you please make yourself more visible to us? That's better, thank you. This is much more than I expected. I think you had something to do with that, Ellen. I'll bet you have some latent powers in your genes that gave the spell some extra *oomph*. You could be a natural witch, you know. That would explain all the positive energy you put into the tea room. It could be a subconscious thing."

Ellen barely heard her, staring. Air was slightly less repulsive than the other three, but only because its outlines were very vague. Ellen shivered, but she tried quell her fear. She didn't want those monstrosities coming any closer for snacks. "W–w–what do we do with them?"

"Well, they're here to do things for us, nearly any kind of thing that involves working with the four elements. We send them back when we're done. Simple as that."

"Send them now!"

"Oh, I'm too tired for now. Look, as long as they're here, let's have some fun."

But Ellen was in no mood for recreational activities. Regaining some measure of inner control, she demanded an explanation from Phylis about the creatures. Phylis was forthcoming with confusing information about different planes and dimensions, interlaced with reassurances that however ugly the things might be, they were harmless.

"At least to us. Now if we sent them to visit your husband, that's another matter . . ."

Ellen paused and considered. "They'd scare him half to death."

"They can do more than that, I'm sure. Don't you want to get him off your back?"

"Yes! But won't it return onto me in some way?" Ellen had overheard enough conversations between the pentacle-adorned students to understand that revenge magic wasn't a wise or constructive thing to attempt.

"Not if it involves a restoration of your balance. He would be getting repaid what he dished out to you over the years. From what you said, I think he deserves whatever he gets. Don't you?"

Ellen bit her lip, staring at three—four—of the absolutely ugliest things she'd ever seen or ever hoped to see. Then she measured them against her ten years of isolated, secret abuse and the prospect of a poverty-stricken future. Should there *be* consequences to her for siccing these monsters on Randall . . . well, they'd be *worth* it.

"Okay," she said. "How do we start?"

Ellen left her part-timer in charge and went off with Phylis, elementals invisibly in tow. "You're sure they're still here?"

"Oh, yes. No one will see them but us, and we'll only see them when we want to. I had to make them understand that."

"Why are they so ugly?"

"I'm not sure. It's atypical as I understand things. Take Water, for example—it should be quite nice-looking. I'm thinking that these turned up looking just this bad because whatever purpose is ahead required them to be like this. Isn't it wonderful how the universe provides? They're smart, like dogs, and loyal, too. I think this bunch really likes you."

Ellen found herself strangely touched. She loved dogs, but, along with a child, Randall forbade her to have one, citing his allergies as the reason. He'd used his allergies to squirm out of everything from the joys of a pet to mowing the lawn or even going to the movies. She felt herself getting steamed again for those wasted years of isolation.

"Take it easy," Phylis warned. You can feed them on a nice roast of anger *after* the job is done."

She and Phylis walked to the town marina, only a few blocks from the tea room. Randall kept his forty-foot boat there. Somehow his allergies were very forgiving of sea air. Ellen had only ever seen the boat from the dock. Randall had convinced her she would break something on it or fall overboard. He also maintained that he needed a "private space" to call his own. "You have your hen parties at that shop, I have my boat," he'd sniffed.

And she'd swallowed it, telling herself that he knew best, and besides, she was too busy with business to go on weekend fishing trips with him. Too late she came to learn his 'trips' always involved other women. She suspected her lawyer might even be one of them. He had suspended philandering for the time being. He was smart enough to play the injured husband role to the hilt right now.

"What a nice big boat," said Phylis.

"It cost more than our house—his house, I mean." Both boat and house would eventually return to Randall, once the divorce was settled. The same went for his hidden savings.

"Oh, that bastard! He didn't tell you how much he made a year?"

Ellen was getting quite used to Phylis picking up her

thoughts. "Not a penny. I earned what I could with the shop, shared that with him because he said he needed it, and all the time he was—oh, I could *kill* him!"

"Yes, betrayal is an awful thing. My ex did it to me, all perfectly legal, too. That's why I turned to my dabbling. I was looking for a way to get some of my life back. What a day it was when one of my little spells activated my mind reading."

"Really? I thought people were born with those abilities."

"I suppose they are. I think I always had the gift, but it got smothered by my upbringing and life in general. Then one day it was like taking out some ear plugs. It was scary at first, but I've learned to trust and control it. Maybe that's what drew me into your tea room, I must have sensed a kindred vibration in its energy today. Come on, let's go save your place."

They walked down a short pier to the boat. It looked huge to Ellen, magnificent.

I helped pay for it and never once enjoyed it.

"You're sure your name isn't on the ownership papers?" asked Phylis.

"He made a point of throwing that in my face."

"That's good, then no one can point an accusing finger at you."

"Accusing me of what?"

"Hm, well, whatever you'd like. Our little friends here are very versatile. Air could blow him off course, Water could make a nasty whirlpool to suck him under, or they could work together as a really violent squall."

Ellen considered these new possibilities, feeling the stretching of her world as an almost physical pleasure. "I wouldn't want to hurt other people who might be out sailing."

"Yes, all right. I'm sure we can find some way to avoid dragging them in. Why don't you test Water out? Look at it, all raring to go."

Water had indeed jumped things, going visible to them and slipping into the normal water next to the pier. It darted around the pilings like an otter. A goat-sized otter with really huge, sharp teeth. Water grinned, made happy gurgling noises, and kicked up little waves. It was quite endearing, really.

"Er, ah, Water?" Ellen felt a little foolish at her diffidence, but the elemental instantly came when called, looking up attentively. "Would you—" what did she want? "—would you please do something nasty to that boat there, if you're able, that is."

Water certainly proved able. Flashing its needle teeth in a joyous grin, it vanished under the pier. After a moment, Ellen heard a deep rolling wash of sound. The whole of the bay seemed to vibrate from it. Then a great watery fist rose thirty feet from the sea and smashed down on Randall's beautiful boat. The craft rocked drunkenly under the assault. The spray from the impact soaked Ellen and Phylis, but Ellen didn't care, and Phylis was cheering.

"Oh, look at it *go*! I bet it'll cost a fortune to have that cleaned!"

The boat's deck was not only awash with water, but with greasy, muddy flotsam dredged up from the bottom. The once-pristine superstructure and fittings were alive with flopping fish, misplaced crabs, shells, foul-smelling seaweed and waterlogged garbage. People from other boats nearby came out to stare.

"We should get out of here before someone recognizes me," said Ellen.

"Yes, you're right, but what fun! Come along, Water, oh, there's a *good* elemental. Who's the dear little creature, then? Who's Mommie's little sweetie?" Water scampered soggily ahead, playing a chasing game with the other three. "That was a wonderful start, Ellen. Have you any ideas of how to use the rest now?"

Ellen did, and she began forming solid plans, much better than her roasting-Randall-on-a-spit fantasies, because she could actually implement them. Or rather her newfound friends could.

From that point forward Randall began to suffer where it hurt the most: his bank account. The following day, after he was advised of the damage to his precious boat and had had time to fully appreciate the wreckage, other disasters overtook him. Ellen was safe in her tea room serving lunch to a dozen witnesses to her whereabouts when Randall's house mysteriously caught fire. A freak wind kept the flames from traveling to any other homes, yet seemed to whip the blaze into an all-consuming frenzy. When the fire trucks arrived, the water hydrants refused to live up to their potential. Water pressure was down to a mere trickle for some reason. This lasted only until the house was reduced to a few charred sticks.

Ellen lost nothing in it. Randall had been careful to box up all her things when he'd thrown her out. She soon learned from gossip that her future ex-husband was stunned, devastated, and gripped in the horrors of utter shock. For every hour of his anguish, Ellen felt months of her own pain falling away from her soul.

Payback was a *wonderful* thing.

Randall retreated to his boat to live on, dead fish

and all. He lost work time from his law office. His partners were not amused. What made things worse was that each day he came home to a renewal of the smelly, filthy mess. Neighbors at the marina told tales of freak waterspouts and strange high waves.

His car was her next target. While Ellen had made do with a wheezing, stuttering wreck that she'd driven since before their marriage, Randall had that year's top-of-the-line Lexus. "Have to let my clients know I can win for them," he'd told her. She'd never been allowed to drive any of his new cars and only rarely got to ride in them.

Again, she was safely serving another tasty lunch to her regulars when a sinkhole opened up in the street in front of her tea room just as Randall was driving past to the marina. The front end of the Lexus plowed into the four-foot deep, eight-foot wide hole at forty miles an hour, stopping the car dead with a noisy and expensive-sounding crunch. All the air-bags deployed. Randall was badly bruised by their unnatural force.

Phylis went to the hospital to check on him, returning with a juicy report.

"He's in a neck brace for at least a week," she said. "And he had some kind of mishap when he tried to take his contact lenses out that scratched his corneas. The doctors had to blindfold and sedate him so he wouldn't claw his eyes out from the agony."

Ellen rocked with laughter and didn't feel a bit guilty. Hadn't he given her a daily dose of pain every day? She still had the visible scars, but she began to lose her shame of them.

Randall tried to bring a suit against the city to replace his totaled car and pay for his hospital stay. He cited shoddy paving as the cause of his mishap, but even his old friend the judge could not rule against a sinkhole in the earth, which was determined to be an "act of God." Odd, perhaps, for this part of the world, but a perfectly normal geologic occurrence.

And one not covered by Randall's insurance.

Ellen rejoiced. She and Phylis celebrated by going to a Mel Gibson film that night and pigging out on chocolate eclairs and satisfaction.

The elementals were now Ellen's fourfold joys. She'd grown very fond of them; she no longer saw them as ugly, but found them endearing, like the little alien from the Spielberg movie. She cooed and told them they were marvelous and fed them servings of Randall's frazzled feelings. In turn, they adored her and Phylis.

"Don't you have anything you want them to do for you?" she'd asked Phylis.

"No, I took care of my ex years ago."

"You used elementals against him?"

"Just one. I wasn't too practiced with summonings back then. All I got was a dear little air elemental. It wasn't very large or powerful, but it was enough."

"What did it do?"

"Well, it's still being done. My ex is in the hospital a lot, suffering from a strange shortness of breath. The doctors are unable to explain it. His lungs are perfectly healthy, but he just can't seem to breathe in enough air. They think he's crazy by now. He's spent a fortune in therapy."

"Oh, Phylis, that's absolutely wicked! I wish I'd thought of that!"

"The condition comes and goes at the worst times, too. I don't think he's had sex in the last eight years.

A fair payback for all the times he was in the mood and I wasn't."

Ellen screamed with delight and made a mental note about it and continued with her fun.

But one day Phylis rushed into the tea room, wearing a worried look. She dragged Ellen to the back and shut the door. "You got trouble," she blurted. "I was taking the kids for an outing in the park across from the courthouse . . ."

Early on they had begun to refer to the elementals as "the kids."

". . . and Randall walked past me! he knows you and I are friends."

"So?"

"So the sight of me sparked off a line of thought with him. It was so loud he might as well have had a bullhorn."

"What was he thinking?"

"It's awful! He's planning to kill you!"

"*What?*"

"He was positively *gloating* about it. I saw everything! He's going out on his boat, then he'll sneak back and make it look like an interrupted robbery. Oh, I've run up against some terrible people, but this one is *diseased*!"

Ellen grabbed the edge of a plastic crate to steady herself, suddenly sick. "B–but why should he? There's no reason."

"I think it's to do with your tea room. He's not going to risk getting only half. He must want it all."

"Have you any proof?"

"I wish I did."

In response to her emotional surge the four elementals swept through the closed door and surrounded her, leaning in close to feed. Impulsively seeking comfort, she reached down to pet them. They fawned even closer, though her hands passed right through them.

"This is too much." Ellen shook off the choking feeling that threatened to take her over. She used to get it all the time, but not lately. She'd almost forgotten what it felt like. *I am not going to go back to it, either!*

"I think this was inevitable," said Phylis. "He's been deprived of all his other resources, of course he'd look on the shop as his last hope of restoring his funds."

"Yes, I'd thought of that. But to take this direction . . . it's wicked."

"Oh, Ellen, we've got to do something! You've got to leave town."

"No! I won't run from him!" Ellen thought fast, and a wonderful, terrible plan blossomed. She almost shivered away from it. Almost. She knew all too well that Randall was absolutely capable of any crime if he thought he could get away with it. But not this time. She regarded the kids—her saviors—fondly. "You little dears. It's been playtime until now, with just a few little snacks. How would you like a *real* banquet?"

They gurgled, growled, rumbled, and wheezed eagerly.

"Who's Mommie's little sweeties? Hmm?"

Ellen was on lookout duty by the front door of the tea room, waiting for Randall to drive by. It was only lunch time, but he always cheated on Fridays, leaving his office early to get to his boat. He finally appeared, in a much less spectacular used Hyundai, the only thing he could get since the insurance company was still investigating the burning of the house. They were not yet ready to dismiss arson as the cause of the blaze, and there was a problem with the house being in his old friend's name.

Randall saw her and slowed as she stepped outside. They got a good look at each other. Ellen showed no expression. Randall, uncharacteristically, broke into a wide smile and waved, a man without a care in the world.

That decided her. His satisfied grin, rife with confidence, was her proof of his intentions. Had he still been worried over his future, he'd have sneered.

Phylis came to stand next to her. She went sheet-white. "Oh, God. It's tonight. He's going to break into your flat with a crowbar and . . ."

"It's all right." Ellen softly called the kids over. "See the car? See the man inside? Go *get* him!" she whispered.

They surged joyfully past, chasing the vehicle down the street like a mismatched wolf pack seeking easy quarry.

"How I wish I could watch."

"There might be a way," said Phylis. "I've been reading a lot lately about scrying. Have you a black bowl?"

They made do with a large blue mixing bowl, setting it on the little table in the back room and filling it with bottled spring water. While the part-timer coped with the rush, Ellen and Phylis lighted candles, placing them carefully so none of their light reflected in the water.

"Now a deep breath," said Phylis. "Concentrate on Randall and let the image come to you."

Ellen breathed deep and waited. She didn't expect much, staring into the dark depths of the still water, then to her surprise an image did indeed surface. It was faint, just a blink, but she saw it like a still photograph: Randall, still in his business suit, climbing aboard his boat.

"Oh! Did you see that?"

"Yes! I didn't think it'd work this well. It must be you boosting the power again. Keep looking!"

Ellen was strongly reminded of a slide show. But this version of vacation pictures was vastly more riveting. More little images came to her in the water. She found she could hold onto them for longer periods, and suddenly one of them showed movement, like a film projector finally grinding to life.

"Are you getting that, too?" she asked Phylis.

"Practice makes perfect. This is *fun*!"

They watched steadily as the afternoon wore away. Randall at the wheel, Randall knocking back a number of beers, Randall taking a leak into the bay.

"What a pig," said Phylis.

"I know. He always left the seat up, too."

"Not any more."

The kids stayed close to him, invisible to his eyes. Air made its presence known by shifting the wind. Randall jumped and cursed as his own pee was blown onto his Armani-clad legs.

"I *heard* him!" Ellen exclaimed. "Oh, I *love* this!"

Randall went below to wash and change his pants. Water followed and saw to his thorough soaking when something went wrong with the faucet pressure. At the same time the toilet backed up.

"I hope you have something for Fire and Earth to do," said Phylis.

"It's coming."

The boat cut farther out into the bay toward open sea. Randall was an experienced sailor and gave a tumble of boulders marking the mouth of the bay a wide berth.

Air and Water had other ideas, though. A sudden blast of wind struck the side of the boat, accompanied by an equally unexpected wave. Two stories tall. Both had a devastating effect on the craft and its captain. The boat heeled over drunkenly, riding the water tipsily toward the rocks. Despite Randall's frantic efforts at hauling the wheel around, he was helpless against the forces of nature.

Or supernature, Ellen silently added. Phylis, picking up the thought, giggled. *What a shame about the boat, though.*

Smashing brutally into the rocks, the forty-footer creaked and groaned like a live thing caught in a trap. Ellen could hear Randall's yells and cursing, a too familiar sound, always directed at her, now directed at the elements.

If he only knew.

As though in response to her thought, all four elementals became visible. To Randall.

Ellen could hear his terrified screams. My, but he was loud. He had every right to be. She recalled her initial shock at seeing them, and they'd been friendly toward her. No such restraints now. All of them did their best to induce the most fear in him, which wasn't too difficult with their looks.

Water finally swept him overboard, then threw him up high so Air could catch him in a miniature tornado. As Randall whirled around in exquisite slow motion, Fire busily dealt with the boat's fuel tanks.

Ellen heard the deep *whump* as the hapless craft blew into a thousand pieces, the fireball rising over the bay like a vast orange and black flower.

"Gosh!" said Phylis. "That's something right out of a James Bond film. You go, girl!"

Air flung Randall toward land. He fell into a spongy area just past the outcrop of boulders. The ground there wasn't *normally* spongy, but that was Earth's doing. Randall had just begun to feebly move when he was sucked down. Water and Earth had worked together to make a wonderfully soupy quicksand.

"Oh!" said Phylis. "That's great! They did it in a Tarzan movie!"

"That's where I got the idea. Come on!"

Ellen led the way to the rear door of her establishment, which opened to a wide, unpaved alley lined with a high fence. None of the neighbors would see. She soon felt a quivering beneath her feet. Moments later Earth opened up, and Randall's torso emerged like an exotic plant. A very muddy one. He slumped over with a groan, gasping for air.

"Ew!" said Ellen. "What a stink! Earth must have dragged him through the sewer lines."

"I didn't know Earth could do that," said Phylis.

"Neither did I, but they've all been getting very strong over the last few weeks."

"Nothing like a steady diet."

"Ellen?" Randall croaked. He stared up, bleary and blinking. "Ellen, help me!"

"Why should I?" she asked, astonished.

"For God's sake, help me!"

"Not this or any other time. You brought this on yourself. You were going to kill me tonight, weren't you?"

Randall's jaw dropped, and he made no reply. His terrified gaze shifted to the elementals that were gathering about him. They *had* grown. "Get me out of here!"

"Apologize."

"What?"

"I want to hear you say you're sorry for—"

Randall was a man quick to assess the fantastic situation and judge his best course of action. He began babbling a series of profound apologies about everything. None were too specific, but all were music to Ellen's ears. When he ran out of breath and began begging for help again, she held up her hand.

"Enough. I know you only said all that to save yourself and you don't mean a word, but it was good to hear all the same. You're a pathetic bully, Randall, and I'm going to do the next woman in your life a favor and make sure she never meets you." At a word from her, Earth sucked Randall under again. The last she heard from him was his abruptly smothered scream as the ground knitted up solidly over his head. The remaining three "kids" swirled up, laughing in their own way, and shot off, heading toward the bay again.

Ellen felt grimly amused and decidedly *free*. "I hope he can hold his breath until Earth takes him out the other side again," she remarked.

"Why is that?" asked Phylis.

"So they find water in his lungs instead of soil. It should look like a natural drowning as a result of the boat accident."

"Ellen, are you *sure*? You can still stop them."

"I'm sure. This is self-defense, pure and simple."

"True. The things I saw in his mind, what he was going to do . . ."

"Well, try to forget it." Ellen straightened, doing a mental dusting off. "I suppose we'd better clean up the scrying stuff."

Phylis gladly seized the change of subject. "Yes. Wouldn't want to leave that lying around."

"Then afterward I'd love to have a look at some of your reading materials. I think I must have a talent for this kind of thing."

"You should explore it, that's how I came to be an artist."

"I have an idea . . ."

Phylis caught the thought and grinned. "About helping others?"

"Lots of women come into my shop with problems. You'd be able to tell which ones were in real need, and then together we could help them. With our four little friends, that is."

"Count me in."

"Besides, I really love the little dears. I'd hate to send them back."

"Oh, no, not when there's so much *more* for them to do!"

"But tomorrow," Ellen said firmly. "Tonight there's going to be a Mel Gibson marathon at the rerun house . . ."

"Great! Let's see if there's any eclairs left!"

UNICORN STEW
by Alan Rodgers

Alan Rodgers' stories are guaranteed to please even the
most discriminating reader. Whether he's writing subtle
fiction where the shocks creep up on you or an out-and-
out screaming terror tale, his command of the genre and
language are a force to be reckoned with. His short fiction
has appeared in such anthologies as *Miskatonic University*, *Tales from the Great Turtle*, *Masques #3*, and *The
Conspiracy Files*.

Cab Callolee got to the village just as the castle's
hunting party emerged from the forest. He
should have taken a hint from that, and from the
abomination that was tied to and hanging from their
game rack, but no, more fool he, he didn't buy the
clue.

Later he regretted that, in the bittersweet way we
all regret the things we love too much. But at that
moment, in that place he never meant to be, he
thought it was the finest jest! Oh, a gift from God,
that joke; a unicorn strung like so much venison
upon a game rack, its once-lively semiequine features
(there is something *human* in the eyes of a unicorn,
and everyone who's ever seen such a creature know
it), all slack from murder.

How Cab would tell the tale of that day, far and wide! That was what he thought when he first saw it: the slaughtered unicorn was a tale that would wine and dine him months along the road, and handsomely at that.

"Ho, Cab," the castle's huntsman called to him across the common, for he knew Cab, and had listened to him more than once across the years at firesides and tables. Afterward, he'd tell everyone "That was Cab Callolee. He's the taleteller, and you and I would know him in our hearts even if we'd never heard him speak."

Now he said, "We've brought a tale in from the forest. I say you'll tell it, like as not."

Cab Callolee laughed an uneasy laugh and allowed as he might tell the tale of how the hunt of the Castle Sundown slew a unicorn.

"You've took it for the masters' larder, eh?" asked Cab, jesting—for surely the unicorn's carcass was meant for a proper burial, and not the roasting spit.

The huntsman grew grim.

"Too right," he said. And then he slapped Cab on the back, spurred his horse, and hurried on his way.

When Cab saw that unicorn, he thought it was a tale he'd always tell.

But the truth, by the time it came to him, was different. Though he didn't know it then, when that unicorn met his final fate, he'd changed poor Cab forever and made him into a thing he never meant to be.

And given him a tale he'd never tell.

"Unicorn stew!" cried the cook deep in his kitchen. Cab was there to hear him, earning his repast the way he always did when he arrived in that castle, by telling tales among the serving maids and seeing what they'd do to please him. "There's the rub," said Cook. "The damned thing's too tough to broil, and too lean to roast. But I'll wager half a fortune we'll take his virtue from my pot."

That was when Cab Callolee first got a notion of what the tale had become. He did not yet have the sense to be afraid, though in hindsight clearly he *should* have been afraid. Cab Callolee was a brave man, and because he was so brave he didn't notice when his fate had found him, and he walked into it, full tilt.

A body must admire that, I say. No matter how we miss him.

"You're going to cook that poor bastard? Really, cook him?"

Cab Callolee stood in the kitchen of the Castle Sundown, looking into the unicorn's warm, dead eyes. It wasn't human—no . . . *he* wasn't human. Cab wasn't sure what made a creature a person and what made one something not a person at all, but when he looked at the unicorn, he knew it was people, and he knew that cooking the poor damned thing was cannibalism.

Everybody knows the rule that made it so: If you can talk to it, you mustn't eat it. Plain and simple.

"Of course I'm going to cook him," Cook said nervously. "You think I want to hang in the larder myself? The Prince of Castle Sundown is a hard master. I would not cross him, not so long as I prize my life."

"But, Cook," said Cab, "surely there's confusion here. The prince can't have told you to cook a thing that might just as well be a man. Think twice! It isn't right. He can't have asked it. Someone's making a mistake."

"Oh," said Cook, "it's a mistake, sure enough. But it's no matter of confusion. The prince has made strange pronouncements, lately, many of them. And those of us who prize our lives have come to know the wisdom of them, that's for certain."

Cab frowned. He wanted to say, *Cook, listen to me, you've misunderstood something, here, you're about to make a terrible mistake*—but then Cook leaned close, and whispered to him desperately, that desperation so intense it left Cab Callolee stunned and speechless.

"Listen to me, Cab," he said. "It's not the anthropophagy that's the worst of it. By far! What terrify me are the rumors. Rumors! They say that the horn will cleanse a poison, and the monster's blood will cure all evils of the flesh. And if the horn and blood have got that kind of power, what will the flesh of the beast do to my kitchen? What will it do to this *castle*, heaven help me?"

Cab blinked.

"I have a guess," Cook said. "That there's fire in those bones. Fire in it that burns forever! And if the creature's murdered, the fire burns so powerful and pure that it will sear away all evil that should touch it, all of it, you hear me, Cab? When I cook this thing, things will happen here in this haunt they call the Castle Sundown. Get your own carcass out of here if you plan to keep it breathing."

By then it was too late for Cab to leave, of course. He was expected in the castle's tap hall within the hour. The Princess Gwendolyn was to be there, in attendance.

He had a royal audience expecting him, and one does not decline a royal audience within the halls of Castle Sundown.

Not if one values one's life.

That's only half the tale, however: unicorn stew. The other half, of course, is love.

It's a known and certain fact that Cab Callolee never intended anything untoward, unseemly, or uncouth in regard to the Princess Gwendolyn. He was a decent man, all in all, and she was a married woman! He wasn't that sort of fellow—and she wasn't a woman prone to anything unprincipled herself.

But the moment came upon them, and it changed them both forever. Some moments are like that, aren't they? They bind us and remake us, as if they were a steaming bowl of unicorn stew.

The old washerwoman had words for Cook as Cab was about to make his leave.

"Don't do it, Cook," she said. "You'll put a curse on all of us through all our days. Better one or two or us should die at the master's hands—how much is one life, in the end? How many are three? You'll bring a doom on all of Sundown if you put your kettle on the fire, mark my word."

Cook scowled.

"Easy enough for you to say, Matilda," he said. "It's not as if it's on your head."

The washerwoman shook her head. "It's on all our heads, Cook," she said. "It's the end of all of us and ours you've got there on the carving table. Don't be selfish with your life, Cook."

"Oh, that's you, Matilda," said Cook. "Ever the generous one where it comes to sacrificing me. A fine thought, that is, isn't it? Eh. Devil take it, I say. I'm not dead yet."

It was dusk when Cab Callolee reached the tap hall of the Castle Sundown. It was dim, as it is always dim in inside that room; the tap hall of the Castle Sundown is a big tall windowless chamber with a ceiling high as a cathedral's. The only light there ever is inside that place comes from torches poised like roosting ravens high up all around the walls. They light that place enough for such business as it does, but they do not light it well at all.

Perhaps that's why none took notice of Cab Callolee as he made his way past the busy ale counter (with its three wide, fast taps) to take his place up on the platform.

When he began his first tale—it was the tale of the Broke-Winged Birds, and Cab had told it many times before, as it was a favorite of his—when he began his tale it seemed at first that no one heard him. But then he realized that there was one listener, out there in the shadows, deep and dark. He could barely see a pair of eyes that watched him intently, carefully.

It took Cab Callolee quite a while to realize just whose eyes they were. He should have known them instantly; they were eyes he'd seen before, and the watcher held his fate in her heart. But maybe because of the darkness, maybe because of the rueful memory of the unicorn, maybe because of the darkness or for no damned reason at all—maybe just because he wasn't meant to—Cab Callolee took the longest time to realize it was Princess Gwendolyn staring at him from the shadows, *listening* to him.

Listening intently and with a purpose poor Cab Callolee never would imagine. And so he continued with his story:

Once there was a pelican, who came inland from the sea.

The pelican is a sacred bird, you know. When Christ comes to us, he comes in one of four forms: he comes as the man he was when he walked among us, or as a unicorn, or a pelican, or a lamb. This pelican was not Our One True Lord, but he once had seen the Christ take wing to soar among his kind, and he took the wrong lesson from the Glory and mistook himself for something other than what he truly was.

This pelican, in his hubris, flew inland for hours upon hours, till he reached the mountain Forest of the Moon. There he came low to fly too close and fast among the trees; he flew that way for hours, till he was full of thrill and confidence, and then he became careless.

And clipped his good left wing into the sharp trunk of a shattered tree, smashing every bone inside it.

The name of this pelican was Crayne. When he struck that tree he fell from the air unconscious, and lay there dead to the world for three hours and a day.

Till sundown next, when the buzzing of flies woke him, and he struggled to his feet desperate to find a shelter.

He found one soon enough—the loft in the barn of a dairy farm just beyond the edge of the edge of the Forest of the Moon.

Pelicans draw a special nurture from the lofts of barns. It's not so much a magical or natural thing among them as it is a bit of folklore: there is a tale they tell their children of a lost pelican who grew up in a barnloft, nurtured by the pigeons. In the story that pelican grew up to be Byrne, the pelican that Christ used to speak his gospel to the fishermen of Calais.

So the pelican Crayne took himself into the barnloft, and shivered there for days and days inside his misery. Till he woke one day to find another pelican there with him in the loft, staring at him in his misery from a place beside the far wall of the loft.

"Who are you?" Crayne asked, but he knew already when he asked. She had Byrne's colors in her wings, a half-star of feathers blue and brown and green. She was a royal princess of the pelicans, and her pinfeathers were clipped.

"I am Lanytte," she said. My sister cast me from the sky."

Crayne snorted.

"Your royal sister feared you, eh, milady?" he asked. His words and his manner were rude and impertinent, but he felt his death upon him, and he felt no need for courtesy when he was already doomed. "I am Crayne. The harm that's come upon me—my undoing—is my own. I flew reckless as a fool, and now it's certain I will die."

"I never hurt my sister!" said Lanytte. "She's just jealous 'cause I'm prettier, that's all."

The fallen princess was a beauty, that's for certain. A beauty, that is, if your taste runs toward pelicans.

Crayne nodded. "Yes, milady," he said, recovering the sense to show some courtesy. "As you say."

"You're dying? Really?"

"My wing is shattered, down and deep," said Crayne. "And every hour makes the inflammation more intense."

"Let me tend to you," she said. "I will give you back your sky."

And she went to him, and set the shattered bones inside his wing, and held him till he healed. There is some magic *in the royal line of Byrne; it's no vast wonder she could heal him.*

Even in his condition, she could save his life.

She had that gift, and more, Lanytte did. She could find his broken bones and ragged sinews and tie them back around themselves; she could find the hurts and inflammations and salve them with her heart till they were whole.

What she didn't have was gift enough to make him fly again.

She nursed him to his health, feeding him on wild honey and stolen mare's milk, 'til Crayne's fever and his inflammation faded, 'til he could stand on his legs and walk a straight line without falling over dizzily from pain.

But no matter how good she was (and she was very good indeed), he did not have gift enough to make him as he was when he first touched the sky.

Crayne took wing in the loft, and tried to fly out of that barn—but instead of flying he plummeted to earth.

If there had not been a great soft pile of hay beneath him, he surely would have broke his elfin neck.

That's the truest thing about the greatest wounds: No matter how we struggle to surmount them, they still own us in their way. And the plain fact is they always will.

Somewhere in the course of the tale, Cab realized, he'd picked up an audience. It wasn't just the princess listening (he'd recognized her, to his discomfort, half-way through the tale); now there were more and more listeners out there in the dark. Squires, guards, and generals gathered at their tables; gentry hangers-on at court, the kind one finds in every castle, trading on their station; out there deeper in the dark, quiet in the shadows, plain working folk who tended to the castle.

All of them listening intently—and, strangely enough, with a focused impatience, as though there were something in his tale that compelled them to listen, and yet despite that they found his story deadly dull.

A great hulking man, a solider, probably, stood up at his table and hoisted his stein at Cab. "Enough of that prissy fancy stuff, Cab Callolee," he called. "Give us a *real* tale! Tell us of the wards that made the land!"

Cab laughed.

"All right, then," he said.

And he told the tale of the wolf and the lamb.

Sometimes when Christ comes to us, He comes in the form of a lamb. When He does, He means that we should listen to the meek and helpless, setting all our needs aside.

The craven-wolf of Armorica never learned the truth of that. How could he? He was a coward, and he was convinced his wits were keen enough to let him use the world as he saw fit. He saw no need for compassion, justice, or the Grace that comes from fairness; he made his way with lies and perfidy.

One day a shepherd of the seaward hills lay dozing, and at his side his dogs were dozing, too. The craven-wolf, seeing his chance, crept up on the flock and whispered to the old ram who led them all.

"Why should there always be this fear and slaughter between us?" said the craven-wolf to the old ram.

The ram regarded him uneasily, but not uneasily enough. He was the eldest and the wisest of this flock, but that was nothing much to boast of. Sheep in the seaward hills of Armorica are a dim lot, even among sheep.

And so the craven-wolf continued. "That evil dog has

*much to answer for. He always barks whenever I approach
you. He attacks when I have neither done nor mean you
any harm. If you would only dismiss him from your heels,
peace and harmony would reign among us. We could rec-
oncile and live as brothers, all in all."*

The ram, wise fool that he was, took this sentiment
to heart.

"I will," he said. And so he went to his master's side,
and woke the shepherd dog with rude jolts from his horns.

"Ram," the dog said, "what are you on about?"

The ram glowered at him.

"It has come to me that you and yours are the reason
why my people live in fear. Be gone from my flock, and
do not cast your shadow on this meadow ever once again."

The dog looked away, snickering.

Dogs don't carry the cunning that wolves and foxes do,
but beside a sheep a dog seems clever indeed. This is a
fact as apparent to the dog as it is to anyone—and few
dogs fail to let sheep know how dim sheep are.

"You are a fool," said the shepherd dog. "A fool who
ought to learn good manners, too. Go back to your grass
and leave me to my nap, old ram."

The old ram took such umbrage at this condescension
that he backed three steps and charged the shepherd dog,
butting him so hard the poor dog rolled senseless head
over paws for a dozen yards.

When his head cleared, the dog got to his feet, growling
something threatful at the ram—

Who was already charging him again.

And what could the shepherd dog do? The same thing
you and I would do in that circumstance.

He ran for his life.

That is how the craven-wolf came to reside among the
sheep of the seaward hills.

What he did among them is much worse.

For even as the old ram took up business with the shepherd dog—even as the shepherd himself rolled over in his sleep and bellowed, demanding silence from his flock—even then the craven-wolf was on about his evil.

The craven wolf found himself a lamb who had wandered from the tending of its ewe, resolved to find some plea that might justify to all the flock the wolf's right to consume him.

This lamb was one of the most innocent, touched as many lambs are by the Grace that comes from Christ.

Remember: often when Christ comes to us, he comes wearing the form of a lamb.

"Lamb," said the craven-wolf, "last year you snubbed me. I grieve at the way you called my honor into question."

"I never could," the Lamb bleated in a mournful tone of voice. "Last year I was not yet born."

The wolf scowled.

"You fed in my pasture, leaving nothing for me in the field," the wolf said.

"No, good sir," replied the Lamb, "I have not yet weaned. I have never eaten any grass, not yours nor man's nor God's."

The wolf snarled. "You drank my well, and left it dry."

"Never!" said the lamb. "I am still so innocent my mother's milk is both food and drink to me."

"Well!" said the wolf. "Argue all you like, you urchin. I am too sly to be impeded by the wit of one dim lamb."

With that the wolf tore off the lamb's hide and swallowed him skinless but whole.

None other of the flock witnessed this. If they had they might have indicted the wolf when he came among the flock, wearing the hide of the lamb and pretending to be one of their number.

But they did not see, and sheep are dim creatures who can be fooled by wolves in lambs' wool.

The shepherd might have recognized him, if he'd been paying any mind. But he was bleary eyed, unsettled from his interrupted nap. When evening came he led his flock down from the pasture, not noticing that one of his own was a wolf in lamb's clothing.

When they reached the shepherd's cottage, he herded his sheep and the wolf among them into the fold, closed the gate, and secured it.

Late that night the shepherd returned to the fold to cull a lamb for slaughter.

The sheep, dim creatures that they are, know what it means when the crook comes in the darkness, and when it came they sidled from it speedily. But the wolf knew nothing of the fold, and when the crook came it took him easily.

When the shepherd saw what he had taken, he slaughtered the wolf immediately.

Sometimes evil comes to us cloaked in the robes of Christ. But no deception can conceal its nature forever, and righteousness will always have its hour.

The way Cab Callolee told that tale, it was even longer than I tell it here. He told about the creatures and the personalities, the love and the losses and the grief and all of that, adding many a homily you've heard oftener than these. I only pass the gist of his tale to you, to give you a small sense of the evening. It was important to Cab's story, after all; the Princess Gwendolyn was still listening to him, out there in the darkness, and the way she listened and the reasons that she did are exactly the stuff that make the story here at hand.

Anyway, by the time Cab finished · telling of the sheep and the wolf, and how they'd only just survived, it was late into the evening, and many in that room were deep into their cups. Cab himself was sober, though—it's important to remember that, it makes a difference later. He'd sipped his ale, as necessary, to keep his palate wet; but for all that he sipped at it for hours he hardly had enough to make a child dizzy.

"Another tale!" somebody shouted. "Tell about Lyonesse! Too many here remember that too well."

It was a great time when the Prince of Sundown led the armies of Armorica over the narrow sea and into Lyonesse. Great forces were about the lands: It was the end of the only age the world had ever known; it was the beginning of the age we live in, and every foot that fell that year echoed mightily through all of time, and back again.

Everything about us, about the world, the land, the people, the nature of our circumstance—everything was in flux. But the thing we noticed most about it was the war. As well we might! Who among us had no reason to fear for life and limb that year? Who among us did the battles spare?

None. Not a solitary one.

When the war had raged its way into Lyonesse so close to us across the sea, every solitary person in the Kingdom of Armorica knew in his heart that it was time to stand and fight. Some fought for ideas, and some fought for booty; others said they fought because the king's gold paid them. But the truth is that we all fought for our lives, and desperately, for if we'd lost the war, every solitary one of us would have died, and everything we knew and loved would have died with us.

And then the great Prince Rupert of Sundown called us all to arms, and led into our ships, over the water to Lyonesse.

The numbers weighed against us, there. We faced the vast and victorious Saxon army, legion upon legion of fearsome warriors bent on the conquest and destruction of our world and all we knew within it.

We met them there, and, oh, but the battle was a grievous bloodbath! Here, look at me, I hold my good left hand up before you—no, it is no longer good, this is the hand that the firesword touched, where it stole two fingers and my thumb.

The Saxons said that they were supermen, inheritors of the world, and they fought us grievously. But their advantages were in numbers, not in kind. We were fresh, and we had a resource the Saxon army could not imagine: Prince Rupert.

There are those who say Prince Rupert is a hard man, and those who live in fear of him. There are those who say the King himself owes his throne and his life to the Prince of Sundown, and probably they're right. But none, no matter how they feel toward the prince, no one could deny he is a military genius.

A genius.

He split our army into two. One flank he landed at Torquay, Cornwall, to fight the Saxon army where it expected to be fought, at the Bitter Pass that leads from Cornwall into Lyonesse. But the greater part of our strength remained at sea ten days more, sailing all around Lyonesse and Cornwall to the south coast of Cumbria.

They landed there at Cardiff, fresh and rested. And they marched by dark of night into Lyonesse from the north.

When the battle at the Bitter Pass was at its thickest, when the enemy had concentrated his forces against our people at the pass, Prince Rupert led us screaming into the enemy's flank.

Oh, how Lyonesse ran red with blood that day! Some say we stained the vast lake at the center of the Lyonesse plateau, stained it with the Saxons' blood, and others say the water there still runs red, and always will.

Just after noon the Saxons who still lived broke and ran. We gave no pursuit; there were too few of them alive to ever menace anyone again.

"What became of them, Cab?" the princess asked. There was no one else still waking; the soldiers, the hangers-on, the courtiers—all of them had collapsed into their ale cups.

All but a few had faded out halfway through the story of battle of Lyonesse—passed out drunk. Partly because they'd heard it all before (too many times, though none of them dared say so) or, worse, lived it just scant years ago.

But partly also it was because of the castle's infamous black honeyed ale—sweet, rich, powerful stuff, that ale, known to make drunkards of the largest and most steadfast men.

At the very end, only the Princess of Sundown was still alert. She was as drunk as anyone else . . . Cab had watched her drinking all night long, but she held it very well—so well that it came to Cab that the princess had to be a lush.

"Those who survived the retreat, milady," said Cab, "took refuge in the east, at Anglia. It's said they still abide there."

Cab took a long look at the princess. Yes, she was

a lush, he thought; she had a look about her of a woman who drinks mightily to salve a deep wound of the heart.

Her guards were all utterly asleep, drunk and snoring.

"You make my husband sound like a prince," said the princess.

"He is a prince, milady," said Cab. "He is Prince Rupert of Sundown, hero of the Battle of Lyonesse."

The princess snorted. "My husband is an un-manned pig," she said. "He is the beast that murders unicorns in the forest and sends their bodies home to fill his larder."

"Surely his huntsmen and the game-bearers misunderstood, milady," said Cab. "The hero of Lyonesse could never descend among the anthropophagi."

The princess shook her head. "You could never be more wrong," she said. "Every day it's worse. Last year it was brutal raids among the Gaulish folk who would pay no tribute. How many of them are there now alive? A handful, no more, surely, and those who live hide from the face of the sun like battered curs. This year he hunts the forest, killing everything he can pretend is not a man—a unicorn yesterday, three infidels a week ago. And what will come next year? Will he hunt our own peasants in their fields, and grind their bones for bread? In my heart I know he will. He is no man, my husband, but a monster on two legs."

Cab was speechless. Partly stunned—how could she speak of the Prince of Sundown this way? How could she dare? No matter that she was the princess here, matron of this castle, she took her head in her hands when she spoke those things.

And surely, *surely*, Cab did not dare respond.

The princess gestured at the drunken guards impatiently and shook her head. "No better than their master," she said. "Follow me."

A drunken guard stirred in his stupor. Sat up.

Groaned.

Collapsed.

The rest of the room was still.

The princess was on her feet, weaving unsteadily among the tables. In a moment she was beside Cab, and now she took his hand and repeated: "Follow me."

Cab had an awful, fateful yearning in his gut, then. A sense that he ought to turn and run and at the same time a longing for the moment that was upon him.

Oh, he never would have said a thing like that, then. He never could! And, if he'd had the sense God gave a rock, he would have run for his life then, while there was still so much less for anyone to hound him for.

But the sad thing is that none of that mattered worth a damn. Because Cab Callolee was already trapped and pinned, caught in a moment he never could escape—

—as Princess Gwendolyn of Sundown took his hand and pulled him off the platform, to lead him out of that tap hall, now bereft of all cognition and perception, to a place in the back of the hall where the princess touched three broken stones in sequence to make a great section of the wall swing free on hinges, as if it were a cupboard door.

She grabbed a torch from off the wall and led Cab through the apeture.

There is no real way Cab Callolee could have refused her. She was the matron of the castle; her request was law, and if he had tried to deny her it would have meant his head.

Which was the trap exactly: if Prince Rupert heard tell of him in the company of the princess, that would have meant his life as well. The prince was a vastly and famously jealous man, and more than once he'd taken the life of a man he had no real reason to suspect.

"Where are we?" Cab asked, nowhere near as nervous as he ought to've been in the circumstance. "I never knew this passage of the Castle Sundown."

The princess snorted. "Of course you didn't," she said. " 'Tis a secret passage, after all."

Cab snorted. He almost said, *Aye, and what other secrets am I to learn tonight?*—but held his tongue for prudence's sake.

Now they cam upon a place where the passages opened out into a lighted room, and Cab saw they were passing near the kitchen.

"Do not fret," the princess said. "Cook and his helpers are my creatures. We have nothing to fear from them."

Even so she let go of his hand before she led him into the kitchen.

"Ho, Cook," said the princess. "Tell me your fortune."

Cook was standing at a great cauldron, a pot larger than a man—a pot large enough to cook a unicorn whole. He looked up from his work when the princess called to him.

He looked uneasy and unwell. He blinked, surprised, when he saw the princess; blinked twice more when he saw Cab Callollee.

"Milady," he said. There was terror in his voice. "Cab Callolee."

Cook's leathery skin had begun to peel in the hours since last Cab had seen him; there was a new stain in his hair, too—a color now sifting through the grey that Cab would have said was youth returned to him if common sense hadn't told him that such a thing never could be.

"Unicorn stew," the princess said. "Stars and hills, what other abominations has that bastard got inside his heart?"

"Milady," Cook said, ignoring the question that he could never dare to answer. "Milady, I am in terror. The tales are true, I can see that now. There is a quality of sorcery inside the carcass of that thing. Look what it does to my kitchen!—and I myself, I feel quite strange, I feel—it is a mortal thing, I think. I feel my life before me."

Cab looked—really *looked*—at the kitchen for the first time and noticed now the strangeness Cook spoke of. It was nothing that he ever would have guessed, not a destruction or a mayhem, not a menacing at all, in fact. It was more as though some strange principle had reversed the wear on everything. The walls, which should have borne a thousand years of grease and soot, were clean and pristine, now, like fresh cut stone; the pots, which should have hung all black and battered, looked new as they must've on the day the smithies forged them.

Even the floor, which should have borne an age of filth and footwear, even the floor had grown immaculate.

It was a wrongness, Cab knew. But he was not sure it was an evil thing. He wasn't sure at all.

"What happened here?" the princess asked. "Tell me everything that happened, Cook."

Cook shook his head. "Nothing I could describe to you, milady. I tend my pot; the stew does simmer steadily. And as the vapors rise up off my pot, they . . . change things."

The princess nodded. "I'd like to see what they do to that bastard husband of mine," he said. "Peel away the evil part of him, I'd guess, and there'd be nothing left at all."

"The tale goes that it purifies," Cab said. "That's what the crones will whisper if you ask them for their lore."

Cook licked his lips uneasily. "Milady," he said, "I beg you, please. Free me tonight, give me leave to run. I know that I will not survive the night if I remain."

The princess winced.

"Forgive me, Cook," she said. "I cannot. My husband would not honor my word if I freed you. He would hunt you down, as he hunts down all of those he claims."

Cook closed his eyes. "Then I am doomed," he said.

"I'm sorry, Cook," the princess said. There was grief in her voice, and guilt there, too.

And then she led Cab Callolee away.

She led him back into the secret passage—up now, up and up, till finally she led him into her private chamber through a doorway made out of a mirror.

I don't belong here, Cab thought. *Dear God, what have I done?*

He was a dead man then, and he knew it. There was no escape for him, none whatever. Unless he pleaded with the princess? *Give me leave, milady, while I still have it, let me run for my life while I still breathe.* She had a heart, he thought. She would free him if he begged.

And he tried to.

He tried to ask the princess for her leave and her forgiveness; he tried to speak the words that would have saved his life.

But he never could.

There was something in the moment that would not let him free. Something that dictated that he stand away, listening and watching as the princess sat on the edge of her bed and began to unlace her boots. . . .

She asked about the pelicans, then. "Did you know them?" she asked. "Have you seen them?"

"I know them well, milady."

"What are they like? As creatures, not as characters in a story."

Cab frowned. "Oh, I like them well enough. Not that they don't have their faults. We all have our faults, don't we? It's a dull bird who has none, I say." He put his hand on his chin, remembering. "The bigger one is always ill-tempered in the morning, and the little one will squawk piteously when she is afraid. And she often is afraid. But I love them, in my way. They are very dear to me."

"Did they have a future? After the story, I mean, could they really live that way, broken like that?"

"Last I saw them, they got on well enough. He took up residence in the attic of an inn, where he lives on rats and bugs and things better not considered. It isn't the fisher's life a pelican is born to, but it's a good life, touched by a strange unnatural sort of grace, I'd say. She helps him when she can. They rue the death of all their drams, but they live a good life and live it decently enough. God knows, they may be happier this way than they might have been if they could fly among the stars as they were born to do."

There was something building in the air as they spoke, Cab thought. A tension, yes, a tension made out of desire. Fierce and consuming, hard to understand.

Cab Callolee was a man of restrained passions, but there was something about the moment, the circumstance, and most especially in the princess herself—something that had him all but trembling with need. He wanted her, he realized—wanted her intensely.

But because he was a man of restrained passions, he kept his peace. Oh, it wasn't all gallantry on his part; he stepped back and rested his back against the wall because he was a gentleman, but also out of self-preservation. It would mean his head if he were caught here, and if he were caught here in the throes of passion it would mean an even slower and crueler end.

The plain fact was, Cab Callolee restrained himself because he was terrified.

The princess, on the other hand—the Princess Gwendolyn was a woman without fear. Or . . . at least at this moment . . . scruples!

There was a moment, while he whispered on and on about the broken pelicans, there was a moment when she looked at him with a bright light in her eye, and Cab knew just exactly what that was about.

It meant that there was something in him that she wanted and that she meant to take it, no matter what it cost them both.

Cab Callolee wasn't willing, not all in all. He wanted her, and wanted her intensely, but not nearly so intensely as he wanted to keep living.

Later it was different. But right then, right there— Cab Callolee was a coward.

And a fool.

"Sit beside me, Cab," the princess said. "I want to listen to you closely."

And maybe, just maybe, in the end Cab wasn't such a coward after all. Because he went to her when she called him, and he sat beside her there.

"Hush, now," she said.

And she told him her own tale for hours in the dim light of her chambers.

Cab Callolee was unsure of his desire, his moment, and his circumstance. But he wasn't nearly unsure enough to run.

He could still have tried that, then. For those long moments as he sat beside her on that bed, he could have stood up, hurried through the mirror, and tried to run for all his life.

It might have worked.

But that moment only lasted for so long, and then he *was* lost, deep down inside where we all really doom ourselves, Cab Callolee was lost.

For the longest time it was just talking between them, whispering as close and intimate as passion, but quieter and more intense.

She told him stories of her life and her adventures, of who she was and how she came to be the person

that she was. She fed him oranges and salted flatbread, she gave him wine fortified with something
so heady it made the world around them spin.

They talked and drank and traded stories late into
the night.

When the hours were small and the castle all
around them was as still as stone, the princess began
to look exhausted.

"I should leave you, milady," said Cab Callolee,
"Before I lose all my restraint, and take you in my
arms."

The princess smiled hungrily.

"You mustn't touch me," she said. "We both know
you never should."

She kissed him, then. And took his hand to wrap
his arms around her.

He touched her lightly, caressing her, not meaning to.

It got confusing after that. And wonderful, too.
Somewhere in the midst of it Cab wondered what
the prince would do when he heard of it, and he
realized that he could no longer care, realized that
he wanted her, and even loved her in the way we
love those with whom we've shared our darkest secrets and our fears.

He wanted her more than he wanted everything,
anything, anything in the world. No matter what the
consequences, no matter what the fate that fell upon
him, he knew how right the moment was, and there
was no way he ever could deny it.

This is adultery, he thought. *Not even mere adultery.
The prince will call it treason. I would never do a thing
like this if I were in my right mind. I never have. It's
always seemed—just wrong, that's all.*

But then and there, it seemed exactly right. He wasn't certain why.

They made love for hours, on and on. She brought things out of his heart and his desire—a quality of hunger—that astounded him.

They had only just collapsed at cockcrow when someone rattled at the door.

Someone rattled at the door, trying to get in.

"Oh, damn," the princess said. "Huelga with my morning tea."

Cab sat up, terrified, looking for a place to hide, to run. But there was none.

"Don't worry," the princess said. "The door is locked."

Just then, Huelga rattled a great ring of keys, found the right one, and unlocked the door.

She opened it and entered unannounced.

How long is a moment? Some moments go on forever, Cab Callolee would say. It was a moment like that when the lady Huelga took in the scene that was her mistress's chamber—that moment went on and on and on before poor Huelga gasped, blanched, dropped the tray she was carrying.

The servant turned tail to hurry from the room, letting the door slam closed behind her.

"Oh, double damn," said the princess.

In a moment she was on her feet, pulling on her shift.

Hurrying out the door after Huelga. Cab (buck-naked and entirely disheveled) followed her as far as the door, and when she closed it after her, he opened it just wide enough to peer through.

He could see the princess grab the girl's shoulder.

Stop her in her tracks in the hallway and speak to her.

Cab listened to her closely, at once terrified and yet remarkably unafraid of what was about to come upon them.

"If you breathe a word of what you've seen," the princess told Huelga, "I'll slit your throat myself."

Huelga trembled at her mistress, cowering. "Not so much as a solitary whisper," Huelga said. "I swear to you my silence, please, milady, I beg you for my life."

The princes shoved the girl away.

"I bind you to that, Huelga," she said. "I bind your oath to all your days and all of your descendants. If you break it there will be no end of it for you and yours."

And then she let the poor girl go.

And returned to Cab, who waited in her chamber.

Kissed him twice.

Closed, bolted, and barred the door behind her.

"We have an hour left to our lives," she said. "My husband owns us soon enough. Make your peace with God, Cab Callolee."

Cab blinked.

"But she swore a profane oath to you, milady. Surely . . ."

"My name is Gwen, Cab. You are my lover and I am about to die. If you call my 'milady' one more time, I will strike you down, I swear it."

"—she *swore*—"

"The child is a liar and a spy. We're dead, Cab." A pause. "Say my name before we die, Cab."

"Gwen," said Cab. "I love you, Gwen."

The princess smiled. "I love you, too, I think," she

said. "Perhaps I'll die happy, now. That's something, isn't it?"

Cab Callolee rolled his eyes. "Die happy, Gwen? Devil take that," said Cab. "Let's run."

"Run! Where?" The princess asked. She scowled. "There's no point, Cab. The monster I married will hunt us to the ends of the earth. And when he finds us, it will be an awful death, a cruel and lingering death."

"Which will be even more likely to occur if he catches us here, like this," said Cab. "We're running."

"He would follow us to hell, if we could find our way there."

"Then let him hound us," said Cab Callolee. "For every hour that he must hunt us is an hour we have stolen from him."

After a long moment, the princess began to laugh. And then she dressed herself, and gathered the three things from that place that were precious to her heart, and led Cab Callolee out through the secret passage from her room.

The secret egress from the castle led out the same passage they'd taken to reach the princess' chamber, back out through the kitchen, just as they'd come.

Cook was still in the kitchen when they got there. He was still alone.

The kitchen had continued to transform in the hours since last they'd passed through it, till now it was utterly pristine. There was a powerful newness about everything, a quality of fierce unraveling of— time? Some powerful and abiding alchemy had burned away the kitchen's events and history, till now the walls themselves were innocent of everything that had passed through them.

Cook himself had transformed even more violently. He was years younger, somehow, his skin peeled away to reveal a ruddy newness, like a baby's skin, black stubble on his balding gray brow, a high boyish quality to his voice. He was not the same man either one of them had known.

"Unicorn stew," said Cook to Princess Gwendolyn. "It has burned the years away from my kitchen—it has burned the years away from me, as well. If you partake of it, perhaps it will burn away the things that plague you, too."

He took a great soft round of flatbread from the steamer and set it on his carving table. Ladled stew inside to fill it, and folded the bread up like a pillow. When he was done he pressed it into Cab's hands.

Cab looked at it dumbly.

"Put it in your rucksack, Cab. Mind me! You will need that stew. If you will not eat it here and now, you will partake of it later. Don't argue with me! Do it!"

The princess ignored the two of them; she wasn't about to deal with anything as grotesque or as unseemly as unicorn stew.

Besides, she had more pressing things on her mind.

Like Huelga.

"Huelga," she said. She bit her lip. "The rumors have started already, haven't they?"

The cook frowned sadly. "I have heard a tale, milady," he said. "I think that you should run as fast and as far as you can."

The princess nodded.

"We mean to," she said.

Cook nodded in turn. "There is a ship down at the docks, by the river," he said. "The captain there is in my debt. Go to him quietly, while darkness still holds. Mention my name, call in my chit, and he will carry you away."

The secret passage took them out of the castle near took them out of the castle near the place where the castle's sewage trough emptied into the river. It was stone, like the door in the tap hall, but secreted still further by a thicket of scrub trees and tall grass. It didn't open easily at all; it had been years since anyone had used it, and in that time thick roots had grown into the crevices around the doorframe. They made it very difficult to open. But it did open, after a little effort, and then they were walking by the river through the moonless night, seeking out the ship Cook had named for them. It wasn't easy, since there were half a dozen ships in port; Sundown is not a busy harbor, being a river port, but it does business enough.

"The *Moonlord's Daughter*," Cab said. "There she is."

"You can read that in this darkness?"

Cab shrugged. "A storyteller gets an eye for detail. I try to see everything I can."

He grabbed hold of the mooring line—there was no plank or ladder, not at this hour in an uncertain port like Sundown—and climbed it to the ship's railing.

"Ho, watch," he called in a whisper. "Rouse your captain for me, and be quick about it."

The watchman—a boy, really—the watch was half asleep, sitting on his rear with his back against the mast, all but snoring.

"What?"

"I said good evening, boy," said Cab, not exactly accurately. "Wake your captain. He owes, and I'm calling the debt."

Cab pulled himself over the railing and lowered the ladder to Princess Gwendolyn.

The captain stumbled out of his cabin just as the princess made her way up the last of the ladder.

When he saw her, he gasped.

"Princess Gwendolyn," he said. "To what do I owe the honor—?"

"Hello, dear Captain," the princess aid. "I am here to call in your debt to the cook of Castle Sundown. We sail at once, in haste."

The captain blinked, clearly torn between fear of the distant king and fear of the queen before him. Proximity triumphed.

"As you say, milady," he said. "As you say, milady, it is done."

Two hours before sunrise, they were on the open sea.

When they were out of sight of land, Cab took the bunk they'd offered him—it had been the first mate's bunk, they said, but he was a guest of the captain and was welcome to it—when they were out of sight of land, Cab took the bunk they'd offered him and let sleep take him.

It was the first sleep he'd had in two days, since he'd made camp in the forest north of Sundown, and he should have slept hard because he was exhausted. But the way it happened was the opposite: He slept fitfully with battered fiery dreams that rocked him like the sea.

Perhaps it was the sea that rocked his dreams. Perhaps. He was no seafarer, that's for certain; surely the unaccustomed rocking of the waves did it's part to stir his dreams.

Cab woke at dusk unsettled and confused—so disoriented that for a long hard moment he forgot who and where and what he was, till he stumbled from the bunk on deck all doubtful of the world around him.

"Cab Callolee," the ship's mate called to him. "There is dinner left waiting for you in the galley. If you hurry after it, it may still be warm when you reach it."

"Galley," said Cab. "Galley?" In his defense, he was still exhausted and had darned few of his wits about him.

The mate gestured at a door a few feet to Cab's left, "Over there, Cab Callolee," he said, laughing, and Cab stumbled toward it, still groggy.

There was one man in the galley, and Cab knew that man. He was Petersen Flint, and when they'd been boys together in that village west of Sundown, Petersen had dreamed that he would someday grow up to be a wizard.

"Petersen!" said Cab (for no matter how disoriented he might be, he had always clear memories of his youth). "What in all the world are you doing here?"

Petersen smiled broadly.

"I'm the ship's navigator, Cab," he said. "Not bad for a country boy, eh?"

Cab laughed.

In those days before men learned to navigate by reckoning the sun and moon and stars, navigation

was a black art in the truest sense. A ship's navigator
was in no wise a wizard, but he was a good deal
more than a than a seer and, often as not, a damn
fine sorcerer.

"Well, I'll be," said Cab. "It's good to see you,
Petersen." He took the seat across from Petersen,
opened the covered dish that'd been left there for
him, and began to eat.

"And you, Cab? What's become of you?"

Cab shrugged. "Look at me," he said. "I am the
man you see."

Petersen laughed. "Not by half," he said. "They
tell of your tales far and side, Cab—in ports you
never would imagine."

Cab smiled. "Do they, now?" he asked. But in its
way the question was a lie, because he knew good
and well that it was so.

Petersen snorted, and then he leaned close. "Tell
me, Cab," he said, "is it true what they say? About
the Princess Gwendolyn?"

Cab flinched, as though he'd been struck. *"Petersen!"* he said. "What sort of a question is that?"

Petersen pulled back in his seat.

"Sorry, Cab," he said. "I ought've thought before
I asked, I guess."

He left after that, and Cab Callolee finished his
meal alone, in silence.

They sailed three long, hard days with the wind
full in their sails, hurrying toward a port in Albion,
where the Princess Gwendolyn had kin and certain
sanctuary.

At dusk on the third night, the watch went up into

the crow's nest and spotted pursuit on the horizon behind them.

"Sail hard, boys," the Captain called. "We've got a chase."

And they sailed on into the night.

At moonrise there was shouting, and Cab stumbled out of his bunk to see the mate dragging Petersen across the deck by his hair.

"I heard this galley rat in his cabin, mumbling sorcery," said the mate, "and opened the door to find him talking to his mirror."

The Captain and the princess were on deck now, too. So was most of the crew.

"And what of that?" asked the Captain. "Man has a right to talk to himself, I say. Mad or not, he's our navigator."

The mate snorted. "Well enough," he said. "But it wasn't him in the mirror. 'Twas Prince Rupert, his own self! This rat is the little monster who told him where to find us."

"Petersen," Cab asked—or blurted, more exactly. "Petersen, I've known you all my life. How could you betray me?"

Petersen looked up at Cab with wide, guilty eyes.

"He owns me, Cab," he said. "I got no choice. He owns my soul."

The Captain's face reddened, and the crew was near as angry. But the really striking thing that moment was the blood rage in the princess's eyes.

"You did *what*?" she asked Petersen. "*What* did you do?"

She walked toward the navigator as she spoke, trembling and angry.

Petersen tried to answer her, but he never had a

chance. Because the princess was upon him, inches from him.

She grabbed the dagger out of the mate's belt.

Whispering her question one last time, she pressed the point of the dagger into the soft flesh underneath the navigator's chin.

"What did you tell him? How much did he promise you?"

Petersen whispered, "Please. I can't tell you! It will mean my life if I do . . ."

"And if you don't . . ." she said. When he refused to speak another word, the princess pressed the dagger up into poor Petersen's skull.

There was a lot of blood. An *awful* lot of blood.

When the body stopped twitching, the Captain heaved it overboard and left it for bellies of the sharks.

It was Prince Rupert himself at the helm of the corsair that overtook them at midnight.

"Surrender, sailors!" he shouted as he drew up along side them. "Submit to me now and you will all die quickly and mercifully."

"Go to hell, you man-eating pig," the Captain answered. "We'll feed your sorry gullet to the fish if you don't go away."

"It's a fight to the death, then," the mate whispered to Cab and the princess as the prince's ship pulled up alongside and the battle began. "I've a notion we're to die, but we'll drag the king's men to hell along with us."

Cab, the princess, and the mate stood on deck, near the wheel, as far from the fighting as they could be and still remain on the ship. The mate held the wheel, but he held it uneasily, as though he would rather be fighting.

"Perhaps we'll die," said the princess. "But we aren't dead yet, and while we live, we have hope."

The mate nodded. "There's the spirit," he said. "Look how the crew fights the bastards! Aye, they're my lot. I love them all."

"Give us swords," said the princess, "and we will fight the enemy, too. And, if need be, die at our own hands, not theirs."

Prince Rupert was on the deck of the corsair, now, looking for an opportunity to join the fray.

"I suspect it will come to that, milady," said the mate. "The melee goes quickly, and not well. You'll have to steal a weapon from one of the dead—they'll have no use for it now, after all."

"Here," said Cab, "I've a dagger in my rucksack." He took the bag from his back, opened it, and looked inside.

Found the dagger—and something else entirely.

What he found was the thing that the cook had given him, hot and steaming, days ago.

The bread wrap filled with unicorn stew.

Cab remembered what Cook had said, just before they'd left his kitchen.

It has burned the years away from my kitchen—it has burned the years away from me, as well. If you partake of it, perhaps it will burn away the things that plague you, too.

"Cab," said the mate, "I can't stand here watching my friends die out there another moment. Take the wheel for me."

"Not yet . . ." Cab Callolee'd meant to take his dagger and dive into the fray himself—he would already have done that, in fact, if he had not found the still-steaming food wrapped up inside his bag.

"Princess," he said, drawing the wrap out of the bag, offering it to her, "Princess, take this, the stew from Cook. Eat it—you saw the cook. Perhaps it can save you."

The princess blinked, and blinked again.

"I'm not eating unicorn, not even to save myself," the princess said. "It would turn me into the same kind of monster my husband is. Besides, he knows what I've done and knows that I'm to blame—and he's right. I enjoyed every minute of it! Damn him anyway! I can hardly wait to tell him what I think of him to his face! So let's get on with this. Get rid of that thing!"

So Cab did.

Pitched the packet full of unicorn stew as hard as he possibly could.

Pitched it straight at Prince Rupert.

High up over the deck at the prince, who was boarding from his corsair—caught him right in the eyes, Cab did.

And the strangest thing happened when the unicorn stew touches that man.

As Prince Rupert of Sundown raised his hand to wipe the steaming, reeking, roiling stew from his face, it burst afire.

He burst afire.

He burned like a bonfire, Prince Rupert did.

The prince was an evil, evil man and the impurity in him burned as fiercely as hot lard burns in an ordinary fire. He burned so hot, so angry, so intensely that everything around him burst aflame in turn; the ships, first, both ships were afire, burning brighter than a unicorn in the sun.

It happened *fast*, very fast. There was no time for anyone to grab a lifeboat, hardly time for anyone to dive overboard; even Cab and the princess at the far end of the ship were close enough to feel the heat of the flames race toward them.

In an instant they were the last beings alive on either ship as the roaring flames consumed everything in their path. Even the seawater burned where it touched the ship.

"Jump," the princess said. Despite the flames, it was crazy idea: They were in open water, and far at sea; there was no land anywhere to swim toward. "Jump, damn you! Or do you want to die here and now?"

Cab hesitated. "We'll drown," he said.

The fire was so close, now, close enough to reach and touch.

"So?" the princess said. And then she shoved him over the rail.

And jumped in after him into the heated waters.

They swam hard in those first moments, trying to get away from the burning, sinking ships. They swam so hard that after only a few moments Cab was soon breathless. There was no land in sight, no more than there'd been any in sight from the wheel of the doomed *Moonlord's Daughter*; they were dead for certain. But Cab had never given up in his life. He wasn't going to start now.

"We need to slow down and take it easy," Cab said. "Kick off your shoes and anything else weighing you down and swim on your back, slowly.

Watch the stars. Swim in a straight line. If we're lucky, a passing ship will find us."

And they swam for hours and hours, into the night, praying for rescue.

They managed to swim that way for a time. But soon enough, beneath the light of the moon, thirst wracked them and strength failed them. They started to drown.

They almost did drown, too. But they didn't. Because they were off the coat of Avalon, where the sea is tide-shallow for miles and miles off the shore— so shallow that a body can wade through knee-deep water hours from the beach.

When the princess wearied and stopped swimming, her feet touched the sandy bottom almost immediately.

In a moment, Cab saw what had happened and knew where they were.

Then he took the princess's hand. And they walked through the sunrise toward a beach they could not see, until the tide went out to leave them alone on a sandy shore that stretched for miles, as far as either one of them could see.

They began their new life then, walking on the beach in the golden dawn. It was a new beginning for them both, one last gift from a doomed Unicorn.

IN QUEST OF THE BEAST
by Jean Rabe

When not writing, Jean Rabe feeds her goldfish, visits museums, and attends gaming conventions. A former newspaper reporter, she is the author of nine fantasy novels including the *Dragonlance* Fifth Age Trilogy. Her latest novel is *Dhamon: The Downfall*. She has written numerous fantasy and science fiction short stories which appear in the anthologies *Merlin* and *Tales from the Eternal Archives: Legends, Guardsmen of Tomorrow*, and *Warrior Fantastic*.

Clare couldn't afford to be the last one to leave tonight, so she delegated Stewart to finish the Society for Creative Anachronism display. She passed him the permit that allowed them to be in the student union after hours, slipped into her Madison Muskies jacket, and slung her new backpack over her shoulder.

She'd been the last one to leave the past three nights, taking on the proverbial lion's share of the work on the overly elaborate and very time-consuming project—which was only right, as Stewart had repeatedly pointed out.

"Your idea. Your responsibility. Your *thing*," he was fond of saying. Last night he had added, "Besides, you're the ranking SCA member at the college, for crissakes. And you're sleeping with the guy who's gonna be the region's next seneschal." Stewart had more than hinted that all of this was to impress her Milwaukee boyfriend, who would be visiting next weekend. Though she scoffed at his comments and said it was only to help with SCA recruitment, Stewart hadn't been entirely wrong.

I should stay and help him finish, she thought, noting, however, that the display was looking very good and that Stewart should have it done in another two hours or so. He was normally so very much like his SCA persona, only interested in fighting and jousts, a jock in any era. But he'd been a relatively good sport about this.

In fact, she had offered to stay, she reminded herself, though there hadn't been any strength to her words—and Stewart knew it. Stewart poignantly played the martyr, shaking his head and raising a hand, fluttering his long, skinny fingers toward the elevator in a dismissive shooing motion.

"Go already. I thought you said you have a big midterm tomorrow? The Quest for King Arthur's Camelot or some such fusty fictional nonsense." He paused and gave her a lopsided grin. "Just because a moistened tart lobbed a scimitar at young Pendragon was no basis for a form of government." Stewart never correctly quoted Monty Python. "Go."

"Yeah, I've gotta go," she told him, padding down the hall and stopping at the elevator. She gave Stewart a last glance. "Gotta study. Hard. Very hard. I should've been hitting it all week. And I shouldn't've stayed here this late."

Go, go, go, he mouthed to her like a mantra.

She groaned at the prospect of her impending all-night-all-morning session and punched her thumb against the down button several times, as if that might speed the elevator's arrival and get her deep into her textbook faster. Clare loved the subject, but she hated the Camelot course because she hated the professor—with all his winks and innuendos and blatant suggestions that she should come over to his condo when his wife wasn't home for . . . how did the slug put it . . . "mulled elderberry wine and much more detailed and comfortable research." She would've gladly dropped the course by the end of the fifth week, when courses were still dropable without affecting one's grades. But her upcoming Master's Thesis was on Sir Thomas Malory and his *Le Morte d'Arthur* as the source of Arthurian Legends, and so the Camelot course could be useful. And she might actually learn something form the lecherous old beady-eyed dirtbag. But once this semester was over and she had her "A" or at the very worst her "B" in hand, and when the next semester had safely started, she intended to file a scathing sexual harassment report with the liberal arts dean about the slug. At the very least she'd get him fired.

"Professor Mides. Professor Creep," she said, as the elevator finally chimed and the doors hissed open. "Professor Slimeball." She stepped inside and stabbed several times at the "1" button. Clare groaned again when the elevator dropped to the ground floor and stopped, the doors defiantly remaining closed. She balled her fist and struck the doors in the center, as she always did when she lazily rode the thing instead of walking down the four flights. One more properly applied fist-pounding and they opened with a protesting hiss. She escaped into the empty lobby.

It was just past midnight, the union closed to the general student body, and only a few lights were on, reflecting off the myriad tall windows and casting a ghostly glow against the polished tile floor. She hurried outside, the Wisconsin fall wind forcing her to zip up her jacket and whipping her hair so wildly across her face that her eyes stung.

"Wonderful."

There was a single loud crack of thunder and she looked up into a black sky that was shot through with bands of thick gray clouds. A heartbeat later she felt the first drop of rain plop on her cheek.

"Truly wonderful."

Clare glanced back at the student union. The front door had *of course* closed and locked securely behind her, and Stewart and any janitors who were about wouldn't be able to hear her shouting to let her back inside. This late, the Madison city bus came by only on the hour.

Her watch proclaimed it ten past midnight. She wasn't about to wait fifty minutes for the next bus. And she wasn't about to walk a block to the nearest payphone to call a cab that she would have to wait God-knew-how-long for and would take her only nine blocks more, charging her what she'd rather spend on lunch tomorrow. So. . . .

"Time to hoof it," she told herself just as the sky opened up.

The rain was cold and came at her sideways, driven by the wind, the drops hard like tiny darts, like angry insects biting her face and hands. She pulled the collar of her jacket up and held the tips together under her chin, and she started to jog across the campus, her heels clicking rhythmically against the concrete sidewalk.

I'll bet Sir Thomas Malory was never caught in weather like this, she thought. *But he would've never been caught dead in Wisconsin.* Knight, prisoner, scholar, he finished his eight tales of Arthur during the ninth year of King Edward IV's reign in an England that in the early fall was assuredly beset by fog and drizzle—but not by the Badger State's bone-chilling cold rain. *Ah, to be in England,* she mused. *Sir Thomas' land.* She intended to use her thesis as an excuse to join a student trip to London next summer. She might actually even study something when she was there, maybe even visit Sir Thomas' grave.

Sir Thomas loved hunting and knightly tournaments, embraced chivalry, and it was said he thoroughly immersed himself in his readings of Arthurian romance. *Tristan, Quest de Saint Graal, Mort Artu*—she'd read all of Malory's works more than once and looked forward to tackling them again.

However, Clare was not looking forward to immersing herself in the lecherous slug's Camelot textbook that was laying open on her desk at home, a seven-hundred-page monstrosity he'd required all his students to buy so he could impress them while earning hefty royalties. The professor's view of the Arthurian legend paralleled Malory's for the most part, at least from what she'd read so far of the text. But in her mind it diverged considerably in a few critical spots, which made the course—though certainly not the slimy instructor—interesting. The test tomorrow would focus mainly on Pellinore, perhaps the foremost knight at King Arthur's round table, and on Morgawse.

Morgawse, Clare concentrated on that woman to take her mind off the weather. Morgawse was said to have come to King Arthur as a messenger, though in truth she was a clever spy and Igraine's daughter, and thus Arthur's sister. Beautiful, she cajoled the king into her bed and later gave birth to Mordred, the man who was both Arthur's nephew and his son. Incest . . .

Clare shivered at the thought and from the cold.

Morgawse. Clare shivered again recalling that the lecherous dirtbag told her just last week that she was "as lovely as Igraine's favored child."

She was soaked before she reached the next corner, the streetlight illuminating the sheet-like rain that was striking the pavement ever harder—and bouncing back. *Tat-tat-tat*, it sounded harshly against the storm grate and the metal lamppost. From somewhere nearby a dog howled mournfully. *Tat-tat-tat.*

Hail? Clare stared. It was staring to *hail*?

"Well and truly wonderful."

She sped up her pace, crossing the street and jogging down a poorly lit service road that ran behind the liberal arts building. It was a shortcut she'd discovered a few weeks after she moved here. Her heels clicked faster, sounding syncopated now with the ice pellets that were pummeling the road and her, bouncing everywhere and performing a stentorian *rat-a-tat-tat* off a collection of big garbage cans. The dog she'd heard continued to howl. Closer now, she decided it sounded as though there were a couple of them—probably chasing a cat that was every bit as wet and unhappy as she was.

I could've taken my "beater" today, she thought, but that would've entailed parking it on the other side of campus during her afternoon classes and trying to find a closer spot when she went to the union. And parking near the union in the middle of the week wasn't likely to happen, unless she was lucky enough to find a place right out front on the street and was willing to feed the meter until well past dark.

So what's a dozen quarters and some inconvenience compared to getting chilled to the bone? she grumped at her practical self.

She found herself wishing she had stayed to help Stewart, at least for fifty more minutes. That would've put her late enough for the one a.m. bus that would have picked her up just across the street from the union and that would have—after a meandering few-mile course—spit her out within a hundred yards of her place.

What would the fifty minutes have hurt since I'd stayed so blasted late anyway?

"Nothing," she answered aloud. It wouldn't have hurt anything. It would have saved her time, actually. Now she would be arriving home thoroughly cold and thoroughly drenched and in need of a hot bath and a hot cup of chocolate that would keep her from the dirtbag's Camelot for at least another hour.

"Three blocks down," she muttered. "Six to go." Clare felt around behind her to make sure her backpack was tied shut. It was green leather, a gift from the soon-to-be-seneschal, and was probably getting ruined because she hadn't been willing to spend the quarters at the meters out front or the blasted fifty minutes to help Stewart.

"Fifty goddamn minutes. I should've stayed in the

union," she said as she passed the far corner of the liberal arts building, where she would be taking her Camelot test in just under ten hours. Light spilled out from a second-floor window. Some professor working late, she thought, someone who had a car conveniently parked right in this lot that she was now crossing.

There was only the one car, she noted, and the hail was loudly *tat-a-tat-tatting* off it and probably scratching the glossy black paint that had been applied in a German factory. Looked expensive.

Clare hadn't bothered to glance up into the window, nor had she registered just which window it was. And so she hadn't seen the professor watching her. He craned his neck to follow her progress across the lot and past his car, and he opened the window so he could hear the hail and the sound of the hounds, the latter most pleasing and familiar. He smiled. It wouldn't be long now.

She darted onto the next street, cutting down a long alley that led past a squat brick apartment building. She had briefly considered renting there three years ago because of its proximity to the liberal arts building, where most of her classes were. But the rooms had been far too small, and her SCA friends rented at the slightly more upscale place that she was now practically running all-out toward.

It was darker away from the campus, but the alley was blacktopped. Slick with water and icy shards, it gleamed in the lights that spilled out of the squat apartment building's windows. Students in their microscopic rooms either studying or partying, Clare thought—probably the former as she didn't hear any obnoxiously loud music drifting out.

Only the constant and annoying *tat-a-tat-tat* and the howling dogs.

"Five blocks down. Five to go," she reassured herself. Clare stopped at the end of the alley and cocked her head, listening to the hail pound the metal roof of a garden shed behind an old Victorian house, strike the street that T-ed in front of her, and patter off her probably-ruined leather backpack. The top of her head was sore from its onslaught. She'd need aspirin with that hot cocoa now.

Those dogs were still howling, even louder it seemed, not caring about the weather and still after that unfortunate cat. There must be an entire pack of them, Clare guessed, as she headed east through an aging residential neighborhood, slowing her pace now because the walk was completely icing up. Everyone was asleep, the windows all dark, the only light coming from the lampposts that were being *tat-tat-tat-tatted* against on every corner.

So loud—the hail and the dogs. *Were they after something else?*

Something niggled at her brain, then, something about the dogs. Something she'd read recently in the slug's textbook and long ago in Malory's writings . . .

. . . something about the howling. About Morgawse and Pellinore and Arthur.

A shiver raced down her spine. She'd definitely been reading too much lately—especially about King Arthur and medieval England and France, about the legends and . . .

So loud.

Reading too much and sleeping too little. Spending too much time on SCA and too many weekends with her boyfriend.

She urged herself faster despite the ice, her feet slipping and slapping against the sidewalk, her eyes darting to the houses, halfway hoping there would be a light on in one of them to signal that someone else was still awake at this hour.

The dogs were certainly baying loud enough to wake up the entire neighborhood—to wake up all of Madison, for that matter. They sounded close. Too close. Her breath caught at the notion that perhaps they were chasing her.

"God, I should've stayed with Stewart," she said. Then she laughed at her nerves and again slowed to a walk, as if her pace would make her calm down and realize how silly she was being. She grabbed her side, which was aching from her run, and she continued to scan the block in front of her for even a front porch light. Ah, there was a light, on a second floor about two blocks down. Another light flicked on a few houses closer, perhaps someone wanting to see what all the barking was about. Maybe they wouldn't mind if she stood on their porch, just to get out of the hail for a few moments and to let the dogs pass.

The howling was so terribly loud now, much louder than the hail, and so wrongfully out of place. Dogs didn't run in packs inside the city limits of Madison. This was Wisconsin, so it was undoubtedly hunting season for something. But not in Madison's city streets. So close, they sounded. Close enough that she should be able to see them. Clare threw her hands over her ears and spun around, nearly losing her balance on the slick pavement.

Where are the dogs?

Nothing. She saw nothing but the hail and the dark

houses, the lampposts still being *tat-tat-tat-tatted* against. And in the distance she saw a soft glow, which was coming from the myriad streetlights on the campus.

Where are the dogs?

There had to be a few dozen of them, she thought by the racket they were making. *Thirty? Forty?*

Forty. Another shiver shot down her back.

Maybe they were in someone's backyard, she thought, giving herself a slight measure of relief at the thought that they wouldn't venture onto the street. Maybe they'd treed the cat they were chasing and would stay put, would not come out where she could see them and make her feel as though she were their target. She laughed again, the sound brittle this time. The dogs—however many there were and no matter where they were—would most certainly leave her alone, she told herself. This was middle-of-the-road, middle-of-the-state Madison, Wisconsin. She was near the university. She was in a peaceful and quiet residential neighborhood a couple of blocks from her apartment. Weird things like hunting dogs going after people didn't happen here. Maybe she should just start running toward home again. Maybe . . .

"What is that?" She hadn't meant to voice the words, or the one following. "Omigod." Her mouth dropped open as her mind tried to put a name to the thing she saw. It was at the edge of her vision, cutting across the old Victorian's front yard and not close enough to truly make out. But it was large, she could tell that, and it moved quickly, gracefully, seemingly heedless of the hail and seemingly heading straight toward her.

As it passed beneath the streetlight, Clare

screamed—her cry of terror drowned out by the hail and the howling—by the pack-of-dogs sound which was coming from just one creature.

"It can't be. It's n–n–not possible. It's n–n–not real!" *It never existed,* she told herself as she turned and ran, her prized leather backpack slipping from her shoulder and hitting the pavement with a *smack!*

"Not real!" she cried as her feet pounded the sidewalk in time with her rapidly beating heart, then struck against the street as she darted across it and toward the closest house with a light on. She took in great gulps of air, pushed her hand against her aching side, and forced herself to move faster still. It would be all right. Someone was up and would let her inside where she'd be safe from the beast.

The impossible beast that lived only in pages written by Sir Thomas Malory, T.H. White, and a few others.

That creature was a thing of fiction, her mind screamed, as the beast screamed. The baying of forty hounds echoed off the homes in the night-dark Madison neighborhood.

She risked a quick glance over her shoulder.

"No!"

The creature was indeed closing in on her and was better revealed in the glare of the streetlight she'd just passed. Her feet were instantly anchored to the ground in terror, her fear holding her in place as surely as if she'd been nailed to the pavement.

The beast certainly didn't look real, though it was clearly moving and breathing and coming right at her. *Nothing that looked like that could be real,* she thought. *It couldn't exist.*

The nightmare creature was at once magnificent

and horrifying. It was longer than a car, its body that of a leopard, spotted coat slick from the rain and hail, sleek muscles rippling under the glow of the streetlight. From its shoulders sprouted the head of an impossibly large snake, green and brown scales glistening, dark eyes sparkling, blood-red forked tongue flicking out. Its maw was open, and the frightening sound of forty hounds that seemed to rumble about in the thing's gut was deafening. The creature slowed its pace to practically a crawl, "clacking" as it neared Clare, the sound of its deer-like hooves crisp against the pavement, its lion's hindquarters quivering.

It was stalking her.

"The Questing Beast," Clare whispered.

In response to her soft words, the snakehead cocked and raised; its thick lizard tail twitched, making it seem catlike.

She'd seen the creature, or renderings of it, depicted in paintings and drawings, illustrations of the beast described by Mallory several times in his *Le Morte d'Arthur*. A symbol of incest, it was said to be, its varying parts symbolizing chaos and anarchy. It was birthed by the Devil upon a princess who had unjustly accused her handsome brother of rape. Her brother hadn't touched her, had rejected her advances. But he died, killed by the beast. Hundreds of years ago.

How could it be here?

Arthur was said to have seen it, according to Mallory. After laying with Morgawse, the king had a dream that all of his people were killed by griffons and great serpents. And when he awoke from the dream, he and some of his knights went hunting.

Arthur followed an impressive stag, chasing it until the horse he was riding died from exertion and he was forced to summon another. While Arthur waited at a fountain, still determined to pursue the stag, a strange creature came to drink. It was the Questing Beast. Pellinore brought the fresh horse to Arthur and saw the creature too. Then Pellinore pursued it, but he was never able to catch it. After Pellinore's death, Sir Palamides, the Saracen knight, chased it.

But that was myth. And hundreds of years ago.

"You're not real," she told it. "Not at all."

For the briefest of moments Clare was sure that it truly wasn't real—that she was dreaming. That she'd fallen asleep in the student union and that she would wait for the bus and then would go home and study for the damnable slug's Camelot test.

That she would be safe.

The creature's tongue flitted out again, tasting the air. Its dark eyes were locked onto hers, holding her in place as surely as any vise. It crept closer, its muscles bunching and releasing, every movement liquid.

"Beautiful," she hissed. Transfixed, she found herself admiring the thing, her mind replaying all the tales of it she'd read and reread. French folklore claimed it was birthed by a woman who'd been torn apart by hounds. It was called *Beste Glatissant,* or the barking beast.

In White's *The Once and Future King* the creature was pitiful and misunderstood. There was no good reason for Pellinore to hunt it, and the knight doing so pointed out that chivalry was often meaningless. But Clare tended to think Malory was right, that the creature had been called into being by the Devil and by a vengeful sister who'd been spurned by her brother.

The creature stopped a few yards from her, perhaps studying Clare as she was studying it. The hail continued to pelt both of them, and the sound of the baying hounds continued to issue from the Questing Beast's belly.

A light flicked on behind her, and she faintly heard the sound of a door creaking open.

"What's all the racket about?" It was a man's voice.

The Questing Beast cocked its head and snarled. The muscles of its back legs gathered themselves.

"No!" Clare screamed as she swung about and bounded down the sidewalk and then up the steps of the house behind her and right into the path of a startled old man.

He was dressed in a rumpled bathrobe, his face creased from sleep, and he held the door handle firmly.

"See here, young woman. You can take your dogs and . . ." he paused and narrowed his eyes, trying to look past her.

The sound of the hounds had stopped. Clare glanced over her shoulder. The Questing Beast was gone. Perhaps it had never been there.

"I'm s–s–sorry," she stammered. "I was just walking home from the student union and . . ." she searched for the words. ". . . and something started chasing me."

The man shook his head. "I don't see anything. Heard some dogs, though."

"It wasn't a dog." The words came quick now. "It was a mythical creature. The Questing Beast. It was part leopard and snake, and it was making the baying sound you heard. I think it was after me, but . . ."

"Drugs," the man said, disgusted. "College students and drugs. You get outta here or I'm going to call the cops on you."

Clare tried to insinuate herself into the doorway, but the old man closed the door in her face until a mere slit of light remained.

"Get out of here. Now."

"No. You don't understand," she pleaded. "I'm so afraid. Could I come in? Just for a moment. I'll call a cab and . . ."

"I'm calling the cops." The door slammed, and she heard a bolt slide into place.

She turned and looked around, terrified. Nothing out of the ordinary . . . She sagged against the side of the house, shaking.

"It's gone."

She looked again. The creature really *was* gone.

"I was dreaming," she said with a sigh of relief. Clare tromped down the stairs once more and started walking.

"Three blocks to go," she grumbled. "Ah . . ." she remembered her dropped backpack and headed out into the street, intending to get it. She stopped when she heard a dog bark. Then another barked, and another . . .

The baying resumed, and from behind a parked pickup truck came the Questing Beast.

She ran, faster than she believed possible, the ache in her side a memory as her feet churned over the sidewalk, then over the curb. She was running in the center of the street now, where the pavement was flat and where she could see better. Her heels *click-*

clacked against the road, just like the hooves of the creature flying along behind her.

"Why are you after me?" she screamed. "Why me?"

The beast didn't answer. It simply bore down on her, leaping with its front legs extended, its deer hooves striking her back sharply and beating the wind from her burning lungs.

Clare screamed as she was driven forward and down. Her head hit the icy street, and the world around her spun and wavered for an instant.

The baying continued, mixed with an odd wuffling sound as if the creature were sniffing her. It pawed at her, turning her over.

She fought desperately against the wooziness engulfing her and tried to get to her feet.

She managed only to make it to her knees, putting her eye-to-eye with the thing's head. It looked at her sadly, if that was possible for a monstrosity, if such a hell-born creature could display anything like remorse.

White was wrong, she thought vaguely. The Questing Beast was not misunderstood and was not a thing to be pitied. It was a killer to be feared and hated.

"*Why?*" she breathed.

A heartbeat later she had her answer. The creature edged forward, its dark eyes wide and mirror-like. Reflected in them was a visage—not hers, but one she knew. *Her slug of a professor's . . .*

She opened her mouth to scream again, but the beast's snakelike maw snapped opened and shot forward, its needle teeth piercing her flesh and ending her life.

And all the while it bayed like a pack of forty hounds.

There was a polite knock. "Professor Mides?" Another knock. "Professor Mides, this is the police. We'd like to speak with you."

The man who opened his door for the officers was distinguished looking. He was markedly handsome, with a complexion that was sun-bronzed, though it was well into fall. He gestured the two officers inside. Both wore plainclothes, marking them as detectives.

The woman flipped open her badge case. "Lieutenant Anders," she said as way of introduction. "And this is my partner, Lieutenant Hoskins."

The professor nodded to each and spread his hands. "May I ask why you've intruded? I was just on my way to my class. I'm giving a midterm at ten."

Lieutenant Anders thrust out her chin. "One of your students was killed last night, Professor. A Clare Kinsley."

He scowled and put on his "sad" face. "Oh, no. A good student," he said. "She was majoring in medieval studies, I believe."

"It seems she was torn apart by some wild animal," the lieutenant continued. "Less than a mile from here."

The professor tsked. "Sorry to hear that. The class will be devastated."

"We'd like to ask you a few questions about Clare and you."

He raised an eyebrow.

"Where were you late last night?"

"Here," he said, gesturing to a desk filled with

opened books and curling papers. "Until after two or so." He cleared his throat. "Why are you asking me this? If a wild animal . . ."

"We have our reasons. Last year about this time another young woman was killed."

He stroked his chin. "Ahh . . . I seem to remember something about that."

"She was one of your students, too."

"Kathy Wilkers," he said. "Kathy had other professors. So did Clare."

"And so did Ellen and Mary Hammerlund," Lieutenant Anders added, checking her notebook. That twin murder dated back four years, to her first year at the university.

A shrug. "So? A coincidence."

"I don't believe in coincidences," the lieutenant replied.

"And what do you believe in, Lieutenant Anders?"

She laughed, the sound pleasant, like crystal wind chimes. "I believe in murder." She gestured to the books surrounding them. "King Arthur and Camelot? I don't believe in those, Professor. But do I believe in finding out what or who killed your students."

"You admit they studied under other professors, too." Mides puffed out his chest. "All of them. They weren't just my students."

"But you're the one thing they have in common. The one thread that binds all to them."

"You can't possibly believe I was involved with Miss Kinsley's death . . . And with the deaths of those other women . . ." He put on his best shocked expression.

Lieutenant Anders answered with a shrug and

scribbled a few notes in her book. "Do you own any pets, Professor Mides?"

"A few calico orandas. They're goldfish," he answered. "And actually, they belong to my son."

She scribbled a few more notes. "We'll be back, Professor." She turned to leave.

"Has anyone ever told you that you're beautiful, Lieutenant Anders?" After she was well down the hall and out of earshot, he added, "As beautiful as Igraine's treasured daughter."

Mides glided to his desk, to the ancient books there written in Old English and French. He turned a page. There was a woodcut, of King Arthur resting against a willow tree, which was shading a fountain. Drinking from the basin was a singular creature. It had a snake's head and a leopard's body, the hooves of a deer and the hindquarters of a lion. He traced the outline of the thing with his index finger.

"They call you the Questing Beast because you are sought after. After and after and never caught." He told it. He sighed and closed the book. "I can't catch you. But I can summon you, and you can be controlled."

Just as his knightly ancestor Palamides sought the creature and discovered that, while he could not catch it, he could use a dark pact to control it.

"Just as my son will someday use you, too." the professor reverently placed the thick tome on the shelf, and followed it with the others he'd used last night to call forth the beast and to send it after the comely young woman who had spurned all his advances. His distant relative.

Perhaps, he mused, if Lieutenant Anders was clever enough, she might just discover that he was vaguely related to Clare, a tenuous family-tree thread that could at best be called "shirt-tailed cousin." But it was a thread nonetheless, a suggestion of improper love and incest. And the same thread ran to Kathy Wilkers and Mary and Ellen Hammerlund. It ran to a freshman whom he would soon convince to take his Camelot course next year. The men in his family had been guilty of many extramarital transgressions, making the family tree a veritable forest.

The thread did not run to Lieutenant Anders, not that he knew of, anyway. But he would consult his genealogy texts to be certain. Perhaps he could find her in the family forest. However, if he could find no thread, perhaps the Questing Beast could be persuaded to hunt her anyway.

The professor smiled slyly and headed out the door, stack of tests in hand.

Through his still-open window, he heard the bark of a dog.

MIDNIGHT SONG
by Carol Hightshoe

This story is Carol Hightshoe's first professional sale, and she's still bouncing off the walls because of it. In her day job she works as a Deputy Sheriff in Colorado and divides her free time between writing, spoiling her two dogs, spending time with her husband and son, and being a Star Trek fanatic.

How many times have I come here? I can no longer count the days, months, or years. The passage of time has no effect on me. I remember other, older times, when I would rise each day with joy to greet the morning sun. In those days, dawn brought hope in the brightening sky and warming earth. Now, I am banished to the nadir of night. In the darkness I inhabit, hope is only a dream.

It was a year ago, perhaps two, when the priests came and laid their blessing on this place. This small valley was sanctified and made anathema to me, or rather to what I have become. Despite this, I am still compelled to be here. Each night I sit beside this stone marker and sing of my sorrow. The moon and stars listen to the pain in my soul as I tell them about the loss of my beloved Adairia. I take some comfort in the silence of the night, a silence that only listens and does not judge.

My song awakens the priests. They stand at their small windows saying prayers for protection. I shudder at the sharp, bittersweet smell of their fear and hatred.

Tonight, as I sit here and raise my gaze to the moon, I feel a stirring in the air. Something is happening. Nothing like this has ever occurred before. My spine tingles. The hair along my neck stands on end. My claws grasp at the dirt. I whine softly.

Looking closely, I see a shimmering before me. A shape forming from wisps of the night, not wholly there. My nose detects only the dustiness of the earth and the biting scent of the trees surrounding this area, but the shape begins to solidify. Suddenly, the perfume of heather fills the air. I inhale deeply. Heather was always her favorite flower.

It is her! I have not seen her since that horrific night so long ago. The night the curse struck and she vanished from my life.

She is much as I remember her—tall, with dark eyes and dark hair. Her delicate features are gently lit by the glow surrounding her as she stands next to the stone bearing her name. Her eyes meet my own, and there is a deep sadness reflected in them.

A soft creak comes from the door of the small church. I see one of the priests step outside. Startled, I rise and turn to flee. She begins to fade.

"Wait," he calls. "Please stay. I am Father Gregory, I mean you no harm."

I glance up at her and she nods slowly, so I sit back down and look at the approaching priest. He is an old man whose eyes, even in this darkness, glow with an inner light. Despite the signs of age in his steps, his movements are confident. As he approaches us, he holds out both his hands to show he is carrying nothing.

I smell his fear, but the scent is accompanied by something else—a fragrance both soft and strong, carrying with it something of the smell of flowers in a meadow, of rain, of a sunrise. It is the scent of love, compassion, and hope.

Father Gregory glances at the misty form, then at the stone marker with a single word scratched into its surface. "Adairia?" he asks.

She nods. Glancing at me, Adairia smiles that small, wistful smile I have not seen in so long.

I nod my understanding of her unspoken request. Closing my eyes, I concentrate on triggering a change I have not experienced since the day I lost her.

The change comes slowly, and I whimper as I feel my limbs lengthen and my nose flatten. I find myself stretched out on the ground as my senses return. Slowly, I push myself into a sitting position. Every joint in my body feels as if it is on fire. I had forgotten the pain.

The night air is chill against my bare skin as I stand, and I shiver. Father Gregory hands me his cloak, and I wrap myself in its warmth. I look at my hands and frown. The smoothness of the skin is strange after all these years. Sniffing the air around me, I can no longer discern the fragrances of the night as before, yet the scent of heather lingers in the air.

I see Father Gregory watching me closely, his right hand holding the cross on the chain around his neck. Something seems to be required between us.

I extend my hand to him. "I am Leathan."

He returns my handshake in a strong clasp.

Gathering the borrowed cloak around me, I sit on the damp ground. Adairia sits beside me and lays her hand on mine. There is warmth in the contact. Looking at her, I see color in her face. I reach up and caress her cheek, and she smiles at me. We look at each other for several minutes, savoring the feel of our shared closeness.

"Forgive me, Father, for I have sinned," she says, turning back to the priest. "It has been too many years since my last confession."

"It was this sin which condemned you to remain here?" Father Gregory asks, his voice nonjudgmental as he looks from her to me.

"Yes." She sighs softly. "It condemned Leathan, also."

Listening to her talk to Father Gregory, I think back on that day so long ago. The day we were married.

The wedding ceremony and celebration had continued until late in the night. The midnight hour had been fast approaching when Adairia and I finally made our way back to the home we were to share. The lantern I carried illuminated the sprays of heather I'd woven around the door to welcome her.

"Leathan, they're beautiful," she said, taking one of the sprays and holding it close to her face.

"Lady Adairia, if I may?" I held my arms out to her.

"Of course." She kissed me lightly as I started to lift her. The light of the full moon washed over us.

A sudden burning coursed down my limbs and engulfed my whole body. Adairia stepped back and dropped the spray of heather.

"No!" I heard her cry as I fell to the ground on top of it.

Just as suddenly as it had started, the pain stopped. The crushed spray of heather lay at my feet, its soft lavender now faded to gray. I tried to stand, but could not. Fur covered my limbs and I realized the truth of what I had become. But it was impossible. How could this have happened to me? The curse had already struck my family this generation. It shouldn't have been able to strike again, not so soon. I should have been free to love and live a normal life, free of care.

I glanced around for Adairia and saw no sign of her. I tried to call her name, but only a howl came from my throat.

Not knowing what to do, I ran. Throughout the night I ran, until I came to this small valley. The scent of the heather reminded me of Adairia as I sat and sang of my sorrow.

With the rising of the sun, I felt the fire consuming my body again as the wolf form I had worn during the night left me. I remained alone here in the forest the rest of the day. I could not return to Adairia, not like this. Harailt had vowed vengeance when she chose me over him. I could only guess that this was the form his attack had taken.

Moonrise found me still here. I raised my voice to the moon, singing of my loss to the watching stars. My throat was sore, my grief overwhelming, when my song finally faded away.

After several minutes of watching the heather sway in the breeze, I reached out and rubbed my paw on the soft sandstone, my claws leaving a visible mark. With more effort, the scratches dug deeper in the rock. Very slowly, I used my claws to scratch Adairia's name into the rough surface. When I finished, the letters were firm and strong. The racing, tumbling beat of my heart was not evident in the straight, clear lines I'd labored to produce.

The next morning I fought the change back to human form, and have remained a wolf ever since. It was the form most suited to my sorrow and solitude.

"Leathan, I'm sorry," Adairia says, bringing me out of my memories.

"Why? I was the one who left and never came back."

"It was my fault, though," she says.

I look at her and she looks away. Reaching out, I gently grasp her chin and turn her face back toward me. "How can that be?"

Her eyes refuse to meet mine, darting between me and the priest standing quietly. He nods and smiles gently at her.

"I knew what Harailt planned as his vengeance." Her voice breaks as she speaks. "We should have postponed the wedding. Found a way to prevent the curse from striking. Something. Anything, but what you were condemned to." I shake my head to reassure her, hoping my face holds a human expression and not the bared-tooth smile of a wolf.

"Adairia, we both knew about Harailt's threat," I said. "We made the decision to go ahead with the wedding together."

The curse of the werewolf is an ancient one in my family. Earlier that spring my younger brother had been afflicted. As the curse only claims one victim each generation, my family and my wife-to-be believed I was safe.

I reached down and took her hands in mine. She

looked at me, her face wet with tears. "It was a long time ago, and it is something which belongs in the past," I said. "What I don't understand is why we are both still here."

"I did not want to go on without you. In my sorrow, I lost the will to live. A few months after our marriage and your metamorphosis, I died from an illness that I no longer had the strength or desire to fight. My spirit was trapped here, in this valley. We are bound together, Leathan—you and I."

"Leathan," Father Gregory says softly. "There is no way the curse itself can be broken. However, it is possible to release you from your immortality. Once you two are no longer bound together, you will live the remainder of a natural life. You must release Adairia."

My mind races in confusion . . . Release Adairia? But how can I? I hesitate.

Glancing at Adairia, I see her dark eyes watching me closely. Those eyes are filled with love and sorrow. Studying her face, I realize how much she means to me. Just as her love for me caused her to die from her sorrow, my love for her bound her here after that death.

"Adairia, be free," I whisper. I lift her hands to my lips and kiss them gently. Releasing her hands, I stand and step back slowly.

I watch as Father Gregory raises his cross and says something in a language I do not understand. The moonlight grows stronger and bathes Adairia as she begins to fade from view.

"No!" she cries. "Leathan, I do not want to leave you."

The moonlight faded and the mist swirls, concealing her from my sight. When the fog lifts, a female wolf stands where Adairia was. I glance at her and then at the priest. Once again, I trigger the change. This time there is no pain, and I find myself standing nose to nose with Adairia.

"Go in peace, my children." Father Gregory makes the sign of the cross over us. "My blessings and God's on you both. May you always find sanctuary and welcome in this place."

Adairia and I bow our heads to the priest, then leave. Our strides match perfectly as we lope off into the forest together. Always together.

THE DRAGON AND THE MAIDEN
by Pamela Luzier

Growing up, Pamela Luzier read everything she could get her hands on, sampling every genre. But, finding she preferred stories that ended with an optimistic outlook, she narrowed her reading down to fantasy, science fiction, and romance stories, especially those that include a touch of humor. Now an engineer turned writer, she enjoys writing stories that contain as many of these elements as possible. Though she's published seven romance novels and a novella under the name Pam McCutcheon, this is her first pure fantasy story.

Wenda poured her heart and soul into the kiss, twisting to avoid Kleef's groping hands as she pressed her body against his in silent guarantee of delights to come. The knight was cooperating very nicely in this dark corner of the castle, murmuring endearments and the sweet promises she had so longed to hear. Finally, security was in her grasp. With any luck, he'd be so besotted, he'd finally ask her to marry him.

It was about time. She'd been saving herself for just this occasion for years. As a lowly servant, it was impossible to better her circumstances unless she married above her station, and Wenda was determined to do just that. Not for her the backbreaking labor that had sent her parents and sister to early graves. No, *she* was determined to live in comfort the rest of her days.

Kleef would be her admission to that life . . . and it didn't hurt that the burly knight was a fine figure of a man.

A gasp of outrage startled them from their embrace. "How dare you," Egberta, the baron's daughter, screeched. "Unhand my betrothed at once."

"Betrothed?" Wenda backed away from Kleef in surprise.

He shrugged and gave her a sheepish look that made her want to kick him, right where it counted. Damn him—he was just like all the others. He'd been leading her on the whole time, hoping for a tumble while promising her the moon.

"Yes, my betrothed," Egberta said. "Father just gave him my hand in marriage. We are to be wed within the week."

"I didn't know," Wenda protested, seeing the spark of battle in Egberta's eyes.

But the homely noblewoman was in no mood to hear it. "That decides it," Egberta said shrilly. "*You* will be the dragon's sacrifice." She pointed at Wenda and addressed the two hulking brutes behind her. "Bind her!"

Sacrifice? Uh-oh.

Wenda tried to bolt, but the men caught her easily and tied her arms behind her back, hauling her around to face Egberta.

Wenda regarded the woman in disbelief. "Why?" she asked desperately. "Why me?"

Silly question—she knew why. She had committed

the cardinal sin of being a great deal prettier than the high-ranking woman. But she didn't understand why Egberta resented her so much. Wenda might be fair of face and form, but Egberta had what really mattered—position and security.

Egberta's gaze turned mocking. "It's nothing personal. But this new dragon is terrorizing the countryside, and we must sacrifice a maiden to satisfy him. You *are* still a maiden, aren't you?"

Wenda seethed as she regarded Egberta's smug face. Of course she was. Egberta knew it and so did everyone else. Wenda had been fending off the village boys since she was old enough to fill out and attract more than her share of lusty glances. But she'd spurned all ignoble advances and made no secret of the fact that she was saving herself for marriage— and not merely the promise of marriage, either.

Now, the only weapons Wenda had available at this juncture were those feminine attributes Egberta despised so much. In desperation, she turned them on her captors. Shaking her thick blond hair out of her face, she turned an imploring gaze on first one man, then the other. But they ignored her pleas, staring at her heaving chest instead. Her bonds had pulled the material of her clothing tight against her bodice, thrusting her breasts out in unintended invitation. No doubt they hoped her attributes would burst free and give them an eyeful.

Stupid men—they were all alike. She would offer them a glimpse of what they so longed to see if she thought it would save her from the dragon, but she knew it wouldn't. They would probably take what they wanted, then feed her to the beast anyway.

Still, this was no time for pride, not when her life was at stake.

"Please, let me go," she begged, trying to look helpless and seductive all at the same time.

"Stop that," Egberta commanded. Removing her own cloak, she swirled it around Wenda to conceal her figure. "You should be honored to be the sacrifice that will save us all."

"If it's such an honor, you can have it," Wenda said. "Unless *you're* no longer a maiden?"

Egberta slapped Wenda so hard, her head rocked to one side. "Enough. Take her to the dragon."

Some girls might have given up, weeping and wailing on their way to their fate, but not Wenda. Instead, she saved her breath and fought the entire way out of the castle and down the bluffs to the dark, forbidding cave at the edge of the sea.

What seemed to be the entire population of the castle and the village tagged along behind her. But Wenda knew better than to expect any help. The women were all jealous of her comeliness, and the men were all peeved because she wouldn't succumb to their blandishments. No doubt the few virgins among them were only too glad that she was the one to be sacrificed.

Her captors dragged her kicking and cursing to a huge, craggy rock outside the cave where the dragon dwelt. As they untied her hands and bound her arms to the rock, holding her spread-eagled on her back against it, she tried to break free, but the men holding her were too strong.

Even after they let go, she struggled against her shackles. She was well and truly in desperate trouble. And all because she had been too proud to let a man take her, at least out of wedlock. She paused, panting for breath, and considered her options.

There was one way out . . . if she wasn't a maiden, she couldn't be a sacrifice. She eyed Kleef and the two servants standing beside him speculatively, wondering if she could convince one of them to take her now. Was it worth her life to give up what she had hoarded so carefully, hoping for a better future?

No, Wenda decided. She couldn't bear to provide entertainment for the entire demesne. Even if they let her go afterward, which she doubted, everyone would have witnessed her humiliation. There was no way she could attract a high-born husband after that.

Wenda tugged on her bonds again, to no avail. She was doomed. Soon, night would fall and the dragon would come out to forage for food, just as he had every night this week. Unfortunately, this time he wouldn't have to go far to find his meal.

As dusk approached, the village folk grew visibly nervous and Wenda lost all patience with them. She was the one about to be served up as the main course for a dragon's feast, not them. Well, she couldn't do anything about that, but maybe she could do something about them. She glanced toward the cave, recoiled in pretended horror, and let out a scream.

That did it. Every last one of them fled for their lives.

Good. At least she wouldn't have an audience for her ignominious end. And with any luck, she might be able to free herself before the beast emerged. Frantically, she rubbed the shackle holding her left wrist against one of the sharp protrusions on the rock, hoping the dragon had dined well the day before and would delay his nocturnal expedition.

Once again, her luck was out. With a slither and a roar, the dragon emerged from the cave and glared down at her, steam escaping from his nostrils.

Wenda froze in disbelief. Was this the dragon? It certainly didn't resemble any dread beast she'd ever heard of. He was beautiful—scarlet with golden scales on his belly, four short legs underneath a long, wyrm-like body, no wings, and tendril-like whiskers flowing back from his huge horned head.

As he lowered that massive head toward her and opened his mouth, Wenda couldn't help it—she screamed and braced herself, squeezing her eyes shut to block out the sight of her approaching demise.

To her shock, nothing happened. No pain, no crunching of bones, no certain death . . . nothing except for a deep voice saying, "Go away."

Her eyes flew open in surprise. Had the dragon spoken?

"Could you repeat that?" she asked in disbelief, her heart pounding.

"Go away," the dragon repeated. Then, apparently having said all it was going to say, the beast made a sinuous turn and looped back on himself to return to the cave.

Wenda's terror faded, but she was still all churned up inside and not in the mood to be chastised by the beast who was supposed to have made her into dragon droppings.

"Wait," she cried. "I can't leave. I'm tied to the rock."

The dragon ignored her and continued undulating into the cave.

Of all the nerve. Frustrated, and having a great deal

of pent-up emotion with no other way to express it, Wenda screamed a few choice words in frustration.

The great head swiveled toward her. "Stop that noise immediately," it ordered.

"I won't unless you release me," she said, beginning to feel as if she might have a chance of surviving this situation.

She opened her mouth to scream again, but the dragon forestalled her. "What do you want of me?" it asked.

"Nothing—I just want you to let me go."

The dragon scowled. "If you want nothing, why are you here?"

"The others left me here."

"Why?"

"For you," Wenda hedged. No sense in giving him any ideas.

The dragon scowled. "Well, it's too late. I don't want you. You may leave."

Too late? What was he talking about? Thoroughly exasperated now, Wenda said, "I can't leave, remember? I'm tied to the rock. If you'll just untie me, I'd be glad to leave you alone." And the rest of the benighted village, too. Seeing he was wavering again, she said, "If you don't, I'll keep on screaming."

"No, not that horrible noise." The beast shuddered and lowered his head to examine her. "Why did they think I would want you, bound as you are?"

Realizing he was regarding her more as a distasteful dish than a tasty treat, Wenda decided to tell the truth. "They, uh, thought you might want to eat me."

He recoiled in horror. "I don't eat humans. What kind of people are you, anyway?"

At any other time, Wenda would be glad to discuss

the shortcomings of her neighbors, but right now, she just wanted to be free. Though relieved that the dragon didn't seem disposed to dine on her, she realized she faced another danger. The tide was rising and inundating the sacrificial rock. It was already swirling around her knees. If she couldn't get loose soon, she'd drown. "Have you figured out how to release me, yet?"

The dragon scowled again. "I could breathe fire on the restraints, but it might burn you."

Crisped Wenda? Bad idea. "Uh, what about your claws?"

"What about them?" he asked defensively, tucking his feet under his body where she couldn't see them.

"Can't you use them to cut through the ropes?"

"No," he said explosively, breathing out even more steam.

Hmm, the big bad beastie seemed sensitive about his feet for some reason. Wenda didn't push the issue. Instead, she asked, "Then what are we going to do? The tide is coming in, and if you don't do something quick, I'll drown."

The speculative expression on the dragon's face seemed to indicate that he didn't find that as horrible a prospect as she did. Best to nip that idea in the bud, fast. "If I die tied to this rock, my body will start stinking in a few days. You wouldn't like that on your front doorstep, would you?"

"Oh, all right," he grumped. "I'll try to help you, if I must. But you must close your eyes until you are free."

Wenda wondered why, but she didn't ask. Besides, if he had wanted to do something horrible to her, he could have done it by now. Without quibbling, she

closed her eyes and heard him slithering around the
back of the rock. Then came a flash of light she could
see even behind her closed eyelids, accompanied by
a popping sound. A few minutes of tugging, then
whatever he did back there apparently worked, because she was loose.

Another flash-pop, and the dragon growled, "You
can look now."

Gratefully, Wenda rubbed the blood back into her
stinging extremities. But now that she was free, she
had second thoughts about leaving. There was no
future for her here. Who would want a rejected
dragon sacrifice? And what were the odds of remaining alive if Egberta learned of her release?

The dragon, who had begun to glow now that
dusk had fallen, glared at her. "You may leave now."

"But I have nowhere to go . . . and it's getting
dark. I won't be able to see. I'll probably fall and
break my neck." She advanced higher, toward the
cave and the dryness it promised.

"I have enough problems of my own," he said
grumpily. "Leave."

But the dragon's insistence only made her more
determined to remain. Oddly enough, she felt far
safer with this dragon than with her own people.
How could she convince him to let her stay?

Hmm, the best way to keep men occupied was to
turn the conversation to their favorite subject—themselves. Maybe that would work with dragons, too.

"So," she said conversationally as she headed
toward the cave and relative safety, "what kind of
dragon are you? I've never heard of a beast quite
like you."

"Of course not," the dragon said indignantly as he

followed her, his glowing scales lighting her way. "I'm not one of your western dragons—nasty ravaging beasts, all. I am a *ti-lung*, a mighty water dragon from the Far East."

It was just as she thought—the dragon was dying for someone to talk to, no matter how much he protested otherwise.

"Oooh, really?" she asked, trying to sound impressed. "*Ti-lung?* What's that?" And how could she use this to her advantage?

The cave opened into a large cavern, and as she seated herself on a convenient ledge, the beast coiled up next to her.

"The *ti-lung* have dominion over all the waters of the land as well as the weather," he explained. "We are highly revered where I come from." He cast her a baleful look. "People in my land know the *ti-lung* bring great luck, and they gratefully serve us, bringing many delicacies and fine entertainment. Not like your people. You have no concept of the proper way to treat a water dragon."

Ah, that explained his earlier annoyance. He had expected to be worshiped for his good luck. Instead, he had been ignored and offered the one sort of food he refused to consume. No wonder he was grouchy.

"Then why did you leave?"

He made a rippling movement like a shrug. "Each *ti-lung* is responsible for guarding a body of water in my land, but I am the youngest of a very long-lived species. There were simply no suitable locations left. I had no choice but to leave in order to find an appropriate dwelling." He gazed out at the sea outside his cave with a sad but proprietary air. "This cave is magnificent and truly worthy of a *ti-lung*, and the water is superb, but it is nothing like home here . . . and I cannot go back.''

She patted his leg in sympathy. "You poor thing. And what happened to your feet?'' She hadn't been able to discern anything wrong, but he sure seemed determined to hide his extremities.

"Didn't you notice?'' he asked in a small voice. "I lost my toes.''

"Your toes?'' What a strange thing to worry about.

"The dragons of my land are the only ones with five toes—all lesser dragons have fewer. I was warned before I left that I would lose my toes the farther I ventured away from our land, but I didn't believe the prophecies.'' He paused, mournfully. "The ancients were right—my toes shriveled one by one the farther I went. I have none left.''

He looked so despondent, she couldn't help but want to buck him up. "Oh, pooh. That doesn't matter.''

"But how can I be a proper dragon without my toes? No wonder none of your people have come to serve me.''

"That had nothing to do with it. You said it yourself—no one here knows anything about your kind of dragon. They don't even know how many toes you're supposed to have.''

He brightened, making the cavern radiant. "Is that right?''

"That's right.'' She warmed to her subject. "And we've never had any dealings with your sort. How could we know you're good luck and that we're supposed to serve you? Especially when all you've done since you got here is terrorize our livestock.''

He looked a bit sheepish at that. "I have to eat . . .''

True, and since he seemed to prefer mutton to maiden, she couldn't argue with his food preferences.

Suddenly, an idea took root and grew in her mind. "How would you like to have all the food you ever want brought to you by as many human servants as you could desire?"

"How is that possible? You said yourself that your people do not understand the *ti-lung*."

"No, but we can educate them. I have a plan . . ."

Wenda surprised herself over the next several days by making fast friends with the dragon, who was starving for companionship. She dubbed him Ti since his real name was too difficult to pronounce, and they exchanged tales. He told her a little about eastern dragons and she regaled him with as many western dragon stories as she could remember.

To drive her point home, she stressed the dangers of daft knights-errant who sought to prove their manhood by picking quarrels with dragons, implacable army commanders who sought to pull dragon's teeth in the belief that sowing them would yield a crop of soldiers, and crafty wizards who would stop at nothing to take the dragon blood they needed for their spells.

Throughout it all, Ti listened, shocked. "Where do your people get these ideas?" he asked in disbelief.

"I don't know, but it makes it very hazardous for a dragon hereabouts . . . unless you have the right sort of person to help you learn our ways."

When he nodded, she added, "Now, here's what we're going to do . . ."

With the dragon's help and a little of his vaunted luck, Wenda might be able to win Kleef back and get a little revenge on Egberta as well. And the baron's daughter had unknowingly provided the perfect opportunity—her own wedding.

Several days later, Wenda waited until everyone had gathered in the courtyard beneath the bright wedding banners, then triumphantly rode the dragon into their midst. She grinned as they screamed and scattered at the sight of Ti. Sacrifice her, would they? Well, she would see how they liked it when the claw was on the other foot . . . so to speak.

And best of all, there was Egberta and her father in all their wedding finery, cowering behind Kleef who had drawn his sword and bared his teeth.

"Look," someone cried. "Wenda has tamed the dragon."

As the others slowly poked their heads out of their hiding places to see this wonder, Wenda used the dragon's foreleg to climb down. "Yes," she exclaimed, when she was assured she had everyone's attention, "I have tamed the dragon. Now we are the greatest power in the land."

Placing her hands on her hips, she gave Kleef a saucy look. And just in case he didn't get it, she spelled it out for him. "Greater even than a baron. Why, the man who marries me will have a dragon in thrall to do his every bidding."

Kleef paused, a thoughtful look in his eye.

"Don't listen to that peasant," Egberta screeched. Her eyes turned shrewd as she added, "Besides, if the dragon wouldn't eat *her*, he won't eat us, either. He's probably toothless."

Damn—the people were actually nodding among themselves, encouraged and emboldened by Egberta's logic. Before Wenda could figure out how to respond to this development, Kleef advanced toward Ti, his sword out thrust as he commanded, "Begone!"

The dragon stood his ground, glaring down at the knight.

Exasperated, Wenda muttered, "Hey, could you help me out, here?"

Ti just rolled his eyes at her. He had agreed to this plan, but only under the condition that he wouldn't have to hurt anybody. And he remained firm in that resolve, even when Kleef took a poke at him. Instead, all he did was draw back and glare at the crowd, steam escaping from his nostrils.

More wedding guests emerged from hiding, some becoming bold enough to throw rocks and sticks at him. Still, Ti did nothing but growl and glare.

This situation was getting way out of control. "Can't you just scorch them a little?" she asked in exasperation.

Ti scowled and released more steam.

"Some dragon," Kleef scoffed. "And you think I should marry you because of *him*? Why, you're nothing but a common doxy. I wouldn't marry you if my life depended on it." With that, everyone jeered, Kleef and Egberta egging them on.

Wenda sagged in defeat. It was over. Nothing had gone as she planned and she was back where she started—no marriage, no security, no prospects. And Ti was in trouble, too. It was only a matter of time until some stupid knight came after him and skewered him. Humiliated and with her plans in ruin, she looked around for a safe way to retreat so they could lick their wounds in private.

But Kleef wasn't done with them yet. "Look," he

exclaimed, pointing down at the dragon's feet. "No claws. He's not only toothless, he's toeless, as well. What good is a defenseless dragon?"

As the villagers howled with laughter, Ti grew deadly still.

Uh-oh. This time they had gone too far. Ti was mighty sensitive about his toes.

The dragon opened his mouth and roared, "You want teeth? I'll show you teeth!" He bared his impressive incisors and expelled a great jet of fire that sent flames licking over the pretty banners Egberta had erected for the occasion.

The wedding guests cowered and Wenda's hopes rose. Maybe they could at least retire from this situation without humiliation.

As the banners burned brightly in the breeze and everyone marveled about the novelty of a talking dragon, Ti spoke again. "Marry her," he boomed, fixing Kleef with a steely glare.

But the knight's honor was at stake now, and Wenda knew he would never back down.

"I cannot," he declared, drawing himself up in a self-righteous pose as he drew Egberta close. "I am promised to another."

Yeah, right. Like that had kept him from trying to sample Wenda's charms a week ago.

"Never mind," she told Ti. "He's not worthy. I don't want him I-I'll find someone better."

"Really?" Egberta jeered. "Like who? No one would have you—you might as well marry the dragon."

Once again, the crowd guffawed.

Surprisingly, the dragon nodded. "An excellent idea. Even the lowliest among us is a lord of great power. By becoming my wife, Wenda will outrank even you."

Huh? Wenda took advantage of everyone's shock to pull his ear down to her level and whisper, "You're a lord? You never mentioned that."

"There are many things I haven't mentioned," Ti rumbled.

"So why did you offer to marry me?"

"You have been my friend in an unfriendly land— the only one who did not laugh at me or try to hurt me. And since a high-ranking marriage seems to mean so much to you, it is the least I can do to repay your kindness."

Gratitude, confusion, and hope warred within Wenda's breast. Could she marry Ti? If she wanted security, marriage to a dragon would certainly provide that, but . . . marriage was about more than security. Could she live as a maiden the rest of her life, without knowing the touch of a man?

She had been silent too long, so Egberta reentered the fray. "By all means, marry the dragon." She wrapped a possessive arm around Kleef's waist and gazed up into his handsome face. "It seems only fitting that I should marry the beauty while you make do with the beast." Turning to the priest, she proclaimed, "We shall have a double wedding ceremony. Father Joseph, marry them!"

Cowed by the baron and the knight, the priest was uncertain. "Only if it's all right with you, my dear," he assured Wenda timidly.

Wenda made up her mind. Ti was the only one who had treated her with consideration. Who cared if she remained a maiden the rest of her life? At least she would have kind and thoughtful company.

"Yes," she said in ringing tones. "I will marry the dragon lord."

She gave Ti a tremulous smile, grateful that he had offered her an honorable way out of this predicament.

But to her surprise, and that of the wedding guests, judging by their exclamations of shock and dismay, Ti suddenly shimmered with coruscating radiance. With a blinding flash and a pop, the dragon disappeared. In his place now stood an elegant man dressed in scarlet and gold robes. Peering closer, Wenda saw that the stranger was as beautiful in human form as he was when he was a dragon, with golden brown skin, exotic dark eyes, and lustrous black hair.

"Ti?" she asked in disbelief.

He smiled at her. "I told you there were still things you didn't know about me," he murmured for her ears alone.

Wenda nodded, utterly captivated by this handsome suitor, so much more attractive than the brutish Kleef. And in this form, Ti seemed to have all his fingers and toes. "So that's how you untied my ropes—by changing into a human."

"Yes. I haven't spent much time in this form so I apologize if I was a bit awkward." He bowed and offered her his arm with a smile. "Shall we?"

"Oh, yes," she breathed as Egberta looked on in envy. "And I didn't tell you everything about my people, either." She took his arm and steered him toward the priest. "In this part of the world, we have this marvelous custom called the wedding night . . ."

COMING TO AMERICA
by Susan Sizemore

Susan Sizemore lives in the Midwest and spends most of her time writing. Some of her other favorite things are coffee, dogs, travel, movies, hiking, history, farmers' markets, art glass, and basketball. You'll find mention of quite a few of these things inside the pages of her stories. She works in many genres, from contemporary romance to epic fantasy and horror. She's the winner of the Romance Writers of America's Golden Heart award and was a nominee for the 2000 Rita Award in historical romance. Her available books include historical romance novels, a dark fantasy series, *The Laws of the Blood,* science fiction, and several electronically published books and short stories. One of her electronic books, the epic fantasy *Moons' Dreaming,* written with Marguerite Krause, was a nominee for the Eppie, the epublishing industries writing award. Susan's email address is Ssizemore@aol.com, and her webpage address is: http://members.aol.com/Ssizemore/storm/home.htm

"Will you be going down to watch the fires, Da?"

Mum's long and lovely hand landed on Aril's shoulder almost before the words were out. With a quick glance back at Da, seated silent and surly at the kitchen table, she turned Aril toward the door.

"It might do some good," he ventured to say to his mother.

"He doesn't want to hear your notions. Go out and play, lad. Your father and I need to talk."

Da looked faded, and the sight frightened Aril enough so that he did as he was told without another word. He'd thought Da would enjoy a fire festival, as fire was his element, that it might bring some light back into his golden eyes, but maybe it was best he should leave the elders alone.

"He's a changeling, I think," Aril heard his father say as the door closed behind him, muffling any indignant answer his mother might make.

Aril's stomach rumbled as he rushed down the dark, narrow stairs. There was a smell of boiled cabbage and onions out in the hallway, but the mouth-watering aroma didn't come from the Sheen kitchen. No one seemed to notice when he was hungry. At least, Mum hadn't put any supper on the table tonight. Maybe there was no food in the flat, or maybe she'd just forgotten. She did sometimes. His sisters could live on air, perhaps, but he was hungry. He wasn't like the others, having been born on water between the Land of Troubles and the New World and after the death of all but one of the family his family had traveled across the ocean with. Nobody of mortal flesh believed in him, and none ever had, so he made do believing in himself. He didn't know how much longer the strength of his own will was going to last. He *knew* he was real, and he was lucky that he had one friend who agreed with him.

They played together in the streets of the slum,

dodging the horse-drawn wagons, hitching rides on the backs of trolleys and elevated trains. They were chased by boys from rival street tribes and by blue-coated cops waving nightsticks when they were spotted hustling fruit from pushcarts. They roamed the city to swim in the Hudson River, to watch tennis players in Central Park, and had found a spot to watch on a hill above the Polo Grounds where Giants did battle with sticks and balls.

"Hey, Adolph!" he called as he rushed onto the tenement's stoop and saw his friend carrying a load of scavenged wood to add to the pile in the center of the street.

Adolph turned a smile on Aril and pointed toward the basement, where he'd been helping his grandfather collect wood for the fire festival for weeks. Aril nodded and ran to follow his friend to help as soon as Adolph dumped the wood onto the growing pile. Other kids in the neighborhood were bringing their stashes for the bonfire as well.

Adolph always wore a turtleneck and a cast off bowler hat he'd stolen from somewhere, but tonight he'd added a worn woolen overcoat to fend off the November chill. He was a skinny, undersized kid, shorter for his age than even Aril, with big eyes and a disarming smile. He didn't go to school, and nobody seemed to mind. He and Aril had that in common.

Adolph had lots of brothers, and they all looked alike, while Aril was afflicted with many sisters, each more beautiful than the other, and all more beautiful than he. Adolph's father was a tailor who worked at home. Aril's father searched the streets of New York, but Aril couldn't say exactly what it was the lord of the hearth did. Adolph's mom was always busy, working outside the house. Aril's mother flitted about from room to room looking sad and lost. She also sang sometimes while his sister played music, and she danced up on the roof in the moonlight with Aril's sisters. Adolph's grandparents and lots of other relatives lived with Adolph's family as well, just like Aril's huge family. Actually, Aril had a family with numerous members, most of them quite small. Adolph's family had come from Alsace Lorraine, and they were human. Aril envied him that.

Aril refused to feel sorry for himself for long, and he worked hard to help Adolph and his grandfather with the wood, using hardly any magic at all in the transport. The kindling was made up of broken bits of furniture, mostly; there weren't many trees in the city. Aril had never known the Green Land where the Troubles drove his people out, so he was happy with brick and concrete, streetcars and the never-ending noise of the crowds.

Da and the others missed green woodlands and sometimes talked of escaping the city. But it was agreed that the ancient Grandmother who slept the rest of her life away wouldn't last long if the family moved from the shelter of manmade buildings to dwell in the depths of Central Park. From overhearing some of the songs crooned in her ear, Aril was grateful they had to stay in their apartment, but he suspected the last mortal that'd come from the Green Land with them was under a deep sleep spell. They needed the ancient Grandmother to believe in them, even if only in her dreams, or—

Aril gulped with terror and pushed away the thought. He noticed how high the woodpile was by this time, and how the light of the sun was nearly all gone from the sky. Anticipation and excitement scented the air along with cabbage from the tenements and cheap cigar smoke from the men who'd gathered on the stoops to talk among themselves. Da never joined the men, and no one ever seemed to notice. Maybe if Da tried talking to someone, they would actually hear him; but Da seemed to have given up hope of belonging in this new land at the turn of a new century. It disturbed Aril, who wished more than anything that his family could be like all the other immigrant households in the neighborhood. It didn't help that they weren't Jewish, like most everyone else in the rundown red brick building and on the rest of the block, but straight off the boat from Ireland.

They'd settled in the tenement on 93rd Street because the old woman they cared for had no strength to go any further when they came into the city. She'd barely managed to rent the apartment before her wits wandered and she settled into the long sleep that would probably go on forever. His mother thought that if they'd settled into an Irish neighborhood, things might have been easier for the fair folk of his clan. At least things would be more familiar to the rest of his family. Maybe not, his father had argued. It was belief they needed, and there was precious little energy left over for faith in the existence of fair folk among immigrants who worked hard to forget the old country and gave themselves up to the belief in the American Dream.

Da said the words like a blasphemy that burned his tongue as he spoke, but Aril liked the American Dream. In the old country his kind were caught too much in dreams that gave them no more substance than spiderwebs much of the time. Here the dream was much tougher than that. Aril thought that if Mum and Da and his sisters could only learn how to shape this substantial dream, then everything would be all right. But Da didn't like to listen when Aril tried to talk to him, so Aril ran on the street with the other neighborhood kids, though only Adolph ever noticed when he was around.

Adolph and his grandfather stood on the sidewalk, and Aril joined them as the bonfires up and down the street were lit. A shout went up as a line of fires climbed toward the sky. Aril leaned his head close to Adolph, to be heard above the shouting and hiss of growing flames. "A fine celebration," he offered.

Adolph turned a wide grin on him. "Yah."

"The gods of the place will be pleased."

Adolph's grin wavered. "Huh?'

"The Tammany of the great hall your grandfather speaks about. The fires are to celebrate their yearly victory, yes? I heard him tell you that to keep in favor with the Tammany the fires must be lit on every street."

"For winning the election, yah. Grandpa and dad voted two or three times for the mayor today."

"That was kind."

"Did your dad vote?"

"Alas, no. He is not an American citizen."

Adolph shrugged. "Neither is Grandpa, but he always votes for Tammany Hall."

"Ah." Aril nodded his understanding, though he did not understand at all. The ways of mortals were even stranger than those of the fair folk, and he found those confusing enough. It was hard, being part of both worlds but belonging wholly in neither.

Were the Tammany gods to be praised and placated or not? He suspected that perhaps they were not, and that made the fires burn a little dimmer to his eyes. But at least the light and warmth did not fade completely to faint grayness. He hated the grayness, and shivered in fear of it.

"You look hungry, boy." The old man's hand landed on Aril's tin shoulder as he spoke, solid and heavy and infinitely reassuring.

That the old man saw him and spoke to him surprised Aril only a little; it pleased him mightily. Adolph's grandfather had been a traveling magician in the old country; now he mended umbrellas for a living. He had no real magic in him, not the way Aril knew it, but there was a light in his wise mortal eyes that registered a knowledge even he didn't know he had. Aril looked into those eyes and wanted to ask if the old magician believed in him. But, of course, believing in him was easy, since Adolph was beside him to lend Aril reality. Besides, Aril was almost as much of the mortal world as mortals themselves. It was Mum, and Da, and all the others who needed—

"Are you hungry?" the old man asked again. Aril nodded. "You look hungry." He reached his other arm out to snag Adolph by the shoulder as Adolph stepped back from the bonfire. "There's a meal waiting," he told his grandson. "Your uncle Al said he might be by tonight, so let's get the meal out of the way and the pinochle game started!"

"Can I play?" Aril asked as the old man led them up the stairs. He liked gambling, for it took only the lightest magic to win. He wondered if Da had ever considered—

"No," Adolph's grandfather answered, and swept them before him into the noisy, crowded apartment that was in almost every physical way exactly like the apartment occupied by Aril's equally huge family. *One is the shadow of the other*, he thought, not at all confused about which was where he would rather be. Guilt, yes, but no confusion.

Over in one corner Adolph's oldest brother, Leonard, was playing the piano, accompanied by a younger brother who sang in a sweet, high voice as he played. These brothers were apprentice bards, if Aril understood what Adolph had told him rightly. Adolph looked at the battered instrument longingly. There was money for only one son to have music lessons, and Adolph had not been the one chosen. There was no magic in the music, but Aril felt the pleasure the boys took in what they did; and those in the bustling, crowded room who paused to listen felt a warm glow of pleasure, and that pleasure flushed the boys with pride in what they did. That was mortal magic, he supposed, and enough for creatures such as these.

The arrogant superiority of his own thought caught him painfully, for it reminded Aril that he was not of this world, though he was closer to it than the rest of his kind. The problem was, he *believed* he could be of the mortal world if he tried hard enough—but where would that leave his family? To force away melancholy, Aril gravitated toward Adolph's mother. She sat in the center of the crowded room, a busy, cunning little woman, as full of life and fire as a small sun, and very much the energy that ran this boisterous family's world. His own mother could be as commanding when she roused herself, but that happened less and less as she faded away at home.

"The act needs more class," she was saying to the young woman seated beside her. "Something to get the attention of bigger booking agents. The boys have talent." She glanced toward her musically inclined sons over by the piano.

"We need a gimmick," the woman beside Adolph's mother said.

"We want to make a mark in show business, get picked up by a circuit, we need a classy gimmick. The singing and mandolin playing aren't enough to go big time."

"But what can we do, Aunt Minnie?"

Adolph's mother looked intensely thoughtful, and happy to face the challenge. "I've got a line on some paper roses I could pick up cheap. We could use those in the act."

"How?"

"We'll make a set. You could do the act in front of a trellis covered in vines and roses. That'll add class. All the big acts have sets." She nodded thoughtfully. "Yah. I like that. My kids are going to break into big time vaudeville."

The girl was mesmerized by the other woman's force of will, as was Aril. He drew closer as the girl said, "You'll get us there, Aunt Minnie. Maybe I should try a blonde wig. What do you think of that?"

Adolph's mother studied the girl. She was another one of the numerous family cousins. Aril had often heard her practicing music and singing with Adolph's brothers. She couldn't sing very well, but she was pretty. Not pretty as his sisters were, but Aril found her pleasant enough to look upon. The adored uncle whose arrival was happily anticipated by the family was also a singer. There were many bards in this large family. The uncle, it seemed, was the only one skilled enough to have found the patronage of a lord of the land. He, Adolph, had proudly told Aril, was smiled upon with favor by a lord known as the Great Zeigfeld. It seemed Adolph's mother coveted such an exalted position for others of her line, as well.

Aril knew that Adolph feared that any day his mother would draw him into her schemes and his free life of roaming the streets would be at an end. Aril dreaded that day, for when Adolph went away, he'd lose not only a true friend but the one mortal who utterly believed in his existence. Aril *thought* he could survive in the mortal world without belief, but he wasn't *sure.*

He sighed.

"You look sad," his friend's mother said, turning her bright smile and lively eye on him. He jumped in surprise, and glowed with delight at her notice. "No one's allowed to be sad in my house, boy. Let's get you some food." She tapped him on the head as she spoke. She stood as she made the gesture. The movement caused Aril's hat to fall off.

He bent down quickly to snatch up his ragged felt cap, but the damage was done. When he straightened, he saw that she saw.

The girl saw as well, and jumped up with a squeak, but the matriarch of the clan did not look in the least bit abashed. Aril stared at her in terror, unable to put a glamor on her to make her forget, though he tried with all his might. He would have smashed the hat back onto his head, but she snatched it away with a quick hand before he could hide his secret once more beneath battered black felt.

"Hey," she said, fingering the delicate skin. "You've got pointed ears."

Aril couldn't stop the shiver, or the giggle. "That tickles!"

Adolph was suddenly at his side. He took Aril's hat from his mother. "Yah, he's got funny ears." He put an arm around Aril's shoulders and looked around the gathering crowd belligerently in defense of a friend. Aril had not known that Adolph knew, knew and accepted him even though Aril looked like a freak without his hat. Others in the room snickered and laughed, but Adolph focused his gaze on his mother, who stood before them with her hands on her hips. "He's my friend," he declared. "Nothing wrong with being funny looking."

"You'd know," one of Adolph's brothers called out.

"Don't tease your brother," Adolph's mom answered automatically. She tapped a finger against her chin, and reached out to touch Aril again, but Adolph pulled him away.

"Leave him alone."

"I won't hurt him. I don't think you're *too* funny looking," she said to Aril. "Can you sing?"

"Of course I can sing!" Aril declared indignantly.

"Don't tell her that!" Adolph warned.

"You're a cute kid," she said, with a grin. She stroked her chin. "You know, those ears might add some class to the act. You want to be in vaudeville, kid?"

Adolph and Aril shared a horrified look. "Run!"

Adolph said, shoving Aril toward the door. "Before she puts you in show business!"

"Ma, not everybody wants to be in vaudeville."

"Of course they do," she said as she preceded Adolph up the stairs. "I remember how your uncle Al told me he didn't want to go into show business. I got him some songs, a partner. I *believed* in him—and look how well he's doing now."

It was true. When his mother believed in something, she made it happen. God help anyone who tried to stand in her way. He argued with her that Aril didn't want to show off his funny ears to the world. "He didn't even think I knew about 'em," he said. "People'll laugh at him."

She'd said, "And he'll make money off the rubes as they laugh."

Ma had pointed out that God wouldn't have given the kid funny ears if he wasn't meant to use them to entertain people. Coming from her, it made sense. But his family wouldn't want him to go into show business, Adolph had argued next. They will, she'd asserted. After I've had a talk with them, was her answer. With that, she'd made him take her two floors up the dark, rickety stairs to show her where Aril lived.

There was no way Aril was going to get out of going on the stage. Adolph knew it was only a matter of time until she had him standing in front of an audience making an ass out of himself too. He dreaded that day with all his heart. He knew he didn't have any talent, not for singing like his brothers, at least. He desperately hungered to play music, though not to perform in front of a crowd. He had even taught himself to pick out a couple of songs on the family's battered piano. He also knew that without any real training a love of music wasn't going to save him from humiliation once his mom finally decided to bring him into the family act.

Better Aril than him, he supposed. If she concentrated on turning his friend into a vaudevillian now, it kept his neck out of the noose for a while. "Yah, ma," Adolph agreed, with a sigh. "Sure Aril wants to be in showbiz."

"He just doesn't know it yet," she said, with a cunning smile that told him she knew exactly what he was up to. "What apartment did you say your friend lives in?"

Adolph pointed. Aril had never brought him up here, but Adolph had followed him a couple of times. There'd been faint music coming from inside the apartment once. Beautiful music, like angels played. He'd thought he'd only stood with his ear pressed to the door listening for a few minutes, but when hunger pangs drove him downstairs for dinner, Grandpa had complained about his staying out until after eleven. His brothers had long since eaten his dinner, and he went to bed hungry. He'd dreamed about the music, though. It had been in his head for a long time after. He'd sneaked up to listen other times, but all he'd ever heard were faint echoes of sound from inside the apartment, more like memories of music than music itself.

"They're strange," he warned his mother as she boldly rapped on the warped wood of the apartment door.

"Everybody in show business is, son," she answered, flashing him a smile. "That's why I love it."

She rapped again. "I know you're in there. I can hear you moving. Don't worry, it's not the landlord's agent come for the rent."

"But, Ma, they aren't in show bus—" Adolph started, but clapped a hand over his mouth as the door very slowly swung open with a creak that sounded like a moan. It was more than a little spooky. He didn't see anybody standing inside the doorway. Adolph took a nervous step back.

"Good morning, Mrs. . . . Sheen, is it?" His mother held out her hand. "Perhaps we're related. Not really, of course. My brother's in vaudeville. His stage name's Shean. You've heard of him, of course, Al Shean. And my sons." She gestured vaguely toward Adolph. "Some of my sons, that is, are part of a singing quartet. We've been so successful lately that we think it's time to turn the act into a review and move into larger theaters. That's why I'm here. To discuss a proposition that's of mutual benefit to our families. I'm very fond of your son, Aril. Such a talented boy."

She spoke fast, brisk and cheerful, as she did to gruff theater managers and booking agents, even though Adolph could have sworn there wasn't anybody there at all. While she talked, she took small, firm steps forward, as though she were backing someone blocking the entrance out of the way.

Adolph squinted hard, trying to get a look at whoever his mother was talking to, but all he could make out were moving shadows. He was suddenly scared and cold, and he shivered as though somebody'd walked on his grave. He didn't want to be here, but his mother was now inside the apartment of Aril's very strange family. Maybe they were dangerous too.

He quickly ran in after his mother, determined to defend her to the death, to—

There wasn't anybody in the room except his mother. Not much furniture, either. The place was cold, colder than any cold water flat had the right to be, even though it was early November. And it was gray in here, kind of like everything was covered in a fog, or spiderwebs. It seemed bigger than it ought to be, too, as though the walls stretched out to forever but were somehow shrunk back in on themselves. It made him sick and dizzy to try to look at anything straight on. So Adolph slid his gaze sideways to look at his mother.

Where she stood the living room looked perfectly normal. It was as though she stood in the light of an overhead spotlight, illuminating her and the worn floorboards on which she stood. Only, the light came from her, rather than from the ceiling, Adolph realized. It was as though she carried some special light inside of her.

"Magic," Aril said, coming suddenly out of the spiderweb shadows. He was staring at Adolph's mother, looking both scared and happy. Then his gaze shifted.

Adolph looked where his friend did. He could make out the figure of a small woman standing just out of the light his mother cast. "Your mom?"

Aril nodded. "Like calls to like! Your mother's talking to me Mum!"

Aril sounded as though this was some kind of wonderful surprise. "My mom talks a lot," Adolph said. "Everybody knows that." In fact, his mother was talking right now, and the little woman was edging closer to her, nodding at everything his mother said. For a moment Adolph thought he saw something with wings standing on the little woman's shoulder, but when he blinked, the little creature was gone.

Aril looked at Adolph, a beaming smile on his narrow, freckled face. "Our mums aren't having any trouble talking to each other."

"My mom's doing all the talking."

"No. My mum's answering yours, but not with her voice." He gestured. "You see what we're like."

Adolph knew very well that you didn't always have to say anything to get your point across. He wasn't much of a talker himself. He guessed Aril's mother was managing well enough with nods and gestures. Adolph actually could see the apartment a little better now. His weird dizzy spell had passed. Everything around him was more solid and substantial all of a sudden. The place was as shabby and crowded as his own family's apartment, but different somehow. There were lots of things lying around, great stuff like tree branches and birds' nests and piles of moss and rocks that didn't make much sense being in a New York tenement. And he could swear there were winged creatures flitting around, though he couldn't quite make them out. Butterflies, maybe? In November? He guessed that maybe Aril's mom wasn't strict about not keeping pets and making her kids throw out the things they collected outside.

And he and Aril and their mothers weren't the only people in the apartment. There were some pale little girls with wispy hair and huge eyes playing with fragile looking dolls over in one corner of the living room. They had pointed ears, too. A squat old woman in funny rags, with a huge, warty nose was scrubbing the floor in the kitchen. There was a man standing behind Mrs. Sheen. A tall, thin man, though he stood all bent shouldered and with his head down. He had hair like a lion's mane, but not as scruffy as the lion Adolph had seen at the zoo. His hair was so bright it almost looked like it was on fire.

"Who's he?"

"My dad," Aril answered. He hopped happily from foot to foot. "He doesn't appear for just anyone. Even the fire festival didn't call him forth last night, and he was known as Fire Walker back in the old country. Your mother's called him with a siren song."

"Yah," Adolph said. "Sure." Sirens were what they called the bells on fire engines. His mom could get peoples' attention like that, though he wasn't sure he liked anyone else saying his mom was loud and pushy, even if they used a fancy word.

"She believes in us!" Aril hugged himself tight around his skinny middle. "Oh, the joy!"

What was not to believe in, Adolph wondered, looking at the Sheens standing there, big as life, attention riveted on his mother's wild promises of fortune and fame in the big time. Mrs. Sheen's hair was red, Adolph noticed now, and it was all wild and frizzy and moved around her head as though she were standing in a draft. She was taller than Adolph had thought, and she had freckles just like Aril's. The apartment wasn't freezing cold now, and it smelled like spring. The room wasn't dark at all anymore, though it was still brightest around his own mother. She was still talking a mile a minute.

"Of course it's all magic," she answered a question from Aril's dad. "It's show business! Everything's illusion, but for a few hours every night you walk out onto a stage and the illusion is so real you taste and smell and feel and live it. You and the audience share the magic together. You make them happy, and they give the energy back to you when they applaud. You live for those hours on the stage and the applause. Everything else is just details." She sighed happily, face shining with her love of entertaining.

She truly believed vaudeville was magic. Adolph knew that pursuing the dream of making her sons headliners who played The Palace was the most important thing in her life. From the shining looks on the Sheens' faces, Adolph could tell she was infecting them with the same dream. He sighed, but he didn't dare interrupt. Never mind what his brothers had told him of sleeping on broken down trains and in fleabag hotels; of crooked theater managers that wouldn't pay the acts they booked; of bad food, or no money for food at all some nights; of tough audiences that sat on their hands no matter how hard you tried to make 'em smile. For Mom it was all magic, even the tough parts. The tough parts made the good parts even sweeter for her, he guessed. She could always find a bright side in every disaster.

"So, if we put an act together . . ." Mrs. Sheen spoke very slowly and tentatively, as though she were learning the words as she spoke them. "And we take this act . . . on the road . . . then we will be believed in?"

"By everyone?" Mr. Sheen asked.

"Sure!" his mom told them. "People *want* to believe in magic. That's why they go to the theater."

"And you would take us there, to this theater, and stay there until others saw us?" Mrs. Sheen asked.

"Sure," she answered. "I'll show you and your kids the ropes. You won't make it in the business without me."

The Sheens looked at each other, smiles on their beautiful, otherworldly faces. They were buying it, Adolph saw, every dream his mom was selling. They were going to do it, they were going to go into vaudeville. And she was going to be their manager. "She's good," he murmured, with a pride he wasn't sure he should be feeling.

"Can we bring the old one with us as well?" Aril piped up. "Can you wake her and bring her, too?"

His parents looked at Aril, his dad frowning. "Don't interrupt, lad," he said.

His voice was so stern that Adolph would have ducked and jumped behind his friend, but Aril got behind him first. Aril peered from behind Adolph's shoulder. Adolph heard him gulp, but Aril went on despite annoying his dad. "She deserves our respect, does she not? So you've told me."

"Perhaps she'll be well enough to travel," Mrs. Sheen spoke up. "It would be right, my love," she added to her husband.

"If you respect the old one so much, go and look in on her," his father ordered. He gestured Adolph's mom toward a gilded chair with a purple velvet cushion Adolph hadn't noticed before. "You lads leave your elders in peace while we talk."

Happy to be dismissed, Adolph followed his friend through a bedroom door. The music started as soon as Aril closed the door. Maybe it had been playing all along, but Adolph didn't notice it until he was away from the spell cast by his mother. He was beginning to believe in that sort of thing.

"You have to believe in something in order for it to be real," Aril said, as though he'd read his mind. "At least, that's how it is for folk like us. Maybe it rubs off when you're around us for a while."

Adolph scratched his head. "Maybe," he said, but he couldn't keep his attention on Aril for long. He did notice the old woman sleeping under a fancy quilt in a corner of the room, but she didn't interest him, either. It was the music that meant everything to him. Hearing it made his heart ache, brought tears to his eyes, and worst and best of all, it made his fingers itch. He wanted to find the source of the sound, touch it, make the music himself.

"You are the music," a sweet voice said all of a sudden. "Your heart needs to let it out."

Adolph followed the voice and found a slender, green-haired girl seated behind an instrument made of tautly strung wires. To his eyes it looked as though somebody'd torn a small piano apart and set the insides up on its side. The girl brushed a hand across the strings, making notes pour out of them—like—like a waterfall glistening in sunlight. Each note held its own falling sparkle. Like fire, like—

"This is my sister, Sian," Aril said, with the contempt only a brother could manage for a sister. "She thinks she's smarter than anyone. You don't have to talk to her if you don't want."

Adolph continued to stare at the instrument, but he was very aware of the girl. He flashed her a brief smile, then concentrated on studying her hands as she continued to softly stroke the strings.

"I'll tell your fortune, if you like," she said. Then she laughed, and it sounded like light on water, too. "But I don't think that's what you want."

"Don't tease him," Aril told his sister.

"He's a mortal. That's what they're made for."

"We're leaving the apartment," Aril said.

"I know that." She closed her eyes. When she spoke it was as if she were seeing things behind her eyelids. "I'm to become a famous singer. Then my voice will be silenced for a while when I live in shadows that tell stories. When the shadow shows start to speak, I'll be even more famous. We'll live in a land where the sun always shines and there are more stars than there are in heaven. You'll be there, too," she said to Adolph. "You and your brothers. Your fingers will talk, but your voice will be forever silent. The world will love your silence. This I promise you."

"Cut it out," Aril complained. "He doesn't believe you. You don't really have the Sight."

"And you're jealous that I've captured your friend for my own."

"You have not!"

"Oh, yes. I called him once before, but he wouldn't come. I'm stronger now."

"Because of his mother."

"She was meant to come to us. I saw it."

"Did not."

Adolph barely heard them. He reached out and touched the carved wood of the instrument. All the hunger he'd ever had to make music was in that tentative gesture. "What is this?" he asked the green-haired girl.

"It's a harp," she said. "And what is your name, little boy?"

"Adolph Marx," he answered. "Will you teach me how to play?"

A PHOENIX TOO FREQUENT
by India Edghill

India Edghill's interest in fantasy can be blamed squarely on her father, who read her *The Wizard of Oz*, *The Five Children and It*, and *Alf's Button* before she was old enough to object. Later, she discovered Andrew Lang's multicolored fairy books, Edward Eager, and the fact that Persian cats make the best paperweights. She and her cats own too many books on far too many subjects.

She was born in fire, scarlet and golden. A fiery bauble; a blazing toy; a charming conceit of the capricious beings that created her from madness and mystery, from paradox and dreams.

Seared into perfection in fire's heart, she was raised in a world of gods; a world luxurious, sophisticated, and profoundly decadent. She was bred to please and amuse; to be pet and plaything, light and enlightenment. Every art and grace and brilliance the infant human race could ever hope to possess was already hers. And, since her creator was pleased with this impossible creation, she was bred to be one thing more:

Eternal.

But there are rules even gods must obey. One such

rule commands all things to die in their season—even gods. So a god's creation, too, must die. But there are ways to thwart every rule, and so, although the charming toy must die, that little death, too, would fulfill her function to amuse and enlighten. Born in fire, she would die in fire—only to be reborn from the flames that consumed her.

It was a cheat, of course, and carried a price.

But it was a price that Phoenix herself would pay, and so her creator did not care.

Nor did Phoenix, cosseted and cherished in her jeweled cage. In the sheltered world in which she dwelt, she was pampered, favored, prized. Every desire she could articulate was gratified, every whim indulged.

Then the eternal cosmos convulsed, transforming, and the gods who created Phoenix died. Phoenix died too—and arose, shining with new hope, out of the scented pyre to find her creators and her timeless world gone.

New risen, Phoenix stood in shattered ruins that once had been the sky-tall and Lucifer-proud City of Masters. Her gods and all their works were gone. Wind blew cold and the world was empty, and there was no one to take care of her.

All that remained was what might someday become humanity—and Phoenix.

Phoenix held within her all that the human race would someday become. But there were no humans yet, for the gods had not finished their labors on that promising creation before their eternity ended.

All that existed now were brutes with a great potential. Someday those brutes would be men and women; artists and teachers, warriors and scientists. But now these fledglings owned no language, no science, no civilization, and no understanding that they needed one another to survive.

Feral humanity possessed only an endless future, and Phoenix. Someday men and women might become what she already was. Phoenix listened to screaming on the cold night wind, and shuddered.

Someday was far away.

Phoenix did not know what had destroyed the creators and their world, nor that their destruction had created Time. She knew no more of this new world than did the someday-men struggling to survive in the ruins surrounding her. But now she knew that she had been created from dreams and reborn from fire for this task: to raise the human race, nurturing and teaching, until these new beings soared free.

Phoenix gathered infant mankind under her wings; it was Morning, and she must tell the gods' wild children what to do.

New-invented mankind followed Phoenix as if she were herself one of the vanished gods. Slow time passed, and people learned, and the world grew. More people were born, and still more; more, at last, than the valley of the dead gods could sustain. Some men moved away to see what future they could fashion for themselves, seeking tomorrow beyond the old world's end. Phoenix blessed them and wished them well.

Then the changes began; the Great Ice came. Ice,

and new kinds of animals all the time; strange beasts undreamed-of by the old gods. These things were new, and unexpected, and frightening; Phoenix shivered and pined for the creator's warmth. Seeing her distress, men desiring her favor dared grasp power themselves, and brought her live coals. As she faded, the tribe's new fire summoned her. Seeing its blaze, Phoenix remembered she might die, and rest.

When she burst forth again from the restoring pyre, summers were warmer and longer, and the Great Ice had faded back and released the land. And there was another change, worse than the ice or the beasts. While she had rested, the serpent Envy had bitten mankind, and that poison had sunk deep.

Mankind remembered Phoenix, but now asked why her blessings should belong to everyone. Should not the strongest alone enjoy the Phoenix gifts? An ambitious man browbeat a dozen others into joining him; when they left the valley with their seed grain and their beasts of burden and their women, all of which were theirs to take freely, they took another thing as well, which was not theirs: Phoenix.

Men discovered war. A tribe holding Phoenix flourished; each tribe desired to possess her treasures for themselves alone. Tribes fought for dominion of the Phoenix, for the privilege of caging her.

War meant more change.

At last the tribe owning Phoenix lost, its men and children slain and its women taken. The victors carried Phoenix off in triumph, secure in the favor of their own tribe's gods. For humans had invented religion, too, in an attempt to explain Phoenix, and The

Time When Things Were Different. They were heartily afraid of their idols; her new owner treated Phoenix as well as any human could.

Time passed in its slow-flowing stream, creating small changes: little wars, little inventions, little cities. Thrice the watching Phoenix tired and remade herself in dark flames.

The first time she returned through fire, awed priests built her a temple of squat gray stones, and all the people of that land flocked to gaze upon her and offer gifts. They were good people, industrious and kind; their crops and lands prospered, and they thought it Phoenix's doing rather than their own. When she left them, they did not argue, but watched in awe as she entered the eternal flame.

The second time she rose, she was caged in a temple of gold and ivory, her gifts prisoned for the benefit of the priests alone—and for those who could pay what the priests demanded. She did not stay there long, and her leaving melted the vessels of gold and blackened the ivory walls.

The third time she slumbered longer than she knew. When she entered the world again, the Phoenix, the Bird of Fire, was a harper's legend. Those who once had honored her were no longer even dust; no living man had ever seen her. While she slept, Mankind had planted the seeds of science and civilization, invented art and agriculture.

Mankind had developed its own gifts. No one truly remembered Phoenix or seemed to need her now.

Because she had nothing else to do, and because she was lonely, Phoenix set out to travel the new earth passing time had spread before her. She journeyed across the world until she met someone who knew the ancient legend of the Phoenix and her flames. He knew, and believed, and took her in and cherished her. She stayed until that man's grandchildren's grandchildren asked who she was and why she was there. Then she began walking the wide world once again.

Çatal Hüyük and Babylon. Egypt, Crete, and Troy. Jerusalem and Tyre. Fiery legend wrapped her like a pearl's nacre around a grain of sand. The risen phoenix; the sati queen; the jewel in the fire's blazing heart. She was hope: a goddess, so there must be gods, and more to life than human eyes could see. There must be eternity.

There was—her eternity. Until humans evolved the ability to count such monstrous spans of time, there would be no tools to measure how old she already was. And humans were young—brawling, ardent, and desperate. They were not given to introspection.

Empires became larger. History became longer. Egypt rose and fell, and then Eternal Rome—both, to Phoenix, an indrawn breath and a sigh.

The tide of secular human learning divided from religious myth—rose, crashed, and rose again—a pattern as visible to Phoenix as waves against the sand.

Phoenix was very tired. She was old, and very little was new. The world grew harder for her to endure; now it was an effort to be simple and speak of things humans would understand. They were pretty, they were clever, but their infinite astonishment made her weary.

And humans were so fragile, so ephemeral, so

mortal. It was easiest to let them do what they would. In a thousand years, who would remember these people or the thing that so excited them in this moment of time?

Even now, uncounted years after the golden age of her creation, she was still remembered. Remembered in dreams, in hopes, in faith, a memory fragile as a candle in the wind. The undying Phoenix, granter of youth, beauty, immortality; healer of the sick; bestower of all virtues and grace. Seeking these treasures, some humans still searched for her and offered services. Remembering why she had been created and what she was, she permitted this worship.

But Phoenix herself no longer sought men out.

She grew weary, and rested long in her fire's heart before rising. This rebirth catapulted her into a world changing more and more swiftly; change tumbling over change; raging floods of invention and discovery and war. Change swept over the world faster, and faster yet, until Phoenix was sickened and terrified by time's ruthless passage.

Now she needed human companions to make her way through the swiftly changing world—mayfly creatures who could live at the speed the new world demanded. Creatures who did not carry the infinite memories she did—a fatal trap and burden. Spiraling hopelessly through whirlwind reality, she feared madness if the world continued mutating at such unbearable speed.

Her mortal companions did not live forever, as she did. But tending upon Phoenix, they lived too long, and sooner or later lost their ability to adapt to change; then they died. The pain of losing her mortal companions grew worse as time rolled on; she did not become accustomed to heartache.

When the world's measureless journey became too great for her to bear, her only solace was sleep within the fire's heart. But her rest was finite; after each brief respite she must wake and fly free again. She could not sleep forever; she could not hope to die. Time battered Phoenix, a constant assault against her soul.

The only consolation she knew was that she still fulfilled the function for which she had been created so long ago, in that forgotten time before time. That was the only mercy.

Then mankind discovered a Fire as great as hers, and for Phoenix, that small mercy ceased to be enough.

Phoenix rose again to still another war; another brilliant tyrant slashed the world, remolded it to feed his own ambition. When he was gone, men of both good and bad will attempted to mend what had been marred, but the poisoned seeds the tyrant had planted festered deep.

Three lifetimes later, the Greatest of all Wars flowered from those seeds; a generation of men died in bloody mud. Worse, as the war scorched across the poisoned earth, its venom spawned new cruelties, new ways of killing.

Worst of all, that war killed mankind's hope, although mankind did not know it then.

Phoenix watched this new horror with her last remaining spark of interest in the affairs of men. In all her endless life, she had never seen such tragedy; surely this must be the end of mankind's disastrous romance with death. Humanity had nearly killed its own soul; Phoenix roused enough to summon her long-dormant gifts, certain that she would be called upon to rekindle that precious spark.

But very few remembered Phoenix at all, save as fairy tale and myth. And the legacy forged by a tyrant now a century dead ripened to full fruition. Like an evil Phoenix, a new despot rose from the ashes of the shattered world with a new creation: a global holocaust to glut mankind's hate.

And hate summoned the future.

For while mankind had forgotten Phoenix's gifts, it still possessed dim memories of Phoenix's fire. Now both the new-risen tyrant and his foes desired that inferno for themselves. Desperate to possess its capacity for destruction, they raced to produce the deathless Flame, understanding neither that Fire's true capacity nor its price.

And as that eternal pyre ignited as a weapon over human cities, the last ember of Phoenix's hope for the old gods' children flickered and died.

Phoenix lived on; she had no choice in that. Now she slept within her pyre whenever its flames would receive her; there she denied the waking dreams of horror.

But even her pyre's dark heart gave unquiet rest; within its ardent embrace, she endured nightmares lit by deathless fire.

Plague and famine; war and death in all the jagged shapes of horror. Men and women starved, and hurt, and died, and she did not. She walked away—

—and walked, and walked, until she traveled a darkling plain, with nothing before her or behind.

Overhead stars burned against endless night. She knew what would happen if she looked up and swore each time that she would not.

But each time she did, and the eternal unchanging stars began to dance. Slowly at first, and then faster, and faster still, a great carousel of light spinning round her until she was the center of a dizzying universe of fire and ice that whirled and changed and would never stop—

—save when she awoke after each sleep of years, forced once more from the only home the Phoenix could ever know. Soaring from the eternal pyre into the winds of time, eternally changing and forever the same, rising once more into the cold light of endless morning.

A NESSY MESS
by Dennis A. Schmidt

Dennis Schmidt lives in New York City, right off Central Park, with his wife and two dogs, one of which is a large, obnoxious Rottweiler named Boo. He teaches politics at a private college where he has been known to pull coins from his students' ears. His previous writings include science fiction (the *Kensho* and the *Questioner* series) and fantasy (the *Twilight of the Gods* trilogy).

I was right in the middle of the third phase of a Seventh Plane Invocation when my beeper went off. I automatically cursed whoever made the call with a case of boils. I mean, do you know how long it takes to prepare a Seventh Plane Invocation? Not to mention waiting for all the planets and the other astral bodies to line up in the proper way.

So why be so nasty? Why not just let it slide and get on with my life? Ha! If only it was that easy. First of all, I have a kind of short fuse when it comes to things like being interrupted in the midst of working magic. Some very nasty things can happen to you if you're messing with the wrong kind of spell and lose control. Things with claws and lots of teeth for instance. And second, the problem wasn't merely having to do the whole damn Invocation over from scratch in a few months. No, the problem was that in the meantime I'd have to put up with Boo.

Who's Boo? More properly denominated Boudicca, she is without doubt the most utterly obnoxious Fifth Plane familiar ever invoked by anyone, anywhere, at any time. And I'm the one who did it. My only defense is that she was my very first Invocation on the Fifth Plane and I did badly need a familiar at the time. But, by Hecate, who expected to get a ninety-three-pound Rottweiler as a familiar? And especially one that has a weird sense of humor, a smart-ass mouth, and a most annoying penchant for quoting Kierkegaard? Plus she's always got this huge, sarcastic grin on her snout, as if she knows all kinds of things none of the rest of us know.

Anyway, the beeper went off, I lost my concentration and had to bag the whole Invocation. Boo began to chuckle. " 'Thus it is one thing to think, and another thing to exist in what has been thought.' Old Soren really has a way with words. He once wrote . . ."

"Not a word!" I snarled in a very good imitation of a bull mastiff (the only dog Boo respected). "Not one more damn quote!" I looked down at the beeper to see who had called and instantly regretted the curse of boils. It was Jimmy Walker, the mayor of New York. Jimmy and I went way back to the very first days of the Discontinuity. He'd hired me to do a couple of off-the-books jobs for the city since he'd become mayor. That thing with the rogue covens, you may remember it, that was one of my best jobs.

The problem is, I'm not really officially a Wizard First Class. Sure, I carry a union card, but I never apprenticed. Couldn't stand the idea of sweeping all those floors and toting all that water. And since I saw *Fantasia* when I was a kid, I know the kinds of things that can go wrong if you work the shortcuts. Which I'm afraid I'm guilty of pretty often.

That's what happens when you come to a profession later in life. I mean, if I had applied to the New School for Magikal Research when I was, say, eighteen or so, I would have had plenty of time to learn from the ground up. But I was already thirty-two when the Discontinuity hit. I was a college professor teaching history, a profession that instantly became irrelevant. So since I had always dabbled in magic (I used to pull coins out of students' ears to keep them awake), I decided to go the Wizard route. The field wasn't very crowded at the time, and there wasn't any organization at all until Mike Quill got the union going. I was grandfathered in, but I won't ever have a full Wizard First Class status.

Jimmy never let that bother him, though. Before he became mayor by trouncing Al Crowley in a wild election (they *really* voted the graveyards in that one!), we used to hang in the East Village trying to hit on the Anarchist chicks from the old NYU (now NYD—New York Diversity). Anarchists were really riding high just after the Discontinuity until they realized Anarchism was the Truth now and not a radical position at all. That was a real bummer for most of them. The majority dropped out and became stockbrokers.

Anyway, I gave Jimmy a buzz from my cell phone. "Yo, Jimmy, what up dude?"

"Damn. I got a problem. No, I got two problems. Damn, would you believe I just broke out with the worst case of boils I've ever had? Must be a reaction to the other problem."

"Boils?" I tried to sound as innocent as Sylvester circling Tweety's cage while Granma was watching. "Eat anything exotic for lunch?"

"Naw. Just the usual eye-of-finny-snake sandwich at the Three Weird Sisters Pub. Maybe it's some kind of sick prank. Maybe some of Crowley's Golden Dawn crowd are still pissed about my beating him out for mayor. That bunch really carries a grudge. Can you do anything about it? I can't afford the time to go to HIP and to get a managed-care doctor to look at it. That could take weeks. My primary care physician is an internist. Doesn't know diddly about boils."

"You know I'm not licensed to practice medicine, Jimmy. But, hey, anything for a good friend. Just keep it to yourself. If the AMA ever hears about it, they'll bust me for good." I stifled a sigh of relief. He didn't suspect me. I made the proper hand motion, muttered "Bibbidee Bobbidee Boo," and spun three times windershins. It's a snap to undo your own curse. "How's that?"

There was a pause on the other end of the line. "Geeze, you are good, man, legit or not. You do face lifts? But, hey, boils aren't the reason I called. I, or should I say we (meaning New York City), have a very big problem on our collective hands, and I need your help, old buddy."

I knew I was in for trouble. Jimmy never calls me "old buddy" unless there's some really rotten job he needs done. I gave my best imitation of a patient sigh. "So what's the real deal?"

"Right to the point. We got us a Nessy in Central

Park Lake. He plucked two tourists right out of the Lakeside Café and then ate Miss Bradshaw's entire fourth grade class from the Rudolph Steiner School. Took us two hours to resurrect them all from DNA samples the school supplied. Couldn't do anything for the tourists. That is not for publication, by the way. It could ruin the whole tourist season if word got out."

"A Nessy? In Central Park Lake?"

"Man, you should have your phone checked. There's an echo. Could you get down there and check it out *tout suite?*"

"I thought the City had a contract with the United Wizards' Federation to handle stuff like that. Why call me?"

"The contract doesn't cover anything larger than an elephant or smaller than a cockroach. I argued with Quill for an hour. Hey, maybe that's where I got the boils. Anyhoo, do Uncle Jimmy a big favor and at least check this one out, okay? There's a cool five grand if you take it. Two I'll transfer to your account right away, the rest when the Nessy's gone. Small, unmarked bills, okay? And say hello to Boo for me, will you?" He broke the connection.

"You heard?" I asked Boo. She nodded, a big grin on her smoosh, her tongue hanging out about a foot. "Whaddaya think?"

She paused. "For the life of me, I can't think of an appropriate Kierkegaard quote. A Nessy? In Central Park Lake?"

"Jimmy's right. There is an echo around here. Want to go check it out?"

She shrugged a doggy shrug. "Got nothing better to do. I just finished my latest Louis Armstrong novel, so I'm out of things to read. Yeh, let's go for it. But how about not trying to break any supersonic barriers this time, huh? Remember, I only got paws to hang on with."

One of the problems with having a ninety-six pound Rottweiler for a familiar is that you can't use one of those neat Chevie two-seater brooms to scoot around town. If I'd been smart and settled for a ferret or a mongoose, it would have been cool. (Black cats are just too cliché.) Instead I was stuck with a Mercedes moped and a giant canine breathing and drooling down my neck everywhere I went. And endlessly back seat kibitzing. I'd go by subway, but I don't trust them any longer, not since the Worm Jormungund showed up in one of the tunnels. Damn thing swallowed a whole train. And all the buses were wiped out along with the cars when they rebelled.

The cops had roped off the 72nd Street entrance to the park with yellow crime scene tape, but I knew the sergeant in charge of the detail. I'd worked with him on that little mess when the vampires broke into the blood bank. He waved me right on through.

I parked my moped by the Bethesda Fountain and walked cautiously over to the edge of the water. "Yo, Nessy!" I called out. "You there?"

A head the size of a draught horse came out of the lake, perched atop a long skinny neck. The head was bright fuchsia, the neck a lovely shade of lavender. The mouth was full of teeth about nine inches long. The eyes were small, black, and cold. Just beneath the surface I could make out a huge elephantine body with four large flippers and a stubby tail. "Yessss. Are you dinner?"

Boo laughed out loud. "Whooeee, you are one stupid Nessy! Don't you know that all wizards are tough, stringy, and have a foul taste? And just in case you're wondering, Rotties have a truly disgusting, bitter flavor. What are you doing here?"

"Talking to you two, obviousssssly. Alsssso, I am trying to figure out what to have for my ssssupper. Thosssse children were tender, but not very filling. And the touristsss were Chinesssse. You get hungry an hour later."

Boo was right. This Nessy was pretty stupid. "No. What Boo meant was what are you doing here in this lake right now. Why aren't you home in Loch Ness?"

"Loch Nesssssss? Never heard of it. Though I do like itssss ssssound."

My jaw dropped in surprise. "Never heard of Loch Ness? But . . . you're a Nessy! A Loch Ness Monster. That's . . . that's like a Parisian who never heard of Paris!"

Nessy pouted. "Well, I never heard of Parisss either, ssssso there. Anyway, why are *you* here if you're not going to provide my ssssupper?"

"Uh, I'm afraid I'm here to exorcise you."

" 'Exxxxorcccisssse me? Doesssss that have anything to do with food? Really, do you realizzzze how many caloriessss I burn every minute? I'm warm blooded, you know and thisss damn lake issss very cold!"

I didn't pay any attention to the Nessy's grumbling. I had an exorcism to do and there was no sense in wasting any time. We were losing precious tourist money every minute this monster tied up the park. And I had a cool five that was waiting for me when the exorcism was over.

Nessys are Fourth Plane creatures, so I marked out

a Magic Square with chalk. Then Boo stepped into the center, careful not to smudge the lines. The Nessy watched the whole process, grumbling all the while about dinner. Then I began the exorcism, chanting the arcane phrases in High Esoteric. I'm not half bad at chanting, though I don't hold a bell, book and candle to Kathy Battle.

Part way through, I began to get a sense that things weren't going well. Boo and the Nessy were supposed to change places. Then I would collapse the Magic Square and send the Nessy back where it came from. But Boo was still in the Square more than half way through the chant and the Nessy was still wallowing around Central Park Lake, crashing into some of the boats that had been left tied to the dock at the Boat House.

I finally had to admit it wasn't working. With a sigh, I stopped, smudged the lines of the Square so Boo could get out and sat down on the edge of the fountain to think. Boo sat down next to me, keeping a weather eye out for the Nessy. If it really got hungry, it might decide to chance the taste of a Wizard and a Rottweiler.

Something was very wrong. A Nessy was a Probability creature and should respond to magik. But the exorcism clearly hadn't taken hold at all. How could that be? Or for that matter, how could a Nessy be in Central Park Lake in the first place? And never have heard of Loch Ness in the second place. In the third place . . . I was getting confused and feeling out of place, so I started over, counting on my fingers this time.

Part way through, Boo said, "What if he's not a Nessy after all?"

"Not a Nessy?" I snorted. "If *he* isn't a Nessy, what the hell is?"

She shrugged. "Don't rightly know. I've never been introduced to one. And the only pictures I've seen in pre-Discontinuity books were so fuzzy and out of focus, it could have been almost anything of any size. How do you know he's a Nessy?"

I thought for a moment. "Well, Jimmy said he was."

She chuckled. "Since when is that knucklehead an expert on monsters? Unless they are voting monsters. And who told him anyway? You don't really think he came down here himself to check it out, do you?"

"Hmmmmm. A valid point. Maybe we should go right to the source and ask the monster itself." I stood up and walked over near the water again. The creature was nowhere to be seen. "Yo, Nessy!" I called out. "I got a question."

The head and neck reared out right in front of me, spewing brown lake water all over my clothes. "If it doessssn't have anything to do with food, I'm not interessssted."

"All right. A suggestion. There are fish in the lake. Eat a couple of them."

"Yuck!" the creature replied. "Look at the color of thissss water! Would you want to eat anything that lived in here? Probably tasssssste like muck."

"Good point. Listen, a simple question. How do you know you're a Nessy?"

He cocked its head to the side, fixing me with his cold glare. "How do I know? How? I wasss told, that'ssss how."

"Right. Who told you?"

"One of thosssse little creaturesss with the

wingsss that live in the woodssss on the north sshore of the lake. It got too clossse to the water, so I grabbed it and ate it. I heard it ssssscream to the otherssss 'Look out! A Nessssy'ssss got me!' Sssssince I wasss the only thing that got it, I asssume it meant me. Sssso, are you happy? Will you bring me sssssome more children for dinner? Or maybe ssssomething more sssubsssstantial, like ssssome German tourisssstssss?"

I backed slowly away beyond range of its neck and sat down next to Boo by the fountain again. "We got us a real problem. If he isn't a Nessy, I can't exorcise him."

"What about a Lift and Carry spell?" Boo suggested.

"Are you kidding? I'll bet that thing weighs a good four tons! I'd get one hell of a hernia trying to Lift and Carry that baby. No, Boo, I don't think magik alone is going to work here. We're going to have to use superior intelligence and guile as well."

"We are in big trouble," she muttered.

I thought for a moment. "Do you remember a book in my library? One about dinosaurs?"

"Yeh. It has a blue cover. So what?"

"Fetch it for me."

"What, am I a dog or something? Fetch it yourself." She rolled over on her back, all four legs in the air. "I'm busy trying to think of a Kierkegaard quote." I growled at her. "Oh, all right. That's what I get for becoming a Familiar in the first place." She disappeared in a flash, then reappeared with a pop, the book in her mouth.

I thumbed through it, looking for a particular page. "Ah, there it is!" I pointed to the picture that spread across two pages in glorious color. "Got the skin shades wrong, but the general shape's right."

Boo looked over my shoulder. "Well I'll be a poodle. That's him. That's the thing in the lake! He's a Plesiosaur. Some kind of Dino."

"More specifically an Eleasmosaurus. He lived in the Mesozoic period, sometime between the early Jurassic and the late Cretaceous. And he wasn't a true dinosaur. Some of the most complete pre-Discontinuity remains were found in Kansas, where there was once a shallow sea. The thing ate fish and other sea creatures. No wonder magik doesn't work. He's not a Probability creature at all. He's a damn Mischronism."

Boo held up a paw. "Whoa, fly that one past me again. What in Dog's name is a Mischronism?"

"A creature misplaced in time. Like Jimmy Walker. Look, when the Last Just Man died and there was no one left to guard the Probability Barrier, everything became possible and the discontinuity occurred. But that not only meant that anything that was Probable could become actual. It also meant that anything that had existed, but no longer did, could exist again. Like an Eleasmosaurus from the shallow sea of Kansas."

Boo considered that for a moment. "While we're being wild eyed here, how about another possibility?"

"I'm open to anything."

"Maybe the Discontinuity opened a crack at the bottom of Central Park Lake that leads right down to Pellucidar and this thing swam up through the crack."

"Yeh, and Tars Tarkas and Woola are about to land in a flying saucer at Belvedere Castle. I like my idea better. Besides, there's no indication of any deep crack in the Lake. And if there were, why wouldn't the water just drain away down to Pellucidar?"

She rolled over on her back again, waving her legs in the air. "Okay, okay. It was just a neat idea. So this thing is a Mischronism. So now what do we do?"

I thought for a while. It was hard to concentrate, because the Eleasmosaur was thrashing around in the lake, getting hungrier by the minute, and I wasn't at all sure whether the damn things ever came out on land to grab prey.

"Well," I finally said tentatively, "if he's not a Nessy but instead a Mischronism, that means I can't exorcise him no matter what. But just because exorcism won't work, it doesn't mean all magik won't work."

"What about we just magically poison the lake" Boo suggested. "We could grind the thing up to make cat food out of it."

"No thanks. We'd have to fill out a huge Environmental Impact Report to do something like that. It'd take years. No, magik is the only way."

"Duh. You know as well as I do that magik can't be worked on any non-Probability creature unless it asks for it or cooperates." She cast a worried look over at the Eleasmosaur. "And assuming that that thing is indeed what you say he is, he is looking less and less cooperative by the minute. Do you suppose we could do our thinking a little further away from the water's edge? That thing's giving me some awfully hungry stares."

We moved up to the top of the stairs at the south side of the fountain's plaza. "If he's a Mischronism and if I could get him to agree . . ." I had an idea.

Not a brilliant idea, but it was the only one I had. It all depended on the thing really being what I thought it was. If he really was a Nessy, I was in deep caca. If he was from Pellucidar, I was in the same stuff. We really had to be sure he was a Mischronism and nothing else. Oh, well, nothing ventured, nothing ventured. I moved cautiously back down to the fountain, just out (I hoped) of the thing's reach. Boo backed me up; about ten paces back to be precise. I had to find out exactly what he was before I could do anything.

"Yo, Nessy," I called. He swung his head in my direction. "What's the last thing you remember before you found yourself here?"

He squinted his beady little eyes with the effort. "Water, water everywhere."

"Did it taste like the water in this lake?"

He considered. "No. Thisss water isss muddy and yukky. That water wasss nice and sssalty. And deliciousss fissshessss! Yesssss! I remember them." He moaned. "Oh, I am sssoo hungry! This is much worssse than Weight Watchersssss!"

I turned to Boo and muttered, "Bingo! I nailed it! Salt water and fish! He's an Eleasmosaur!"

She frowned. "Maybe the Loch Ness is salty? How about one last test?" I grunted assent. Might as well be as sure as possible. Boo twirled in a circle and transformed into a Rottweiler dressed in a kilt with a bagpipe across her shoulder. She began to march toward the Nessy, caterwauling on those pipes, coming out with something that vaguely resembled a cross between Danny Boy and a whale in labor. The Nessy let out a shriek and lunged for her, his huge mouth snapping shut on the empty air where she had been strutting the instant before. I could feel her trembling from behind me. "Uh, guess that locks it up. He's definitely not from Scotland."

"Right. Or maybe that reaction to the way you play the pipes proves he is. Anyway, I am firmly convinced he is a Mischronism. Now to see if I can convince him to let me do magik on him." I took a deep breath and stepped closer to the moaning monster. "Nessy, would you like to go back to that salty water with all the fish?"

He reared half his bulk out of the water, sending a huge wave crashing against the shore, swamping the remaining boats at the dock. "YYYYEEESSSSS!" he roared.

"Okay, then here's the real deal. I can get you out of this muddy little lake with its muddy little fish, but only if you trust me and let me do something to you."

He peered suspiciously at me with his beady little eyes. "What?"

"Well, I was thinking of a shrinking spell. You know, bring you down to about seal size. Then we'll cart you out to Fire Island and put you in the ocean. Lots of salt, lots of fish and lots and lots of water. You'll be able to eat and eat. And in a day or so, the spell will wear off and you'll be back to your old size again. How's that sound?"

He blew the raspberries at me. "Do you think I'm that ssstupid? Once you make me sssmall you can put me in a zzzzoo or ssssomething. And how do I know your magik will wear off like you ssssay? Lisssten, busster, I wasssssn't born yessssterday, ya know." He paused to do a little mental calculation. "More like a couple hundred million yearssss ago.

Get lossst. Or do something usssseful and tossss me that Rottweiler for a sssnack!"

I went back and sat down on the rim of the fountain. Boo edged slightly away from me. "Don't get any ideas, boss. No offense, but you aren't much of a negotiator."

"Yeh, so you got a better idea?" I groused.

She gave a huge grin. "Guy like that, you got to offer him something with no apparent strings attached. Ya gotta hide the hook in a big, juicy worm. Something he can grab for right now. No fish-in-the-future for this boyo. He wants something to eat and he wants it now and he wants it delivered. Maybe we should order in Italian for him."

"Oh, great idea," I replied, my voice dripping with sarcasm. "Bring in an Italian and we'll have the Mafia all over us."

"I didn't say *an* Italian, sicko. I said Italian, like in maybe pizza. Wave it under his nose and . . ."

It hit me. "Wait! Hush up a minute! An idea is forming. A scheme. A brilliant plan. A solution to the whole problem." I thought it through carefully. "If the Nessy does something through an act of his own will that causes magik to be worked on him, it fits the rules."

Boo frowned and thought about it. "I guess that's right. It's not quite the same thing as cooperation, but if it happens through an act of his own, I guess that fits the requirements. But how do you get him to do something like that? Take a cattle prod to him?"

I smiled my loveliest, friendliest smile. "We have to offer him something he wants. Then when he goes for it, we trick him. Like the hook in the worm."

"Oh, great. And just where are you going to find a worm big enough to tempt this dude?"

I widened my smile, making it even more luminous and inviting.

Boo sat back on her haunches and held up a paw. "Whoa, buddy. You got that look on your ugly mug. That look that says somebody's familiar is in deep trouble."

"No trouble. Just a little game with Nessy. You let him chase you around the lake. You know, act like very fast food. Do a Gingerbread Boy. Then you lead him past where I'm waiting and wham! We hook him."

She began backing away. "Uh, I think I hear my mother calling. Gotta go back to the Fifth Level now. Bye, been nice knowing you. Barrel of laughs."

"Boo, stay!" I commanded, just like they taught me in obedience school.

She sat down. "Like, wow, man. Whaddya want from me? I can't outswim that thing. The only stroke I know is the dog paddle."

I crossed my eyes, snapped my fingers, wiggled my left ear while raising my right eyebrow, muttered a few patented words and poof! there was a brand new Skidoo sitting there. "That baby can do up to thirty miles an hour on calm water. You should be able to run circles around him."

"Terrific. And while I'm running circles around him, where will you be?"

"Take him out of this area into the bigger part of the lake on the other side of the bridge. Then circle around twice and bring him back in again. I'll have a trap set under the bridge so he can't avoid it."

"Yah. But neither can I."

"Don't worry. It won't be anything lethal. And you know it'll wear off in a couple of days at most." She didn't look convinced. "Okay, okay," I said. "Look, I'll do the shrinking thing like I said before. You know that one wears off in less than forty-eight hours. Now be a good familiar and do as you're told or I'll give *you* a case of the boils."

If she'd had a tail, it would have been between her legs as she slunk over to the Skidoo. "Okay. But you owe me big time for this one." Then she jumped on it, kicked it into roaring life, and took off across Central Park Lake like a Rottweiler with a Nessy on its stump of a tail. "Go, dog, go!" I screamed as I raced for the bridge.

The rest is history. I got my five thou. The papers never picked up a sniff of the whole incident, so the tourist season was saved (except for that little thing with the werewolves). And for two glorious days I had a Rottweiler familiar the size of a mouse.

Oh, yeh, there is one other thing. There was one small hitch I'm not sure I should mention. You see, Nessy wasn't a him. Nessy was a her. And she was carrying fertilized eggs. Which she laid and which hatched. And which grew and spread. And which ruined the whole beach scene on Fire Island for several years.

But please don't tell anybody I was the one who started all this. I can't afford to lose my Wizards' Union Card and my only way of making a relatively honest living. I need the money. You have no idea how expensive it is to feed a full-size ninety-eight pound Rottweiler familiar.

A GIFT OF TWO GRAY HORSES
by Rosemary Edghill

Rosemary Edghill is the author of *Speak Daggers to Her*, *The Book of Moons*, and *Fleeting Fancy*. Her short fiction has appeared in *Return to Avalon*, *Chicks in Chainmail*, and *Tarot Fantastic*. She is a full-time author who lives in Poughkeepsie, New York.

It was in the Mothertime, the dark of the year before the light is born, when Fadring made the gift to Owl Farm.

It was an odd gift, both in the giving and the substance, for Owl Farm was at the very edge of the World, where man's earth gave way to bleak tundra and the black woods of the Wildwold, and Owl Farm was soon to be reclaimed by the Wildwold, for only an old woman and a boy lived there. The man and his brothers had died in battle, and the other wives had gone where there was fire and food, taking the land-bonded with them. But the old woman and her boy would not go, and as no one wanted Owl Farm, they were left to stay. Even Fadring did not want it.

And Fadring was a greedy man, greedy for legend, land, and gold. He was close-handed with the praise-gifts, giving only what he must to avoid being sung down by the bards, and never a useless mouth feasted at his tables, even at Longest Night.

Fadring had gone to raid a rich caravan that a Walking Priest had brought word of—even the old woman knew that. Upon the horizon she had seen the tail of smoke and was not surprised, three days later, to see the war-band pass along the road on the way to the village.

She had spent the morning chipping the ice from the well and setting the pieces in a pan in the sun to melt. When Fadring halted his men in her dooryard, she feared his mischief, for Fadring was a cruel man when it was safe to be.

"Hail, old woman!" Fadring said. "How fares your stead in the long nights?"

The old woman did not answer, for it was clear to any man how it was with her.

Fadring frowned, cheated of his sport by her silence. "Nevertheless, of my charity, I am minded to give you a rich gift, for let no man say that Fadring Brighthair is clutch-fisted or mean with the spoils of his victory."

Still the old woman did not speak, for Fadring did not give one thing save to gain two, and his smile now was a thing of swordblades. Then she saw what he meant to give her.

They were the biggest horses she had ever seen— as big as the southern horses she had seen as a bride, when her husband had taken her raiding in the south. They were sleek as only a rich man's animals were in the Mothertime, rounded and firm with flesh and fat and sinew. Their coats shone in the dim daylight like polished glass, and their coats were the soft shining gray of a mouse's belly.

One had a white star on its forehead, and one had a white sock on its left foreleg. Fadring's man Sorli led them on braided leather halters, and they followed, as docile as sucking lambs.

But for all their worth and gentleness, the old woman could see that Fadring was afraid of these two horses and itched to be rid of them.

"They are yours, old woman," he said. "My Kindling gift to you."

Sorli put the halters into her hand, and still the old woman said nothing. Any words of hers now would be no other than the spark to the tinder of Fadring's anger, for fear and anger are brothers and march to war side by side. But Fadring looked at her no more, turning to his men and calling them all to witness the greatness of his gift. Moments later they were gone, leaving Owl Farm behind them.

When they were gone, the boy came out of hiding. He stared at the horses, his face showing all the shock and amazement that the old woman would not show.

"These are horses for kings!" he said.

"Then we are kings, now," the old woman answered him crossly. "Take you this gift of Fadring's, and see they are well stabled."

The boy watered the animals at the trough where he had smashed the ice that morning, and then led the gray horses into the barn. It was swept clean— there had been nothing to do but sweep, for a very long time—and there was no speck of dirt nor scrap of straw anywhere here. He put the animals into the spaces the oxen had occupied, when there had been oxen, and removed the leather halters and hung them away. He brought the grooming tools and combed out their coats—which did not need it—and their tails, which were as smooth and fine as a maiden's hair. Then he looked to the manger, which was so bare that not even a spider had spun his web there. In the loft there was grain still on the stalk from last year's harvest; they eked it out with straw, feeding the skinny goats, but it would not last much longer— even the Kindling still lay ahead, and beyond that the dark time stretched on for months.

He looked at the gray horses, who were nosing the manger hopefully, and bitter shame filled him that not even an animal should have good guesting in his father's house.

Recklessly he climbed to the hayloft and flung down armfuls of grain until the manger was full, and then he added handfuls of turnips from the barrel that stood almost as tall as he did. Immediately the horses bent their heads and began to feed.

Slowly he walked across the yard back to the wooden house. The long house had been one of the things that they had sold to keep them; his father's great building had been taken down and the timbers erected over another woman's hearth. Of kindness, the men who had taken the forge-stones had erected its walls about the great hearth, and the woman and the boy had covered the small building with turfs cut in the spring; now the woman and the boy lived inside the ring of the great stone hearth, tending their own tiny fire and sleeping with the goats for warmth.

Anger filled him as he guessed the truth behind Fadring's gift. They could feed the horses for only a handful of days, and that only if they themselves ate nothing. They would starve, and the goats would starve, and Fadring would reclaim his prize and enrich himself with the dishonor to their name.

The boy went inside, not wishing to tell what he had done. The old woman was bent over the small fire on the hearth. One of the goats lay dead beside her, and with careful gestures the old woman cut up the meat for the pot. The boy stopped, staring at what he saw. The goats gave wool for spinning and dung for the fire. In the spring there would be milk, and perhaps a new kid. To slaughter any of them now was to doom their future.

"Did you not think I knew how it must be when Fadring holds himself a generous man?" she asked. "Come. There will be food soon. And it is in my mind that a well-fed youngling with two strong horses could make his way south, out of Fadring's lands, to a better place."

"Rather would I die than let it be said that I left my kindred to starve alone," the boy said bitterly. He flung himself down beside the fire, taking the blade from the old woman to finish the work.

They ate to bursting that night, the first such meal for either of them in many days. When they had done, the old woman banked the fire for morning, and the two settled down in their thin blankets upon the cold stone to sleep.

In the morning the boy roused himself at first light. He drove the surviving goats out of the small wooden house to forage as best they could and went to the barn to see to the horses.

They stood quietly in their stalls, the heat from their bodies making the place warmer than the place he had left. He climbed to the loft to throw down grain for the morning feeding, but when he looked down to the stalls below, his eyes grew wide, and he clutched the thunderstone about his neck to ward off mischief.

The manger was as full as he had left it. More—thick-headed stalks of grain were spilled on the floor, and the tramping of the great hooves had winnowed the golden stalks, so that the floor of the stalls were covered with corn. He stood, staring, for he knew the horses had been hungry when he brought them here and should have eaten all he gave them.

He did not know what to think of this. He stared a while longer and then went to fetch the old woman. She came, muttering and grumbling with the ache in the old bones, and stared at what he had seen. After a long moment she spoke.

"Go and get the hearth broom. Sweep up all that is spilled. Feed the goats. But do not take one stalk from the manger."

He swept up enough to fill a large bag. The goats mistrusted their sudden good fortune and had to be coaxed to come to see what he had for them. Once they did, they ate it all and the bag as well, wandering off again with satisfied looks. The boy went back to the stable. He did not know what else to do.

He was relieved to see that there was less in the manger than there had been, for the thought that these splendid animals should sicken and die under his care was unbearable. But they dunged like ordinary animals, and when he got their halters and led them out to the trough and broke the ice over the water beneath they drank like ordinary animals, snorting and blowing and shaking a fine freezing spray of water all over him.

"What are we to do with you?" he asked them

helplessly. The plow was still there, in the corner of the barn, but even if it were already spring he could not imagine hitching such beasts to it and using them as if they were his father's oxen. They were meant for more than that, and he had no more to offer them. So he brought down the brushes again and groomed their gleaming hides until they shone like gray ice in the dim sunlight, and when he left them for the night, he made sure that their manger was filled with the best the steading could offer.

The next morning it was as it had been before. This time he filled his blanket with the spilled grain and the cast-off turnips. There was enough to feed the goats and to thicken the stew, and enough more to leave as an offering to the folk of World's End, for both the old woman and the boy knew there was something not of this world in their sudden bounty, though they did not speak of it. The boy tended Star and Whitefoot (for so he had named them) and gathered wood for the fire, and the short days passed.

And each morning, there was more in the manger than had been put there the night before, and the floor of the barn was covered hock-deep in what the horses had spilled. The horses fed on corn and turnips, and there was bounty enough to fatten the goats and to bait the wily hares that lived on the tundra. The old woman killed no more goats, but still there was meat in the pot and fuel for the fire.

The days grew short, racing toward the Kindling Time, and now a new fear lived with the two in the wooden hut, the fear that Fadring Brighthair would return. For if Owl Farm did not yet flourish, the goats and the boy grew sleek. Word of that would come to Fadring's ear as if carried by Old One-Eye's ravens.

And there were the horses.

"Such horses are not for the likes of us," the old woman said, one night by the fire. It was a larger fire now, for food had brought the boy strength to range farther into the Wildwold in search of wood, and the goats strength to pull the cart to carry it.

"Nor are they for Fadring," the boy answered, and this was a thing that could not be argued.

"Better you should leave. I will not see the spring," the old woman said. But she had said this every winter that the boy could remember and still she lived, stubborn and enduring as the rock beneath the plow.

"There are two horses," the boy pointed out. The old woman could ride. If they killed the rest of the goats and dried the meat, there would be food for the journey, and the halls and steadings of the south would know what was due in guest-friendship to the traveler.

But the old woman turned her face away and did not answer, and the boy knew that she would not leave Owl Farm that her man had gotten for her.

Nor would he go without her.

"You must go," the boy said to the horses. It was Kindling Eve. Tomorrow the sun would start back from the south, and the days would grow longer once more. The old woman had brought the last of their hoarded food from beneath the hearthstone: dried apples, and honey, and a jug of ale strong with age.

The boy fed the gray horses pieces of apple dipped in honey, and when the treats were gone, he clutched the neck of the nearer animal and wept into its mane until his soul was empty of tears, though he could not have said who he cried for.

"You must go. You are not for us. Fadring will surely ride out to see what we have made of his gift, and he will take you away to lives of shame, great though his dishonor will be. Go! Go now!"

He propped the barn door open with a rock and opened the stall doors. He took the braided leather cords and looped them about the necks of the two gray horses and led them away from the farm until he could no longer see the barn or the small wooden house. The last of the sun was a faint pale smear upon the horizon, and soon it would be dark. Then he took the halters from the horses' necks and flung them away.

"Go! Find a master who can honor you as you deserve!"

Whitefoot and Star regarded him with mild dark eyes, and for a moment, in this uncanny place, it seemed as if they would speak. But there was only silence and the thin droning of the winter wind, and the boy shivered in his patched and threadbare clothing. Before he could change his mind, before he could beg the fates to be other than they were, he turned his back upon the two gray horses and ran as fast as he could to the old woman's hearth.

The ale was hot and sweetened with honey. The old woman sang the Kindling Song in her thin, cracked voice and poured toasts to Old One-Eye, and the Thunder-lord, and the Lady of Apples. The boy's head was dizzy and spinning with strong drink before she was through, and when he lay down to sleep that night he did not feel the cold.

*   *   *

The light of full day woke him, and the boy wondered that the old woman had let him sleep so long. But when he sat up and rubbed his eyes, he did not see her anywhere. The fire was built high, and a pottage of turnips and grain waited for him in a bowl at its side. He left it lying there and ran outside.

The goats were in the barn, busy at the manger, regarding him with smug gluttony from their slitted eyes, and he felt a pang of loss that the horses were not there as well, for he had loved them dearly. *Go free*, he said in his heart, a silent, unspoken prayer.

The old woman was not in the barn, nor in the loft, nor at the trough, nor at the well. He broke the ice in the well and filled the trough so that the goats could drink, for on a farm the animals must come first, and then he went in search of her, his heart cold with fear.

Her track was clear, for she had gone out in the deepest night when the frost is heavy upon the ground. He followed her steps out into the Wildwold, and there, where he had left the horses, he found her. Her clothes were folded neatly beside her on the ground where she lay, and her body was stiff and blue with frost. Now and forever, she would not leave Owl Farm.

And now he was truly alone. In his heart, the treacherous, traitorous, confused thought burned: that if only she had done this thing two nights ago, he would not have turned the two gray horses out, would have taken them and ridden them to the south and all the promise that his future might hold.

Sternly, he banished such fantasies. It did not matter when she had died. What he had said at last night's sunset was true: Such horses were not for such as he. It was for the honor of Owl Farm that he had loosed them, and he would not take back the gift he had made, even in his mind.

He walked home again and harnessed two of the goats to the cart. He brought the cart to the Wildwold and bore the old woman's body back to Owl Farm. Then he took the hammer and the axe and spent the rest of the day taking down as much of the barn as he could. He would not think beyond that moment, to what must come after, for he knew—had known since his father died—that in the end it would come to outlawry or slavery. For a fatherless, masterless boy alone in the world there was no third choice. He could not hold Owl Farm all alone, and he had no kinfolk who would open their hearths to him. The old woman had been the last of his blood kin, and now she was gone.

When the pyre was built and the daylight began to go, he placed the old woman's body atop the pyre. The boy climbed down off the top of the pyre and walked over to the goat he had caught and tethered to the skeletal frame. He slit its throat with an economical, matter-of-fact motion and dragged it to the top of the pyre to lay at the old woman's feet, still bleeding. There was not much for him to send with her into the Afterworld, but he swore he would do her honor.

When everything was arranged, the boy went back into the small wooden house and came out carrying a dish full of coals. He placed them in a hollow at the foot of the pyre, and fed their flame with wisps of straw from the manger. As the last of the light left the sky, the wood kindled and began to burn. Soon the whole pyre was alight, a bright gold pillar reaching into the winter sky. Perhaps it would be visible from the doors to Fadring's hall, and he would see, and wonder at the sight. Perhaps he would come to reclaim his rich gift. The boy smiled ferally to contemplate Fadring's wrath when he found that Owl Farm had set beyond his reach that which he had unjustly claimed.

"Hail, Kridi Havnir's-son," a voice said quietly behind his shoulder.

The boy gasped and turned quickly, his hand going to the knife upon his belt. But those before him were not of Fadring's sending. In the light of the pyre he could see them well.

They were seven women, and each rode a gray horse with a coat as smooth as polished glass. Their ring-mail was as bright as fine silver hot from the fire, and their helms were of rich gold inlaid with boar ivory. Their cloaks were of wolfskin and scarlet, and their trews were of the soft white wool of the lamb's first shearing. The boots upon their feet were stamped with gold, and each among them bore spear and shield.

He would have knelt, but he was far too astonished that so many should come upon him unrecognized, silent as the shadows cast by the fire. He had never seen such battle-maidens before, but two of the horses he had seen. One was ridden by the leader of the women and one by the woman at her side.

"Whitefoot! Star!" he gasped. The gray horses nodded their heads as if to acknowledge his greeting.

"Is it well with you, Havnir's son?" the leader asked.

"It is not well," the boy admitted, with the flames

of the old woman's fire warm at his back. "But I have tended your horses well."

"And so you have," the battle-maiden said. "Without thought for your own gain you have cared for them, and upon Kindling Eve you freed them to return to their rightful masters. Fadring came upon them tethered at the edge of a battle he did not fight and spoiled them away who could not have had them by right. This we will remember, my sisters and I. But tell me, Havnir's son, what reward will you have for returning to us that which belongs to us? Would you have wealth and lands? Vengeance upon your enemies? A place at the table of a great king?"

"I would have no more than what my mother wished for me," Kridi answered. "I would have a horse to ride and food for the journey, and I would make my own way in the world."

"That is a man's answer," the shield-maiden said approvingly. She dismounted from Whitefoot's back and walked forward, and suddenly there was a horse beside her where no animal had been before. She led the riderless horse forward, and Kridi could see that the animal was not gray, as Whitefoot was, but a fine dapple such as any man would be proud to claim. The horse bore a good saddle upon his back, with sword and cloak and provision for a journey. There was a mail shirt as splendid as the woman's own tied behind the saddle.

"Take you this horse. It is not so fine as ours, but they are not for mortal man to ride. Take my gift and ride you where you will. And may we not meet again for many years—but when we do, be certain that we will grant you good feasting in our hall," the shield-maiden said. She kissed Kridi Havnir's-son upon the brow, and her kiss burned as if she had set a burning brand there. Then she placed the dapple's rein into his hand and remounted her own horse.

"Come, sisters!" she cried. "The night is short and we have far to go!"

As one the riders turned their horses. First they trotted, then they cantered, all in the silence of falling snow, and then, most wondrous of all, it seemed as if the gray horses spread great swan's wings and rushed into the sky. As their forms dwindled away, they began to glow, brighter and more brightly still, until in a few heartbeats they were indistinguishable from the stars burning in the heavens.

Kridi looked at the horse whose rein he held. Not so fine an animal as those he had tended, but still a fine horse, a horse for one who would make his way in the world as other than wolfshead or slave.

"Come, Gray Swan," Kridi said to the horse as he led it toward the small house erected over the stones of his father's great hearth. "Tonight I will give you good guesting, and tomorrow we ride out into the world."

THE FIELDS, THE SKY
by Gary A. Braunbeck

Gary A. Braunbeck is the author of the acclaimed collection *Things Left Behind*, as well as the forthcoming collection *Escaping Purgatory* (in collaboration with Alan M. Clark) and the CD-ROM *Sorties, Cathexes, and Human Remains*. His first solo novel, *The Indifference of Heaven*, was recently released by Obsidian Books, as was his Dark Matter novel, *In Hollow Houses*. He lives in Columbus, Ohio, and has, to date, sold nearly 200 short stories, many of which have appeared in DAW anthologies. His fiction, to quote *Publisher's Weekly*, ". . . stirs the mind as it chills the marrow."

"Thus have the gods spun the thread for wretched mortals; that they live in grief while the gods themselves are without cares; for two jars stand on the floor of Zeus of the gifts he gives, one of evils, and another of blessings."
—Homer, *The Iliad*, translated by Alexander Pope

The poets called me brute, called me savage; I, who have slept in the caves of the ancients; I, who have fed on flesh in the secret grottos of Daedalus' masterpiece; I, who have walked the soils of Eden and drunk the waters of its four rivers; I, born of Pasi-

306

phaë, wife of Minos, pawn of Poseidon's vengeance;
I, who battled Ariadne's clumsy lover with his tight
fists and silver thread. How I remember the way he
fought, the feel of his blows against my face and
chest, how I was left for dead, stunned by his
strength and power but still alive. My sleep that
night was troubled, filled with pain and longing. I
felt the wind carry me. I blew over the land. I became
a howling river, a torrent of rage, the wings of the
Gryphon, looking down at the fields where men
worked their labors, then up toward the sky where
no gods looked down in pity, love, or awe. The memory of Eden's rivers filled my senses: *Only*, said
Pison; *You*, replied Gihon; *Remain*, followed Hidde-
kel; *Eternal*, whispered Euphrates.

I knew not if this was curse or grandeur.

Then a new crying reached me. Astonished, I
looked down and saw them being bred by men for
their flesh, being herded and tortured, imprisoned
and maimed. They cried out from the moment of
their birth to the hour of their death. Their crying
filled me with anger. It must not go this way. We are
of one animal, except man, who refused to recognize
himself in our eyes but could not deny his reflection
in *my* shadow, my profile, the sight of me.

A voice asked: *Lives there a man who has not dreamed
of being strong as a bull in the fields? Is there a bull who
has never longed to stand as a man and be nearer the sky?*

Then I woke, alone in the labyrinth, the sting of
Theseus' blows still tormenting my flesh.

I remembered the dream, and the wind.

The wind . . .

Since my birth and imprisonment, I had never once
felt the crispness of the wind from above. Oh, there

was wind from the Pits, the grottos, the bottomless bowels where even I dared not journey, but the wind from above had never before filled my lungs, whistled between my horns, dried the sweat under my torso where my four legs ached to set foot upon sungoldened soil.

I remember how, upon waking, the wind from above beckoned me, and I knew then that foolish Theseus, in his haste and arrogance, had left open the secret entrance.

And so I followed the wind, letting it carry me, until I at last reached the world above and moved freely into the light. I looked around through teary eyes and stepped into the thick grass of the fields, shadows in the woods around me shifting position and even darting away as I came near to walk among them. The gods had run here, had spoken and drunk, had unleashed their wrath and made their love, and would continue to do so without another thought of me.

I envied them. I hated them.

I was alone of my kind; nowhere did I find the Chimera, the Manticore, the Kraaken or Gorgon or Centaur; even the mischievous Ladon, the serpent who guarded the golden apples of the Hesperides, left no traces of itself in the soil or the breath of memories.

There was only me, and Man, and his machines.

The fields, the sky, and those creatures who dwelt in between.

And so I made my way into the world of Man, who would face me, know me, who would recognize himself in my eyes, who would cower in my shadow, weep at the beauty of my profile, see in me the strength and glory he wished he himself possessed, and offer me the awe and worship denied me by the gods and the ancient world I had outlived.

He would look upon me and give me reign over the fields, the sky, and all creatures who dwelt in between.

What manner of beast are you? asked the voices from beyond the trees. *You are much like us, yet your face is that of a man.*

I broke into a run, my four hooves kicking soil into smoke, and broke through the trees and foliage into the next field beyond the trees where their herd was grazing.

Never have we seen one such as you, they say to themselves, unaware that I am a thing of glory and legend, and a thing of glory and legend hears every thought of those creatures lower than itself.

I laughed, and raised my arms toward the sun, letting its light bathe my face in splendor.

The time of the gods had passed.

I was alone of my kind.

How I longed for the moment when Man would fall to his knees in worship of me.

I wake to the sounds of moaning and bleating. I blink my eyes and stretch my arms, pulling in the first breath of the day. I nearly choke from the fetid stench of wet straw and urine-soaked dirt. I press my hands into the floor to begin raising myself. I feel something warm and deep. I look down and see the trail of liquid filth that has squittered from the bowels of one of the sick animals chained in this place. Rising, I find a cloth hanging from one of the stable doors and drape it over my shoulder.

Walking outside, I climb the small rise to the side of the building and stop when I reach the well. I work the water pump beside it and soon the spigot spits out a heavy stream of something lukewarm but wet. I lean down my head—careful not to catch either of my horns on the iron—and drench my face and chest. I rub until I feel the filth of the night wash away, then use the cloth to dry myself.

In the distance, from a place just over the rise, I can already hear the groaning of the machinery, smell the metallic smoke rising into the air from the chimneys.

Overhead I hear a crow calling, and there is the faint odor of rotting flesh in the air.

Suddenly one of the men is behind me, prodding me into movement with a long device that cracks and sizzles when it touches my flesh. The electricity jolts through my tail, my legs, and up into my chest.

"Get your ass moving, pal!" he shouts, then holds the device above his head, smiling, filled with glory; Jason showing his Golden Fleece to the masses.

He makes the device hiss and crackle once again. I twirl the cloth like a rope and snap it forward, knocking the device from his grip. It flies out of his hand and lands in a puddle of liquid excrement. Before he can pull his other weapon from its holster, I grab him by the throat and lift him off the ground. He kicks and chokes. It amuses me, the way his dangling feet twist and move. Are you trying to dance on air?

Another voice says, "Please put him down. He's an idiot. It ain't worth it."

I turn my head. The overseer stands nearby. His hand rests on the butt of his holstered weapon, and

I know from his eyes that he does not wish to harm me, but he will if left no choice.

I release my grip from the other man's throat and he drops to the ground with a heavy wet noise. He coughs, rubs his neck, then looks up at me. "I swear to God, I'm gonna kill you one of these days."

"That's enough," says the overseer.

"My ass," shouts the other man, stumbling to his feet. "I don't see why the rest of us should have to put up with this shit—*you're* the freak-lover!"

"One more word out of you and I'll turn him loose. There won't be enough left of you to feed to the pigs."

The other man glowers for a moment, then spits on my front left hoof and begins to walk away.

The overseer looks at the puddle of excrement and says: "Forgetting something, aren't you?"

The other man stops. For a moment it looks as if he might respond in anger, then a shadow crosses his face. In that shadow I see his wife and children, their too-thin bodies, their dirty clothes, the hunger in their eyes.

He nods his head and walks to the puddle. I offer him the cloth. Wordlessly, he takes it, covers his hands, and retrieves his device from the puddle. He leaves without saying another word or looking at me.

"Are you all right?" asks the overseer.

I nod. Long ago I learned that silence is mistaken for respect by these men.

The overseer smiles but there is no joy or relief there.

He begins walking over the rise, and I follow him. Behind me the other animals, the sick ones with whom I share the building, begin their moaning anew.

We see the dance of life, rippling, flying, running by. There was a time when we were part of the dance, before the fields were plowed over and we were taken to these rooms.

I wish that I could find some pity in my heart for them, but I cannot. They are ill, their flesh tainted. They can only wait for the walk to the bloody chamber.

As I top the rise, I look down and see them in the fields. They graze and sleep. Two are by the fence, one mounting the other. They rut and grumble as one lunges into the other. I look away, remembering a story once told me by a nameless, faceless Athenian sent to me for sacrifice:

"One day, Zeus looked down from Olympus and saw a mother weeping over her dead child. Not quite grasping the concept of human suffering, Zeus chose to come down to Earth as a child himself in order to find out more about it. The other gods were irritated with Zeus at this time and so played a trick on him: They turned the Earth while he wasn't looking. He landed in the middle of a desert. He wandered as a child for days, then weeks, and began to weaken from starvation. The gods had temporarily stripped him of his godly powers; he was totally human.

"So he wandered, then collapsed, unable to walk from the sores upon his feet. He crawled until he could move no more. He lay there dying. In what might have been the last moments of his life, Zeus heard a strange weeping sound. He turned his head to see an odd beast lumbering toward him. This beast was a cow who had no one to milk her. Her teats were swollen and painful. She saw this child lying there in the middle of the desert and went to him, positioning her body so that her teats were directly above his mouth. Zeus sucked hungrily, drinking his fill of her life-restoring milk.

"The gods saw this and were strangely moved and so restored Zeus's powers to him. He brought the cow back to Olympus with him and decreed that she and her like were to be considered sacred and would be plentiful upon the Earth so that no child would ever again know the suffering he had to endure and no parent the grief of having to see their children die. The cow lives on Olympus still, grazing in a field beside Zeus's throne."

I devoured his face in one bite afterward. It was a quick death, with little pain. Such was the manner in which I thanked him for the story.

Zeus had always been a selective sentimentalist. Where was the muse of Fate who moved the gods' hearts when I wandered lost and lonely and afraid in the labyrinth?

A loud whistle breaks the still of the morning. Men wander into the fields, each carrying their own device, and begin to prod the beasts into groups, and those groups into lines. They march toward the large building with the smokestacks. The men continue shouting and prodding them until they are stuffed into the corrals. The animals cry out in confusion. Another man walks the length of the rows, tossing handfuls of hay to them. They lower their heads and eat, silently.

At the front of each corral is a large metal door. There are four in all.

A buzzing sound fills the air for a moment, followed by a deafening shriek that momentarily frightens the herds, then is replaced by the chords of soothing music.

The animals, calm again, return to their meal.

I walk to the bottom where the overseer waits. I can hear the voices of the herd.

Our hearts are pounding together. There is not enough room. Is this a face I am standing on? Is my friend dead? Are we all dead, already, or is death still to come? Are we real? Do we exist at all?

I envy them. Their whole purpose is fulfilled just by standing in the field all day, eating, then looking upward at the sky where no gods look down.

The door at the end of the first corral opens. From deep inside the dark place beyond comes a rumbling.

The rumbling room! they think.

One by one, they raise their heads and cry out. More hay is tossed to them, but they do not look at it. All thoughts of hunger have fled. Now there is only fear and bodies pressing together, the crushing weight of one becoming that of many. The wooden rails of the corral make clattering noises as their bodies slam against them, but they do not break. The rails never break. Such is the care given to the construction.

One of the beasts cries out as blood bubbles from its nostrils.

Another releases the contents of its bowels.

Yet another stomps in crimson-colored urine.

Their fear reaches out and grips my horns, pulling my head forward.

"It's time, Capo," says the foreman. This is the name he has given me. I do not know what it means. Pasiphaë never gave me a name, so the overseer's will have to do. Why did you not name me, Mother? Did you ever love me? Did you ever hold me in your arms when I was small and sing a lullaby?

I march forward, my hooves sinking into the mud. I can feel my muscles rippling under my flesh. I have to remember that I am not the same as them. I must remember this. It is important.

I enter the corral gate and follow the path that leads me to the right. I walk a separate path that parallels that of the herd. I reach the end and step up onto the platform that the overseer and his men have built for me. I turn to face them. I take a breath. I raise my arms before them.

They stare at me in awe and wonder. This is how they worship me. How they love me. To them I am a god. Their cud-stuffed prayers are only for me.

I suffer as you do, I say to them. *I have known the loneliness of dark spaces. I have tasted the fruit of betrayal. I know what it is like to stand upright as a man does.*

TWO LEGS! they pray to me. *IF ONLY WE HAD TWO LEGS, WE COULD LEAVE THIS PLACE OF FEAR AND FOLLOW YOU!*

You will never stand on two legs, I say to them. *To stand as a man stands is very hard. Two legs are very hard. Perhaps four is better, after all.*

WHERE ARE WE TO GO? TELL US, SHOW US THE WAY. WE WILL FOLLOW.

I answer them with a cry of my own, one composed of equal parts field-beast and man. They throw back their heads in reply.

I turn on the platform and begin walking inside. They follow.

The platform extends all the way across the rumbling room. I can travel its length and never touch the soil below. I know from before that the platform will empty onto a wooden terrace at the other end, and there I will walk down the ramp, go around the building, and enter the Corral of the Separate Path once again, then twice more after that. Until all the herd have been led into the dark rumbling room.

Then I shall be rewarded.

I step through the doorway into the rumbling room. Behind me, the herd moves as one.

My arms still raised, I gesture for them to come. *Come, my children, follow me.*

They enter the rumbling room four at a time. As they step through the door, men walk up to each of them. These men hold hammers. Hammers smash into heads. Their knees buckle, and with a cry they drop. Chains are dropped from above and secured around their legs. The room roars. The chains are pulled taut and the first four are lifted from the ground. They hang there, in great pain but not yet dead. Another roar, the walls shake, and they begin to move. It is as if they are slowly flying. As they pass by, they look at me. Their eyes are stupid with fear, and I cannot return their gaze. I am not the same as them. I am a thing of glory and legend. They are the sacrifice. They bleed for my exaltation.

Other men approach them now, holding things long, curved, and shiny. They lift their arms, these men, and pass the shiny curves through the flesh.

I whisper to them, *Fear not; soon you too shall graze in the fields by Zeus' throne.*

I have to make them believe this, as I must make myself believe it.

There is no other way to survive in this world of no gods.

The line is moving smoothly now, the beasts entering, the men falling upon them with hammers and chains. The room roars and snarls. I walk on. I reach the end of the platform and turn to see the fruition of my leadership.

The beasts hang there with their stomachs split open and their heads cut off. I smell their open flesh and see their dead hooves. On a metal hook I see all of their tongues, cut out and pierced by the sharp metal, pierced through the root and hanging there, mute and bloody.

I lower my arms.

I see their heads lined up on the floor. Someone is cutting off their cheeks with a knife, slicing through their tender flesh. Once this has been done, he kicks what remains of their heads down through a hole in the floor.

Blade passing through them.

Lives there a man who has not dreamed of being strong as a bull in the fields?

Red running past.

Is there a bull who has never longed to stand as a man and be nearer the sky?

Bubbling up.

Only. You. Remain. Eternal.

Red passing through. The world, this room.

Give to me reign over the fields, the sky, and all creatures who dwell in between.

Split in half, this way and that.

Their cries still screeching through my brain, I climb down the stairs and walk around the building, an abandoning god, and prepare myself for the moment when the sun kisses the ground and the sky bleeds twilight and I am fed on my follower's broiled remains.

To stand as a man stands is very hard. Two legs are very hard. Perhaps four is better, after all.

I touch my sides, wishing to stand on two legs. Two legs gives me a tailor. A tailor gives me clothing. Clothing gives me pockets. A place to hide my hands. To keep my paycheck. To store a key to a room with no straw on the ground.

Lisanne Norman
THE SHOLAN ALLIANCE SERIES

"will hold you spellbound"—*Romantic Times*